UNDER THE SKIN

Also by Michel Faber

Some Rain Must Fall and Other Stories
The Hundred and Ninety-Nine Steps
The Courage Consort
The Crimson Petal and the White
The Fahrenheit Twins
The Apple
The Fire Gospel

UNDER THE SKIN

MICHEL FABER

CANONGATE

Edinburgh · London · New York · Melbourne

This edition published in 2010 by Canongate Books

3

First published in Great Britain in 2000 by
Canongate Books Ltd, 14 High Street,
Edinburgh EH1 1TE.

British Library Cataloguing-in-Publication Data
A catalogue record for this book is available
on request from the British Library

ISBN 978 1 84767 892 8

Typeset by Hewer Text Ltd, Edinburgh
Printed and bound in Great Britain by Clays Ltd, St Ives plc

www.canongate.tv

Thanks to Jeff and Fuggo
and especially to my wife Eva,
for bringing me back to earth

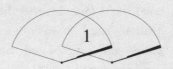

1

ISSERLEY ALWAYS DROVE straight past a hitch-hiker when she first saw him, to give herself time to size him up. She was looking for big muscles: a hunk on legs. Puny, scrawny specimens were no use to her.

At first glance, though, it could be surprisingly difficult to tell the difference. You'd think a lone hitcher on a country road would stand out a mile, like a distant monument or a grain silo; you'd think you would be able to appraise him calmly as you drove, undress him and turn him over in your mind well in advance. But Isserley had found it didn't happen that way.

Driving through the Highlands of Scotland was an absorbing task in itself; there was always more going on than picture postcards allowed. Even in the nacreous hush of a winter dawn, when the mists were still dossed down in the fields on either side, the A9 could not be trusted to stay empty for long. Furry carcasses of unidentifiable forest creatures littered the asphalt, fresh every morning, each of them a frozen moment in time when some living thing had mistaken the road for its natural habitat.

Isserley, too, often ventured out at hours of such pre-historic stillness that her vehicle might have been the first ever. It was as if she had been set down on a world so newly finished that the mountains might still have some shifting to do and the wooded valleys might yet be recast as seas.

Nevertheless, once she'd launched her little car onto the deserted, faintly steaming road, it was often only a matter of minutes before there was southbound traffic coming up behind her. Nor was this traffic content to let her set the pace, like one sheep following another on a narrow path; she must drive faster, or be hooted off the single carriageway.

Also, this being an arterial road, she must be alert to all the little capillary paths joining it. Only a few of the junctions were clearly signposted, as if singled out for this distinction by natural selection; the rest were camouflaged by trees. Ignoring junctions was not a good idea, even though Isserley had the right of way: any one of them could be spring-loaded with an impatiently shuddering tractor which, if it leapt into her path, would hardly suffer for its mistake, while she would be strewn across the bitumen.

Most distracting of all, though, was not the threat of danger but the allure of beauty. A luminous moat of rainwater, a swarm of gulls following a seeder around a loamy field, a glimpse of rain two or three mountains away, even a lone oystercatcher flying overhead: any of these could make Isserley half forget what she was on the road for. She would be driving along as the sun rose fully, watching distant farmhouses turn golden, when something much nearer to her, drably shaded, would metamorphose suddenly from a tree-branch or a tangle of debris into a fleshy biped with its arm extended.

Then she'd remember, but sometimes not until she was already sweeping by, narrowly missing the tip of the hitcher's hand, as if the fingers might have been snapped off, twig-like, had they grown just a few centimetres longer.

Stepping on the brake was out of the question. Instead, she'd leave her foot undisturbed on the accelerator, stay in line with the other cars, and do nothing more than take a mental photograph as she, too, zoomed past.

Sometimes, examining this mental image as she drove on, she would note that the hitcher was a female. Isserley wasn't interested in females, at least not in that way. Let them get picked up by someone else.

If the hitcher was male, she usually went back for another look, unless he was an obvious weakling. Assuming he'd made a reasonable impression on her, she would execute a U-turn as soon as it was safe to do so – well out of sight, of course: she didn't want him to know she was interested. Then, driving past on the other side of the road, as slowly as traffic allowed, she'd size him up a second time.

Very occasionally she would fail to find him again: some other motorist, less cautious or less choosy, must have slewed to a halt and picked him up in the time it had taken her to double back. She would squint at where she thought he'd been standing, and see only a vacant hem of gravel. She'd look beyond the road's edge, at the fields or the undergrowth, in case he was hidden in there somewhere, urinating. (They were prone to do that.) It would seem inconceivable to her that he should be gone so soon; his body had been so good – so excellent – so *perfect* – why had she thrown away her chance? Why hadn't she just picked him up as soon as she saw him?

Sometimes the loss would be so hard to accept that she just kept driving, for miles and miles, hoping that whoever had taken him from her would set him down again. Cows blinked at her innocently as she sped by in a haze of wasted petrol.

Usually, however, the hitcher was standing exactly where she'd first passed him, his arm perhaps just marginally less erect, his clothing (if rain was setting in) just that little bit more piebald. Coming from the opposite direction, Isserley might catch a glimpse of his buttocks, or his thighs, or maybe how well-muscled his shoulders were. There was something in the stance, too, that could indicate the cocky self-awareness of a male in prime condition.

Driving past, she'd stare straight at him, to verify her first impressions, making totally sure she wasn't pumping him up in her imagination.

If he really did make the grade, she stopped the car and took him.

Isserley had been doing this for years. Scarcely a day went by when she didn't drive her battered red Toyota Corolla to the A9 and start cruising. Even when she'd had a run of successful encounters and her self-esteem was high, she'd worry that the last hitcher she'd picked up might prove, with hindsight, to be her last truly satisfactory one: perhaps no-one in the future would measure up.

In truth, there was for Isserley an addictive thrill about the challenge. She could have some magnificent brute sitting in her car, right next to her, knowing for sure that he was coming home with her, and she could already be thinking ahead to the next one. Even while she was admiring him, following the curves of his brawny shoulders or the swell of his chest under his T-shirt, savouring the thought of how superb he'd be once he was naked, she would keep one eye on the roadside, just in case an even better prospect was beckoning to her out there.

Today hadn't started well.

Driving the car across the railway overpass near the comatose village of Fearn, before she'd even reached the highway, she became aware of a rattle somewhere above the wheel on the passenger side. She listened to it, holding her breath, wondering what it was trying to tell her in its quaint foreign language. Was the rattle a plea for help? A momentary grumble? A friendly warning? She listened some more, trying to imagine how a car might make itself understood.

This red Corolla wasn't the best car she'd ever had; she especially missed the grey Nissan estate she'd learned to drive in. It had responded smoothly and placidly, made almost no noise, and had lots of room in the back – enough to put a bed in, even. But she'd had to dump it, after only a year.

Since then, she'd had a couple of vehicles, but they were smaller, and the customized bits, when transplanted from the Nissan, caused trouble. This red Corolla handled stiffly and could be temperamental. No doubt it wanted to be a good car, but it had its problems.

Only a few hundred metres short of the junction with the highway, a hairy youngster was ambling along the side of the narrow road, thumbing a lift. She accelerated past him, and he threw up his arm lazily, adding two fingers to the gesture. He knew her face, vaguely, and she knew his, vaguely. They were both locals, though they'd never met except at moments like this.

Isserley had a policy of steering well clear of locals.

Turning onto the A9 at Kildary, she checked the clock on the dashboard. The days were lengthening fast: only 8:24, and the sun was already off the ground. The sky was bruise blue and flesh pink behind a swaddling of pure white cumulus, hinting at the frigid clarity to come. There would be no snow, but frost would sparkle for hours yet and night would fall well before the air had a chance to get warm.

For Isserley's purposes, a clear raw day like this was good for safe driving, but wasn't so good for assessing hitchers. Exceptionally hardy specimens might go short-sleeved, to show off their fitness, but most would be bundled up in overcoats and layers of wool to make things difficult for her. Even a starveling could look musclebound if he had enough gear on.

There was no traffic in her rear-view mirror and she gave herself permission to pootle along at 40 miles an hour, partly to test out how the rattle was doing. It seemed to have fixed itself. That was wishful thinking, of course. But it was a cheering thing to think when setting out in the morning, after a night of nagging pain, bad dreams and fitful sleep.

She sniffed deeply and laboriously through her narrow, barely patent little nostrils. The air was fresh and sharp, slightly intoxicating, like pure oxygen administered through a mask, or ether. Her consciousness was hesitating at a cross-roads between hyperactive wakefulness and a return to sleep. If she didn't get the stimulation of some action soon, she knew which way it was likely to go.

Isserley drove past some of the usual spots where hitchers were set down, but there was no-one. Just the road and the wide world, empty.

A few stray drops of rain spattered the windscreen, and the

wipers smeared two filthy monochrome rainbows across her line of vision. She squirted bottled water from inside the bonnet, a seemingly endless stream of it against the glass, before she was able to get a clear view again. The manoeuvre left her more tired somehow, as if she'd had to give up vital fluids of her own.

She tried to project herself forward in time, visualizing herself already parked somewhere with a hunky young hitch-hiker sitting next to her; she imagined herself breathing heavily against him as she smoothed his hair and grasped him round the waist to ease him into position. The fantasy was not enough, however, to keep her eyes from drooping shut.

Just as Isserley was considering finding a place to pull in and doze for a while, she spotted a silhouetted figure just below the horizon. Instantly she roused herself and dilated her eyelids attentively, pushing her glasses on straight. She checked her face and hair in the rear-view mirror. Experimentally, she pouted her lips, which were red as lipstick.

Driving past the hitcher the first time, she noted he was a male, quite tall, broad-shouldered, casually dressed. He was using both thumb and forefinger, rather slackly, as if he'd been waiting ages. Or maybe he didn't want to appear too eager.

On the way back, she noted he was quite young, with a very short haircut in the penal Scottish style. His clothing was drab as mud. What he had inside it filled up his jacket impressively, although whether with muscle or fat remained to be seen.

Driving towards him the final time, Isserley realized he really was uncommonly tall. He was staring at her, possibly figuring out that he had already seen her a couple of minutes before, as there wasn't much other traffic. Nevertheless, he didn't beckon to her any more urgently, just kept his hand lazily extended. Begging was not his style.

She slowed down and brought her car to a standstill right in front of him.

'Hop in,' she said.

'Cheers,' he said breezily as he swung into the passenger seat.

Just from that one word, delivered without a smile despite the smiley facial muscles involved, Isserley already knew something about him. He was the type who needed to swerve round the saying of thanks, as if gratitude were a trap. In his world, there was nothing Isserley could do for him that would put him in her debt; everything was only natural. She had stopped to pick him up off the side of the road; fine. Why not? She was giving him, for free, something a taxi would have charged him a fortune for, and what he said to that was 'Cheers', as if she were a drinking pal and had just done him a trifling, perfunctory favour like sliding an ashtray into his reach.

'No problem,' responded Isserley, as if he'd thanked her anyway. 'Where are you heading?'

'South,' he said, looking south.

A long second idled by, then he pulled the seatbelt across his torso as if reluctantly conceding this was the only way to get the two of them moving.

'Just south?' she enquired as she eased the car away from the kerb, careful, as always, to flip the toggle for the indicators rather than the headlights or the windscreen wipers or the icpathua.

'Well . . . it depends,' he said. 'Where are *you* heading?'

She made a calculation in her head, then looked at his face to judge where he might figure in it.

'I haven't decided yet,' she said. 'Inverness, to begin with.'

'Inverness is fine with me.'

'But you'd like to go further?'

'I'll go as far as I can get.'

Another car had appeared suddenly in her rear-view mirror and she had to gauge its intentions; by the time she was able to turn back to the hitcher his face was impassive. Had his remark been impish arrogance? Sexual innuendo? Or just dull matter-of-fact?

'Waiting long?' she asked, to tease out more of his wit.

'Pardon?'

He blinked at her, interrupted in the act of unzipping his jacket. Was the challenge of pulling a zip and simultaneously listening to a simple question more than his intellect could manage? He had a thin black scab etched across his right eyebrow, almost healed — a drunken fall maybe? The whites of his eyes were clear, his hair had been washed in the not too distant past, he didn't smell — was he just stupid?

'Where I picked you up,' she elaborated. 'Had you been standing there long?'

'I don't know,' he said. 'I don't have a watch.'

She glanced down at his nearest wrist; it was big, with fine golden hairs, and two blueish veins passing over onto the backs of his hands.

'Well, did it feel long?'

He seemed to think this over for a moment.

'Yeah.'

He grinned. His teeth weren't so good.

In the world outside, the sun's rays intensified abruptly as if some responsible agency had just noticed they were shining at half the recommended power. The windscreen lit up like a lamp and beamed ultraviolet rays onto Isserley and the hitcher, pure heat with the nip of breeze neatly filtered out. The car's heater was on full as well, so the hitcher was soon squirming in his seat, taking his jacket off altogether. Isserley watched him surreptitiously, watched the mechanics of his biceps and triceps, the roll of his shoulders.

'OK if I put this on the back seat?' he presumed, bundling the jacket up in his big hands.

'Sure,' she said, noting the ripples of muscle momentarily expressing themselves through his T-shirt as he twisted round to toss the jacket on top of her own. His abdomen was a bit fatty – beer, not muscle – but nothing too gross. The bulge in his jeans was promising, although most of it was probably testicles.

Comfortable now, he settled back in his seat and flashed her a smile seasoned by a lifetime of foul Scottish fodder.

She smiled back, wondering how much the teeth really mattered.

She could sense herself moving closer to deciding. In fact, to be honest, she was more than half-way already, and her breathing was quickening.

She made an effort to forestall the adrenaline as it leaked from her glands, by sending calming messages into herself, swallowing them down. All right, yes, he was good: all right, yes, she wanted him: but she must know a little more about him first. She must avoid the humiliation of committing herself, of allowing herself to believe he would be coming with her, and then finding out he had a wife or a girlfriend waiting.

If only he would make some conversation. Why was it always the desirable ones that sat in silence, and the misshapen rejects that prattled away unprompted? She'd had one miserable creature who'd removed a voluminous parka to reveal spindly arms and a pigeon chest: within minutes he was telling her his whole life's story. The brawny ones were more likely to stare into space, or make pronouncements about the world in general, deflecting personal questions with the reflex skill of athletes.

Minutes flashed by and her hitcher seemed content to say nothing. Yet at least he was taking the trouble to peek at her body – in particular at her breasts. In fact, as far as she could tell from glancing sideways and meeting his own furtive eyes, he was keen for her to face front so he could ogle her undetected. OK, then: she would let him have a good stare, to see what difference it might make. The Evanton turn-off was coming soon, anyhow, and she needed to concentrate on her driving. She craned forward a little, exaggerating her concentration on the road, and allowed herself to be examined in earnest.

Immediately she felt his gaze beaming all over her like another kind of ultraviolet ray, and no less intense.

Isserley wondered, oh how she wondered, what she looked like to him, in his alien innocence. Did he notice the trouble she had gone to for him? She straightened her back against the seat, pushing her chest out.

The hitcher noticed all right.

Fantastic tits on this one, but God, there wasn't much of her otherwise. Tiny – like a kid peering up over the steering wheel. How tall would she be? Five foot one, maybe, standing up. Funny how a lot of women with the best tits were really really short. This girl obviously knew she had a couple of ripe ones, the way she had them sitting pretty on the scoop of a low-cut top. That's why this car was heated like an oven, of course: so she could wear a skimpy black top and air her boobs for all to see – for *him* to see.

The rest of her was a funny shape, though. Long skinny arms with big knobbly elbows – no wonder her top was long sleeved. Knobbly wrists too, and big hands. Still, with tits like that . . .

They were really odd, actually, those hands. Bigger than you'd think they'd be, to look at the rest of her, but narrow too, like . . . chicken feet. And tough, like she'd done hard labour with them, maybe worked in a factory. He couldn't see her legs properly, she was wearing those horrible flared seventies trousers that were back in fashion – shiny green, for Christ's sake – and what looked like Doc Martens, but there was no disguising how short her legs were. Still, those tits . . . They were like . . . they were like . . . He didn't know what to compare them to. They looked pretty fucking good, nestled next to one another there, with the sun shining on them through the windscreen.

Never mind the tits, though: what about the face? Well, he couldn't see it just now; she had to actually turn towards him for him to see it, because of her haircut. She had thick, fluffy hair, mouse-brown, hanging down straight so he couldn't even see her cheeks when she was facing front. It was tempting to imagine a beautiful face hidden behind that hair, a face like a pop singer or an actress, but he knew different. In fact, when she'd turned towards him, her face had kind of shocked him. It was small and heart-shaped, like an elf in a kiddie's book, with a perfect little nose and a fantastic big-lipped curvy mouth like a supermodel. But she had puffy cheeks and was also wearing the thickest glasses he'd seen in his life: they magnified her eyes so much they looked about twice normal size.

She was a weird one all right. Half Baywatch babe, half little old lady.

She *drove* like a little old lady. Fifty miles an hour, absolute max. And that shoddy old anorak of hers on the back seat – what was that all about? She had a screw loose, probably. Nutter, probably. And she talked funny – foreign, definitely.

Would he like to fuck her?

Probably, if he got the chance. She'd probably be a much better fuck than Janine, that was for sure.

Janine. Christ, it was amazing how just thinking of her could bring him right down. He'd been in a great mood until now. Good old Janine. If ever your spirits are getting too up, just think of Janine. Jesus . . . couldn't he just forget it? Just look at this girl's tits, blazing in the sun, like . . . He knew what they looked like now: they looked like the moon. Well, two moons.

'So, what are you doing in Inverness?' he said suddenly.

'Business,' she said.

'What do you do?'

Isserley thought for a moment. It was so long since anything had been said, she'd forgotten what she'd decided to be this time.

'I'm a lawyer.'

'No kidding?'

'No kidding.'

'Like on TV?'

'I don't watch TV.' This was true, more or less. She'd watched it almost constantly when she'd first come to Scotland, but nowadays she only watched the news and occasionally a snatch of whatever happened to be on while she was exercising.

'Criminal cases?' he suggested.

She looked him briefly in the eyes. There was a spark there that might be worth fanning.

'Sometimes,' she shrugged. Or tried to. Shrugging while driving was a surprisingly difficult physical trick, especially with breasts like hers.

'Anything juicy?' he pushed.

She squinted into her rear-view mirror, slowing the car to allow a Volkswagen pulling a caravan to overtake.

'What would you think was juicy?' she enquired as the manoeuvre slipped gently into place.

'I don't know . . .' he sighed, sounding doleful and playful at the same time. 'A man kills his wife 'cause she's playing around with another guy.'

'I may have had one of those,' Isserley said noncommittally.

'And did you nail him?'

'Nail him?'

'Did you get him sent down for life?'

'What makes you think I wouldn't be defending him?' she smirked.

'Oh, you know: women together against men.'

His tone had grown distinctly odd: despondent, even bitter, and yet flirtatious. She had to think hard how best to respond.

'Oh, I'm not against men,' she said at last, changing lanes reflectively. 'Especially men who get a raw deal from their women.'

She hoped that would open him up.

But instead he was silent and slumped a little in his seat. She looked aside at him, but he didn't allow eye contact, as if she'd failed to respect some limit. She settled for reading the inscription on his T-shirt. AC/DC, it said, and in large embossed letters, BALLBREAKER. She had no idea what on earth this might mean, and felt suddenly out of her depth with him.

Experience had taught her there was nothing to do about that but try to go deeper.

'Are you married?' she asked.

'Was,' he stated flatly. Sweat was glistening beneath the hairline of his big prickly head; he ran his thumb under the seatbelt as if it were smothering him.

'You won't be so keen on lawyers, then,' she suggested.

'It was OK,' he said. 'Clean break.'

'No children, then?'

'*She* got 'em. Good luck to her.' He said this as if his wife were a distant and repugnant country on which there was no point trying to impose the customs of a more civilized society.

'I didn't mean to pry,' said Isserley.

'S'alright.'

They drove on. What had seemed like growing intimacy between them hardened into mutual unease.

Ahead of them, the sun had risen above the car's roof, leaving the windscreen filled with a harsh unpunctuated whiteness that threatened to become painful. The forest on the driver's side thinned out and was replaced by a steep embankment infested with creepers and bluebells. Signs printed in several languages unknown to Isserley reminded foreigners not to drive on the wrong side of the road.

The temperature inside the car was approaching stifling, even for Isserley, who could tolerate extremes without particularly caring. Her glasses were starting to fog up, but she couldn't take them off now: he mustn't see her eyes without them. A slow, subtle trickle of perspiration ran down her neck onto her breastbone, hesitating on the brink of her cleavage. Her hitcher seemed not to notice. His hands were drumming desultorily on his inner thighs to some tune she couldn't hear; as soon as he realized she was watching, he stopped abruptly and folded his hands limply over his crotch.

What on earth had happened to him? What had brought on this dismal metamorphosis? Just as she'd grown to appreciate how attractive a prospect he was, he seemed to be shrinking before her eyes; he wasn't the same male she'd taken into her car twenty minutes ago. Was he one of those inadequate lugs whose sexual self-confidence depended on not being reminded of any real females? Or was it her fault?

'You can open a window if you're too hot,' she offered.

He nodded, didn't even speak.

Isserley pressed her foot gingerly down on the accelerator, hoping this would please him. But he just sighed and settled further back in his seat, as if what he considered to be an insignificant increase in speed only reminded him how slowly they were getting nowhere.

Maybe she shouldn't have said she was a lawyer. Maybe a shop assistant or an infant teacher would have brought him out more. It was just that she'd taken him to be a rough, robust kind of character; she'd thought he might have a criminal history he'd start to talk about, as a way of teasing her, testing her out. Maybe the only truly safe thing she could have been was a housewife.

'Your wife,' she rejoined, striving for a reassuring, companionable, male sort of tone, a tone he might expect from a drinking buddy. 'Did she get the house?'

'Yeah . . . well . . . no . . .' He drew a deep breath. 'I had to sell it, and give her half. She went to live in Bradford. I stayed on here.'

'Where's here?' she asked, nodding her head at the open road, hoping to remind him how far she had taken him already.

'Milnafua.' He sniggered, as if self-conscious about the name.

To Isserley, Milnafua sounded perfectly normal; more normal in fact than London or Dundee, which she had some trouble getting her tongue round. She appreciated, however, that to him it represented some outlandish extreme.

'There's no work anywhere up there, is there,' she suggested, hoping she was striking a matter-of-fact, masculine note of sympathy.

'Don't I know it,' he mumbled. Then, with a startling boost of volume and pitch: 'Still, got to keep trying, eh?'

Looking at him in disbelief, she confirmed what he was playing at: a pathetic gesture towards optimism, missing the mark by miles. He was even smiling, his face sheened with sweat, as if he'd suddenly become convinced it was dangerous to admit to too much sloth, as if there could be serious consequences for admitting to her that his life was spent on the dole. Was it all her fault for telling him she was a lawyer? Had she made him afraid that she'd get him in trouble? Or that one day she might turn out to have some official power over him? Could she apologize, laughing, for her deception and start all over again? Tell him she sold computer software or clothes for the larger lady?

A big green sign at the side of the road announced how many miles remained before Dingwall and Inverness: not very many. The land had fallen away on the left side, revealing the gleaming shore of the Cromarty Firth. The tide was low, all the rocks and sands exposed. A solitary seal languished on one of those rocks, as if stranded.

Isserley bit her lip, slowly adjusting to her mistake. Lawyer, saleswoman, housewife: it wouldn't have made any difference. He was wrong for her, that's all. She had picked up the wrong type. Again.

Yes, it was obvious now what this big, touchy bruiser was up to. He was going to Bradford to visit his wife, or at least his children.

This made him a bad risk, from her point of view. Things could get very complicated when there were children in-volved. Much as she wanted him – it was sinking in now how much she'd already invested in the idea of having him – she didn't want complications. She would have to give him up. She would have to put him back.

They both sat in silence for the rest of the journey, as if conscious of having let each other down.

Traffic had accumulated all around them; they were caught up in an orderly queue of vehicles crossing the multi-laned tightrope of Kessock Bridge. Isserley glanced at her hitcher, felt a pang of loss at finding him turned away from her, staring down at the industrial estates of the Inverness shore far below. He was appraising a dismal toy-town of prefab ugliness as intently as he had admired her breasts not so long ago. Tiny trucks disappearing into factory mouths: that was what made sense to him now.

Isserley kept to the left, drove faster than she'd done all day. It wasn't just the pace demanded by the traffic around her; she wanted to get this over with as soon as possible. The tiredness had returned with a vengeance; she longed to find a shady bower off the road, lean her head against the seat and sleep a while.

On the far side, where the bridge rejoined the mainland, she negotiated the roundabout with pained and earnest concentration, to avoid being caught up in the town-bound traffic and herded to Inverness. She didn't even bother to disguise her grimace of anxiety as she did this: she had already lost him, after all.

However, to fill the silence of their last few moments together, she offered him a small parting consolation.

'I'll drive you just a bit further, get you past the Aberdeen turn-off. Then at least you'll know all the cars passing you are going south.'

'Great, yeah,' he said passionlessly.

'Who knows?' she jollied him. 'You might get to Bradford by tonight.'

'Bradford?' he frowned, turning to challenge her. 'Who says I'm going to Bradford?'

'To see your kids?' she reminded him.

There was an awkward pause, then:

'I never see my kids,' he stated flatly. 'I don't even know where they live, exactly. Somewhere in Bradford, that's as much as I know. Janine – my ex-wife – doesn't want anything to do with me. I don't exist anymore as far as she's concerned.' He peered straight ahead, as if roughly calculating all the thousands of places that lay south, and comparing that number to what he himself amounted to.

'Bradford was years ago, anyway,' he said. 'She could've moved to fuckin' Mars by now, for all I know.'

'So . . .' enquired Isserley, changing gear with such clumsiness that the gearbox made a hideous grinding noise, 'where *are* you hoping to get to today?'

Her hitcher shrugged. 'Glasgow will do me,' he told her. 'There's some good pubs there.'

Noticing her looking past him at the signs announcing imminent parking areas, it registered with him that she was about to discharge him from the car. Abruptly he mustered a last incongruous burst of conversational energy, fuelled by bitterness.

'It beats sitting in the Commercial Hotel in Alness with a

bunch of old boilers listening to some idiot singin' fuckin' "Copacabana".'

'But where will you sleep?'

'I know a couple of guys in Glasgow,' he told her, faltering again, as if that last squirt of fuel had already sputtered into the atmosphere. 'It's just a matter of running into them, that's all. They'll be there somewhere. It's a small world, eh?'

Isserley was staring ahead at the snow-capped mountains. It looked like a pretty big world to her.

'Mm,' she said, unable to share his vision of how Glasgow might greet him. Sensing this, he made a small mournful gesture, an opening out of his beefy hands to show there was nothing in them.

'Although people can always let you down, eh?' he said. 'That's why you always got to have a plan B.'

And he swallowed hard, his Adam's apple bulging like a real one stuck in his neck.

Isserley nodded approvingly, trying not to let her feelings show. She was covered in sweat now, cold chills running down her back like electric currents. Her heart hammered so hard her breasts shook; she disciplined herself to take just one deep breath instead of many shallow ones. Keeping her right hand clamped securely to the steering wheel she checked the rear-view mirror, the other lane, her speed, the hitcher.

Everything was ideal, everything pointed to this moment.

Noticing her excitement, he grinned at her uncertainly, removing his hands from his lap with an awkward jerk, as if waking up, dazed, to something that might yet be expected of him. She grinned back in reassurance, nodding almost imperceptibly as if to say 'Yes'.

Then the middle finger of her left hand flipped a little toggle on the steering wheel.

It might have been for the headlights or the indicators, or for the windscreen wipers. It was neither. It was the icpathua toggle, the trigger for the needles inside the passenger seat, to make them spring up silently from their little sheath-like burrows in the upholstery.

The hitcher flinched as they stung him through the fabric of his jeans, one needle in each buttock. His eyes, by chance, were facing the rear-view mirror, but no-one but Isserley witnessed the expression in them; the nearest vehicle was a giant lorry labelled FARMFOODS which was far away still, its driver an insect head behind tinted glass. In any case, the hitcher's look of surprise was momentary; the dose of icpathua was adequate for body sizes considerably larger than his. He lost consciousness and his head lolled back into the padded hollow of the headrest.

Isserley flipped another toggle, her fingers trembling ever so slightly. The gentle tick of the indicator lights set the rhythm of her breathing as she allowed the car to drift off the road and smoothly enter the lay-by. The speedometer wobbled to zero; the car stopped moving; the engine stalled, or maybe she turned off the ignition. It was over.

As always at this moment, she saw herself as if from a height; an aerial view of her little red Toyota parked in its little asphalt parenthesis. The FARMFOODS lorry roared past on the straight.

Then, as always, Isserley fell from her vantage point, a dizzying drop, and plunged back into her body. Her head slammed against the headrest, quite a lot harder than his had done, and she inhaled shudderingly. Gasping, she clung to the steering wheel, as if it might stop her falling further down, into the bowels of the earth.

Finding her way back to ground level always took a little

while. She counted her breaths, slowly getting them down to six a minute. Then she unclenched her hands from the steering wheel, laid them over her stomach. That was always oddly comforting.

When at last the adrenaline had ebbed and she was feeling calmer, she re-applied herself to the job in hand. Vehicles were humming past from both directions, but she could only hear them, not see them. The glass of all the car's windows had turned dark amber, at the touch of a button on the dashboard. She was never aware of having touched that button; it must happen during the adrenaline rush. She only remembered that always, by the time she was at this point, the windows were already dark.

Something massive drove past, vibrating the ground, sweeping a black shadow across the car. She waited till it was gone.

Then she opened the glove box and fetched out the wig. It was a wig for males, but blond and curly. She turned to the hitcher, who was still frozen in position, and placed the wig carefully on his head. She smoothed some wayward locks over his ears, pecked at the fringe with her sharp fingernails to help it settle over the forehead. She leaned back and evaluated the total effect, made some more adjustments. Already he looked much like all the others she had picked up; later, when his clothes were off, he would look more or less identical.

Next she scooped a handful of different spectacles from the glove box and selected an appropriate pair. She slid them into position over the hitcher's nose and ears.

Finally she retrieved the anorak from the back seat, allowing the hitcher's own coat to slip onto the floor. The anorak was actually only the front half of the garment; the back had been cut away and discarded. She arranged the fur-lined façade over the hitcher's upper torso, tucking the edges of the sleeves round his arms, draping the bisected hood over his shoulders.

He was ready to go.

She pressed a button and the amber faded from the windows like dispersion in reverse. The world outside was still chilly and bright. There was a lull in the traffic. She had about two hours' grace before the icpathua wore off, yet she was only fifty minutes' drive from home. *And* it was only 9:35. She was doing well after all.

She turned the key in the ignition. As the engine started up, the rattling noise that had worried her earlier on made itself heard again.

She would have to look into that when she got back to the farm.

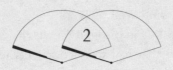

2

NEXT DAY, ISSERLEY drove for hours in sleet and rain before finding anything. It was as if the bad weather had kept all the eligible males indoors.

Despite peering so intently through her windscreen that she began to get mesmerized by the motion of the wipers, she could identify nothing on the road except the ghostly tail-lights of other rainswept vehicles crawling through the noon-day twilight.

The only pedestrians, let alone hitch-hikers, she had seen all morning were a couple of tubby youths with crewcut heads and plastic knapsacks, splashing in a gutter near the Inver-gordon underpass. Schoolkids, late or playing truant. They had turned at her approach and shouted something too heavily accented for her to understand. Their rain-soaked heads looked like a couple of peeled potatoes, each with a little splat of brown sauce on top; their hands seemed gloved in bright green foil: the wrappers of crisps packets. In her rear-view mirror, Isserley had watched their waddling bodies recede to coloured blobs finally swallowed up in the grey soup of the rain.

Driving past Alness for the fourth time, she could scarcely believe there was nobody there. It was usually such a good spot, because so many motorists were loath to pick up anybody they suspected might be *from* Alness. A grateful hitcher had explained this to Isserley not long ago: Alness was known, he said, as 'Little Glasgow', and gave the area 'a bad name'. Illegal pharmaceutical substances were freely available, leading to broken windows and females giving birth too young. Isserley had never been to Alness itself, though it was only a mile off the road. She just drove past it on the A9.

Today, she drove past it over and over again, hoping one of its leather-jacketed reprobates might finally come forward, thumbing a lift to a better place. None did.

She considered going farther, crossing the bridge and trying her luck beyond Inverness. There, she was likely to find hitchers who were more organized and purposeful than the ones closer to home, with thermos flasks and little cardboard placards saying ABERDEEN or GLASGOW.

Ordinarily, she had no objection to going a long way to find what she was looking for; it was not uncommon for her to drive as far as Pitlochry before turning back. Today, however, she was superstitious about travelling too far from home. Too many things could go wrong in the wet. She didn't want to end up stranded somewhere, her engine churning feebly against a deluge. Who said she had to bring somebody home every day, anyway? One a week should be enough to satisfy any reasonable person.

Giving up around midday, she headed back north, playing

with the notion that if she announced resolutely enough to the universe that she'd abandoned all hope, she might be offered something after all.

Sure enough, not far from the sign inviting motorists to visit picturesque seaboard villages on the B9175, she spotted a miserable-looking biped thumbing the watery air in the snubstream of the traffic. He was on the other side of the road from her, lit up by the headlights of a procession of vehicles sweeping past. She had no doubt he would still be there when she'd doubled back.

'Hello!' she called out, swinging the passenger door open for him.

'Thank Christ for that,' he exclaimed, leaning one arm on the edge of the door as he poked his dripping face into the car. 'I was beginning to think there was no justice in the world.'

'How's that?' said Isserley. His hands were grimy, but large and well-formed. They'd clean up nicely, with detergent.

'I always pick up hitchers,' he asserted, as if refuting a malicious slur. 'Always. Never drive past one, if I've got room in the van.'

'Neither do I,' Isserley assured him, wondering how long he was intending to stand there ushering rain into her car. 'Hop in.'

He swung in, his big waterlogged rump centering him on the seat like the bottom of a lifebuoy. Steam was already rising before he'd even shut the door; his casual clothes were soaked through and squeaked like a shammy as he settled himself.

He was older than she'd taken him to be, but fit. Did wrinkles matter? They shouldn't: they were only skin deep, after all.

'So, the one bloody time *I* need a lift,' he blustered on, 'what happens? I walk half a bloody mile to the main road in the pissing rain, and do you think any bugger will stop for me?'

'Well . . .' Isserley smiled. '*I* stopped, didn't I?'

'Aye, well you're car number two thousand and bloody fifty, I can tell you,' he said, squinting at her as if she was missing the point.

'Have you been counting?' she challenged him sportively.

'Aye,' he sighed. 'Well, rough head-count, you know.' He shook his head, sending droplets flying off his bushy eyebrows and abundant quiff. 'Can you drop me off somewhere near Tomich Farm?'

Isserley made a mental calculation. She had ten minutes only, driving slowly, to get to know him.

'Sure,' she said, admiring the steely density of his neck and the width of his shoulders, determined not to disqualify him merely on the grounds of age.

He sat back, satisfied, but after a couple of seconds a glimmer of bafflement appeared on his stubbled spade of a face. Why were they not moving?

'Seatbelt,' she reminded him.

He strapped himself in as if she had just asked him to bow three times to a god of her choice.

'Death traps,' he mumbled derisively, fidgeting in a faint miasma of his own steam.

'It's not me that wants it,' she assured him. 'I just can't afford to be stopped by the police, that's all.'

'Ach, police,' he scoffed, as if she were admitting to a fear of mice or mad cow disease. But there was an undertone of paternal indulgence in his voice, and he wiggled his shoulders experimentally, to demonstrate how he was adjusting to his confinement.

Isserley smiled and drove off with him, lifting her arms high on the steering wheel to show him her breasts.

She'd better watch those, the hitcher thought. Or they'll fall into her Corn Flakes.

Mind you, this girl needed *something* going for her, with glasses as thick as that and no chin. Nicki, his own daughter, was no pearl of beauty either, and to be honest she didn't even make the most of what she'd got. Still, if she really was studying to become a lawyer instead of just boozing his allowance away in Edinburgh, maybe she'd end up being some use to him after all. Like, she could maybe find a few extra loopholes in the EU regulations.

What did *this* girl do for a crust? Her hands weren't quite right. No, they weren't normal at all. She'd buggered them up, maybe, in some heavy manual job when she was too young to handle it and too stupid to complain. Chicken-plucking. Fish-gutting.

She lived by the sea, definitely. Smelled of it. Fresh today. Maybe she worked for one of the local fishermen. Mackenzie was known to take women on, if they were strong enough and not too much trouble.

Was this girl trouble?

She was tough, that was for sure. Probably had been through hell, growing up funny-looking in one of those little seaboard villages. Balintore. Hilton. Rockfield. No, not Rockfield. He knew every single person in Rockfield.

How old was she? Eighteen, maybe. Her hands were forty. She drove like she was pulling a wonky trailer-load of hay over a narrow bridge. Sat like she had a rod up her arse. Any shorter and she'd need a couple of pillows on the seat. Maybe he'd suggest that to her – maybe she'd bite his head off if he did. Probably illegal, anyway. Highway Code regulation number three million and sixty. She'd be scared to tell them where to shove it. She'd rather suffer.

And she *was* suffering. The way she moved her arms and legs. The heating turned up full. She'd done some damage there somewhere along the line. A car accident, maybe? She had guts, then, to keep driving. A tough little bird.

Could he help her out, maybe?

Could she be any use to him?

'You live near the sea, am I right?' he said.

'How can you tell?' Isserley was surprised; she had made no conversation yet, assuming he needed more time to appraise her body.

'Smell,' he stated bluntly. 'I can smell the sea on your clothes. Dornoch Firth? Moray Firth?'

It was alarming, this point-blank accuracy. She would never have expected it; he had the half-smiling, half-grimacing squint of the dull-witted. There was black engine oil on the sleeves of his shabby polyester jacket. Pale scars littered his tanned face like imperfectly erased graffiti.

Of his two guesses, she picked the one that was wrong.

'Dornoch,' she said.

'I haven't seen you around,' he said.

'I only arrived a few days ago,' she said.

Her car had caught up now with the procession of vehicles that had passed him by. A long trail of tail-lights stretched, fading, into the distance. That was good. She dropped back into first gear and crawled along, absolved from speed.

'You working?' he asked.

Isserley's brain was functioning optimally now, barely distracted by the steady pace of the traffic. She deduced he was probably the type who knew someone in every conceivable profession, or at least in those professions he didn't despise.

'No,' she said. 'I'm unemployed.'

'You need a fixed address to get benefits,' he pointed out, quick as a flash.

'I don't believe in the dole.' She was getting the hang of him at last, and suspected this reply would please him.

'Looking for work?'

'Yes,' she said, slowing down even further to allow a luminous white Mini into the queue. 'But I don't have much education. And I'm not that strong.'

'Tried gathering whelks?'

'Whelks?'

'Whelks. It's one of my lines of business. People just like yourself gather 'em. I sell 'em on.'

Isserley pondered for a few seconds, assessing whether she had enough information to proceed.

'What are whelks?' she said at last.

He grinned through his haze of steam.

'Molluscs, basically. You'll've seen 'em, living where you live. But I've got one here, as it happens.' He lifted one cheek of his meaty buttocks towards her, to fish around in his right trouser pocket.

'There's the fella,' he said, holding a dull grey shell up to her eye level. 'I always keep one in my pocket, to show people.'

'That's very foresightful of you,' complimented Isserley.

'It's to show people the size that's wanted. There's piddly wee ones, y'see, size of peas, that aren't worth the bother of picking up. But these big fellas are just fine.'

'And I could just gather them and get money for it?'

'Nothing simpler,' he assured her. 'Dornoch's good for 'em. Millions of 'em there, if you go at the right time.'

'When is the right time?' Isserley asked. She had hoped he'd have taken his jacket off by now, but he seemed content to swelter and evaporate.

'Well, what you do,' he told her, 'is get yourself a book of the tides. Costs about 75p from the Coastguard Authority. You check when it's low tide, go to the shore and just rake 'em in. Soon as you've got enough, you give me a tinkle and I come and collect.'

'What are they worth?'

'Plenty, in France and Spain. I sell 'em to restaurant suppliers – they can't get enough of 'em, especially in winter. Most people only gather in summer, y'see.'

'Too cold for the whelks in winter?'

'Too cold for the people. But you'd do all right. Wear rubber gloves, that's my tip. The thin ones, like women use for washing dishes.'

Isserley almost pressed him to be specific about what *she,* rather than he, could earn from whelk-gathering; he had the gift of half persuading her to consider possibilities which were in fact absurd. She had to remind herself that it was him she was interested in getting to know, not herself.

'So: this whelk-selling business – does it support you? I mean, do you have a family?'

'I do all sorts of things,' he said, dragging a metal comb through his thick hair. 'I sell car tyres for silage pits. Creosote. Paint. My wife makes lobster creels. Not for lobsters – no fuckin' lobsters left. But American tourists buy 'em, if they're painted up nice. My son does a bit of the whelk-gathering himself. Fixes cars too. He could sort that rattle in your chassis no bother.'

'I might not be able to afford it,' retorted Isserley, discomfited again by the sharpness of his observation.

'He's cheap, my son. Cheap and fast. Labour's what costs, y'see, when it comes to cars. He's got a constant stream of 'em passing through his garage. In and out. Genius touch.'

Isserley wasn't interested. If she wanted a man with a genius touch, she already had one on tap, back at the farm. He'd do anything for her, and he kept his paws to himself – if only just.

'What about *your* van?' she said.

'Oh, he'll fix that too. Soon as he gets his hands on it.'

'Where is it?'

'About half a mile from where you picked me up,' he wheezed, stoically amused. 'I was half-way home with a tonload of whelks in the back. Fuckin' engine just died on me. But my boy will sort it. Better value than the AA, that lad. When he's not pissed.'

'Do you have a business card of your son's on you?' Isserley enquired politely.

'Hold on,' he grunted.

Again he lifted his meaty rump, which was not destined after all to be injected with icpathua. From his pocket he removed a handful of wrinkled, dog-eared and tarnished cardboard squares, which he shuffled through like playing cards. He selected two, and laid them on the dashboard.

'One's me, and one's my son,' he said. 'If you feel like doing a bit of whelk-gathering, get in touch. I'll come out for any amount over twenty kilos. If you don't get that much in one day, a couple of days will do it.'

'But don't they spoil?'

'Takes 'em about a week to die. It's actually good to let

'em sit for a while so as the excess water drains out. And keep the bag closed, or they'll crawl out and hide under your bed.'

'I'll remember that,' promised Isserley. The rain was easing off at last, allowing her to slow the windscreen wipers down. Light began to seep through the greyness. 'Here's Tomich Farm coming up,' she announced.

'Another two hundred yards and that's me,' said the whelk stud, already unbuckling his seatbelt. 'Thanks a lot. You're a little Samaritan.'

She stopped the car where he told her to and he let himself out, squeezing her affectionately on the arm with one big hand before she realized what was happening. If he noticed the hardness and thinness of the limb, he didn't let on. Ambling off, he waved once without looking back.

Isserley watched him disappear, her arm tingling unpleasantly. Then when he was gone, she frowned into her rearview mirror, looking for a break in the traffic. She was forgetting him already, apart from a resolution to wash and put on fresh clothes whenever she'd been for a morning walk along the firth.

Indicator ticking, she cruised back onto the road, eyes front.

Her second hitcher was waiting for her quite close to home, so close that she had to think hard about whether she'd ever seen him before. He was young, almost too short, with a beetle brow and hair dyed so blond it was almost white. Despite the cold and the persistent drizzle, he wore only a short-sleeved Celtic T-shirt and military camouflage pants. Vague tattoos disfigured his lean but powerful forearms: skin deep, she reminded herself again.

Deciding, on the southwards approach, that he was a total stranger after all, she stopped for him.

As soon as he'd entered her car and sat down, Isserley sensed he was trouble. It was as if the laws of physics were unsettled by his presence; as if the electrons in the air were suddenly vibrating faster, until they were ricocheting around the confines of the cabin like crazed invisible insects.

'Gaun anywhir near Redcastle?' A sour aroma of alcohol sidled over to her.

Isserley shook her head. 'Invergordon,' she said. 'If that's not worth your while . . .'

'Neh, it's cool,' he shrugged, drumming on his knees with his wrists, as if responding to the beat of an inbuilt Walkman.

'OK,' Isserley said, pulling out from the kerb.

She regretted there wasn't more traffic: always a bad sign. She also found herself, instinctively, gripping the steering wheel in such a way that her elbows hung down, obscuring her passenger's view of her breasts. This, too, was a bad sign.

His stare burned through regardless.

Women don't dress like that, he thought, unless they want a fuck.

The only thing was, she mustn't expect him to pay. Not like that slag in Galashiels. Buy them a drink and they think they can sting you for twenty pounds. Did he look like some kind of loser?

That road in Invergordon with the Academy in it. That was a good place. Quiet. She could suck him off there. He wouldn't have to see her ugly face then.

Her tits would dangle between his legs. He'd give them a bit of a squeeze if she did a good job. She'd do her best, he could tell. Breathing hard already she was, like a bitch in heat.

Not like that slag in Galashiels. This one would be satisfied with what she could get. Ugly women always were, weren't they?

Not that he was the kind of guy who could only get ugly women.

It was just, here he was and here *she* was. It was like . . . force of nature, wasn't it? The law of the fucking jungle.

'So, what brings you out on the road today?' Isserley said brightly.

'Settin' aroond the estate wuz doin' mah heid in.'

'In between jobs, then?'

'Jobs dinnae exist up here. Nae such fuckin' thing.'

'The government still expects you to look for them though, doesn't it?'

This gesture of empathy did not particularly impress him.

'Ah'm oan a fuckin' trainin' schim,' he fumed. 'They says, You go find some old fogies and talk shite tae 'em aboot central fuckin' heatin' and we'll tell the government yir oaff the dole, OK? Fuckin' hush money. Yi ken?'

'It sucks,' Isserley agreed, hoping this was the right term for him.

The atmosphere in the car was growing intolerable. Every available cubic millimetre of empty space between him and her was filling up with his malignant breath. She had to make her decision fast; her fingers itched to hit the icpathua toggle. But she must, at all costs, stay calm. To act on impulse was to invite disaster.

Years ago, in the very beginning, she'd stung a hitcher who had asked her, scarcely two minutes after getting into the car, if she liked having a fat cock up each hole. Her English hadn't been quite as good then, and it had taken her a little while to figure out he wasn't talking about poultry or sports. By then he'd exposed his penis. She'd panicked and stung him. It had been a very bad decision.

Police had searched for him for weeks. His picture was shown on television and published not just in the newspapers but also in a special magazine for homeless people. He was described as vulnerable. His wife and parents appealed to anyone who might have sighted him. Within days, despite the privacy she'd imagined at the time she picked him up, the investigation turned its spotlight on a grey Nissan estate driven possibly by a woman. Isserley had had to lie low on the farm for what seemed like an eternity. Her faithful car was handed over to Ensel, and he cannibalized it in order to customize the next-best one on the farm, a horrid little monster called Lada.

'Anyone can make a mistake,' Ensel had reassured her as he laboured to get her back on the road, his arms smeared with black grease, his eyes bloodshot from the welding flame.

But Isserley's shame was such that even now she couldn't think about her failure without an involuntary grunt of distress. It would never happen again: never.

They had reached a stretch of the A9 which was being converted to dual carriage; there were noisy mechanical dinosaurs and uniformed personnel meandering over mounds of soil on either side of the road. The commotion was consoling, in a way.

'You're not from this area, are you?' Isserley said, raising her voice slightly to be heard above the din of great blades slicing into the earth.

'Nearer tae it than *you*, Ah kin bet,' he retorted.

She ignored this jibe, determined to hold on to the conversational thread which might lead to his family, when he startled her by suddenly, violently, winding his window down.

'He-e-ey *Doug*-eeee!' he yelled into the rain, waving one fisted arm out the window.

Isserley glanced up at the rear-view mirror, caught a glimpse of a burly figure in bright yellow reflective clothing standing by an earthmover, waving back hesitantly.

'Mate ae mine,' explained her hitcher, winding his window up again.

Isserley took a deep breath, tried to get her heart rate down. She couldn't take him now, obviously; she had lost her chance. Whether or not he was married with children had become irrelevant in an instant; on balance she would rather not find out, in case he wasn't.

If only she could stop panting and let go of him!

'Are those real?' he said.

'Pardon?' It was as much as she could do to speak one word without her breath catching.

'What yis goat stickin' oot in front ae yi,' he elaborated. 'Yir tits.'

'This . . . is as far as I go,' she said, veering the car into the middle of the road, indicator flashing. By the grace of Providence, they had reached the comforting eyesore of Donny's Garage in Kildary. WELCOME, the sign said.

'You seid Invergordon,' her hitcher protested, but Isserley was already turning across the lanes, homing her car towards the space between the garage and its petrol pumps.

'There's a rattle in the chassis somewhere,' she said. 'Can't you hear it?' Her voice was hoarse and none too even, but it didn't matter now. 'I'd better get it looked at. Might be dangerous.'

The car stopped moving. Some kind of life bustled behind the cluttered shop windows of Donny's Garage: other voices, the creak of large refrigerators, the clink of bottles.

Isserley turned to her hitcher and gently pointed back to the A9.

'You can try your luck just there,' she advised. 'It's a good spot. Drivers are going quite slowly. I'll get this car looked at. If you're still here when I'm finished, I'll maybe pick you up again.'

'Dinnae poosh yirself,' he sneered, but he got out of the car. And then he walked away, he walked away.

Isserley opened her own door and heaved herself out. Standing upright sent a shock of pain through her spine. She steadied herself against the roof of the car and stretched, watching Beetle-brow crossing the road and slouching towards the far gutter. The frigid breeze thrilled the sweat on her skin, blew oxygen straight up her nose.

Nothing bad would happen now.

She extracted one of the petrol pumps from its holster, manipulating the great nozzle awkwardly in her narrow claw. It wasn't strength she lacked, it was sheer breadth of handspan. She needed two hands to guide the nozzle into the hole. Watching the computerized gauge with care, she squirted exactly five pounds' worth of petrol into the tank. Five zero zero. She replaced the pump, walked into the building and paid somebody with one of the five-pound notes she'd been saving for just this purpose.

It all took under three minutes. When she emerged, she looked uneasily across the road for the green-and-white form of Beetle-brow. He was gone. Incredibly, someone else had taken him.

Only a couple of hours later, it was already late afternoon and the light was failing; that is, about half past four. Chastened by her experience so close to home with Beetle-brow, Isserley had driven about fifty miles south, past Inverness, almost as far as Tomatin, before turning back empty-handed.

Although it was not unusual for her to have days when she made her pick-up well after dark, this depended wholly on her stamina for driving and her appetite for the game. Just one humiliating encounter could shake her so badly that she would retreat to the farm as soon as possible, to brood on where she'd gone wrong and what she could have done to protect herself.

Isserley was wondering, as she drove, whether or not this Beetle-brow character had shaken her that much.

It was difficult to decide, because her own emotions hid from her. She'd always been like that, even back home – even when she was a kid. Men had always said they couldn't figure her out, but she couldn't figure herself out, either, and had to look for clues like anyone else. In the past, the surest sign that an emotion was stuck inside her had been sudden, unwarranted fits of temper, often with regrettable consequences. She didn't have those tantrums anymore, now that her adolescence was behind her. Her anger was well under control nowadays – which was just as well, given what was at stake. But it did mean it was harder for her to guess what sort of state she might be in. She could glimpse her feelings, but only out of the corner of her eye, like distant headlights reflected in a side mirror. Only by not looking for them directly did she have any chance of spotting them.

Lately, she suspected her feelings were getting swallowed up, undigested, inside purely physical symptoms. Her backache and eye-strain were sometimes much worse than usual, for no real reason; at these times, there was probably something else troubling her.

Another tell-tale sign was the way perfectly ordinary

events could bring her down, like being overtaken by a school bus on a gloomy afternoon. If she was in reasonable shape, the sight of that great shield-shaped back window crowded with jeering, gesticulating adolescents didn't perturb her in the least. Today, however, the spectacle of them hovering above her, like an image on a giant screen she must meekly follow for miles, filled her with despond. The way they gurned and grimaced, and smeared their grubby hands in the condensation, seemed an expression of malevolence towards her personally.

Eventually the bus turned off the A9, leaving Isserley tailing inscrutable little red sedans very like her own. The line seemed to go on forever. The corners of the world were darkening fast.

She *was* upset, she decided. Also, her back was sore, her tailbone ached and her eyes were stinging after so many hours of peering through thick lenses and rain. If she gave up and went home, she could take off her glasses and give her eyes a rest, lie curled up on her bed, perhaps even sleep: oh, what bliss that would be! Trifling gifts of creature comfort, consolation prizes to soothe away the pangs of failure.

At Daviot, however, she spotted a tall, rangy backpacker holding a cardboard sign that said THURSO. He looked fine. After the usual three approaches, she stopped for him, about a dozen yards ahead of where he stood. In her rear-view mirror she watched him bound towards the car shrugging his backpack off his broad shoulders even as he ran.

He must be very strong, she thought as she reached across for the door handle, to be able to run like that with a heavy load.

Having drawn abreast with her car, the hitcher hesitated at the door she'd opened for him, gripping his garishly coloured swag with long, pale fingers. He smiled apologetically; his rucksack was bigger than Isserley, and clearly wasn't going to fit on his lap or even the back seat.

Isserley got out of the car and opened the boot, which was always empty apart from a canister of butane fuel and a small fire extinguisher. Together they loaded his burden in.

'Thank you very much,' he said, in a serious, sonorous voice which even Isserley could tell was not a product of the United Kingdom.

She returned to the driver's seat, he to his, and they drove off together just as the sun was taken below the horizon.

'I'm pleased,' he said, self-consciously turning his THURSO sign face-down on the lap of his orange track pants. It was sheathed in a clear rainproof folder and contained many pieces of paper, no doubt inscribed with different destinations. 'It isn't so easy to get a lift after dark.'

'People like to see what they're getting,' agreed Isserley.

'That's understandable,' he said.

Isserley leaned back against her seat, extended her arms, and let him see what he might be getting.

This lift was a fortunate thing. It meant he might get to Thurso by tonight, and Orkney by tomorrow. Of course Thurso was more than a hundred miles further north, but a car travelling at an average of fifty miles per hour – or even forty, as in this case – could in theory cover the distance in less than three hours.

He hadn't asked her where she was going yet. Perhaps she would only take him a short way, and then say she was turning off. However, the fact that she had seemed to understand his allusion to the difficulties of hitch-hiking in the dark implied she did not intend to put him back on the road ten miles further on, with darkness falling. She would speak soon, no doubt. He had spoken last. It might be impolite for him to speak again.

Her accent was not, in his opinion, a Scottish one.

Perhaps she was Welsh; the people in Wales had spoken a little like her. Perhaps she was European, though not from any of the countries he knew.

It was unusual for a woman to pick him up. Women almost invariably drove past, the older ones shaking their heads as if he were attempting some highly dangerous folly like somersaulting across the traffic, the younger ones looking pained and nervous as if he had already managed to reach inside their cars and molest them. This woman was different. She was friendly and had very big breasts which she was showing off to him. He hoped she was not wanting him for a sexual experience of some kind.

Unless it was to be in Thurso.

He could not see her face when she was looking ahead, which was a pity. It had been very remarkable. She wore the thickest corrective lenses he had ever seen. In Germany, he doubted that a person with such severe visual impairment would be approved for a driver's licence. Her posture was, in his opinion, suggestive of some spinal problem. Her hands were large and yet unusually narrow. The skin on the edge of her hand, along her pinkie and down to the wrist, had a horny smoothness that was texturally quite different from the rest, suggesting scar tissue following surgery. Her breasts were perfect, flawless; perhaps they, too, were the product of surgery.

She was turning towards him now. Mouth-breathing, as if her perfectly sculpted little nose had indeed been sculpted by a plastic surgeon and had proved to be too small for her needs.

Her magnified eyes were a little bloodshot with tiredness, but startlingly beautiful, in his opinion. The irises were hazel and green, glowing like . . . like illuminated microscope slides of some exotic bacterial culture.

'Well,' she said, 'What is there for you in Thurso?'

'I don't know,' he replied. 'Perhaps nothing.'

He was, she noticed now, superbly built. Deceptively lean, but all muscle. He could probably have run alongside her car for a mile, if she drove slowly enough.

'And if there *is* nothing?' she said.

He pulled a face which she assumed was his culture's equivalent of a shrug. 'I'm going there because I have never been there,' he explained.

The prospect seemed to fill him with ennui and enthusiasm all at once. Thick grey-blond eyebrows were gathering over his pale blue eyes like a stormcloud.

'You're travelling through the entire country?' she prompted.

'Yes.' His enunciation was precise and slightly emphatic, but not arrogant; more as if he needed to push each utterance up a modest-sized hill before it could be released. 'I began in London ten days ago.'

'Travelling alone?'

'Yes.'

'For the first time?'

'When I was young I have travelled a lot in Europe with my pairends.' (This last word, as he pronounced it, was the first one Isserley had trouble decoding.) 'But I think, in a way, I saw everything through my pairends' eyes. Now, I want to see things through my own eyes.' He looked at her nervously, as if confirming how foolish he'd been to engage with a foreign stranger on this level.

'Do your parents understand this?' enquired Isserley, relaxing as she found her way with him, allowing her foot to sink down a little on the accelerator.

'I hope they will understand,' he said, frowning uneasily.

Tempting though it was to pursue this connective cord to its far-off umbilicus, Isserley sensed she'd found out as much about his 'pairends' as he was prepared to tell her, at least for the moment. Instead, she asked, 'What country are you from?'

'Germany,' he answered. Again he regarded her nervously, as if he expected she might be violent towards him without warning. She tried to reassure him by tuning her conversation to the standards of seriousness he seemed to aim for himself.

'And what, so far, do you find is the thing that makes this country most different from yours?'

He pondered for about ninety seconds. Long dark fields dappled with the pale flanks of cows flowed by on either side of them. A sign glowed in the headlights, depicting a stylized Loch Ness Monster in three fluorescent segments.

'The British people,' the hitcher said at last, 'are not so concerned with what place they have in the world.'

Isserley thought this over, briefly. She couldn't work out whether he was suggesting that the British were admirably self-reliant or deplorably insular. She guessed the ambiguity might be deliberate.

Night settled all around them. Isserley glanced aside, admired the lines of his lips and cheekbones in the reflected head- and tail-lights.

'Have you been staying with anyone you know in this country, or just in hotels?' she asked.

'Mainly in youth hostels,' he replied after a few seconds, as if, in the interests of truth, he'd had to consult a mental record. 'A family in Wales invited me to stay in their house for a couple of days.'

'That was kind of them,' murmured Isserley, observing the lights of the Kessock Bridge winking in the distance. 'Are they expecting you back on the way home?'

'No, I think not,' he said, after having pushed that particular utterance up a very steep hill indeed. 'I believe I . . . offended them in some way. I don't know how. I think my English is not as good as it needs to be in certain situations.'

'It sounds excellent to me.'

He sighed. 'That is the problem perhaps. If it was worse, there would be an expectation of . . .' He laboured silently, then let the sentence roll back down the mountain. 'There would not be the automatic expectation of shared understanding.'

Even in the dimness she could tell that he was fidgeting, clenching his big hands. Perhaps he could hear her beginning to breathe faster, although the change was surely, she felt, quite subtle this time.

'What do you do back in Germany?' she asked.

'I'm a student . . . well, no,' he corrected. 'When I get back to Germany I will be unemployed.'

'You'll live with your parents, perhaps?' she hinted.

'Mm,' he said blankly.

'What were you studying? Before your studies ended?'

There was a pause. A grimy black van with a noisy exhaust overtook Isserley, muffling the sound of her own respiration.

'My studies did not end,' the hitcher announced at last.

'I walked away from them. I am a fugitive, you could say.'

'A fugitive?' echoed Isserley, flashing him an encouraging smile.

He smiled back, sadly.

'Not from justice,' he said, 'but from a medical institute.'

'You mean . . . you're a psychotic?' she suggested breathlessly.

'No. But I almost became a doctor, which in my case would perhaps have been the same thing. My pairends think I am still studying at the institute. They sent me a very far distance and paid a lot of money so that I could study there. It is very important to them that I must become a doctor. Not just a regular doctor, but a specialist. I have been sending them letters telling them that my reezurch is proceeding very smoothly. Instead, I have been drinking beer and reading books about travel. Now I am here, travelling.'

'And what do your parents think of that?'

He sighed and looked down into his lap.

'They don't know anything about it. I have been training them. So many weeks between letters, then so many weeks more, then so many weeks still more. I always say that I am very busy with my reezurch. I will send them my next letter after I am back in Germany.'

'What about your friends?' insisted Isserley. 'Doesn't anybody know you've gone on this adventure?'

'I had some good friends back in Bremen before my studies began. At medical school I have many acquaintances who want to become specialists and drive a Porsche.' He turned towards her in concern, although she was doing her very best to keep calm. 'Are you all right?'

'Yes, fine, thank you,' she panted, and flipped the icpathua toggle.

She knew he would fall against her, turned sideways as he was. She was prepared for it. With her right hand she kept steering straight and true. With her left she shoved his slumping body back into position. The driver of the car behind her would just assume there'd been an attempted kiss and she'd rebuffed it. Kissing in a moving vehicle was universally acknowledged to be dangerous. She'd known that even before she'd learned to drive, had read it in an ancient book about road safety for American teenagers, not long after her arrival in Scotland. It had taken her a long time to fully understand that book, studying it for weeks on end while the television chattered in the background. You could never predict when the television might make something clear that books couldn't – especially when the books came from charity shops.

The hitcher was toppling towards her again. Again she shoved him back. 'Behind the wheel of an automobile is no place for canoodling, necking, or "petting",' the book had said. For someone new to the language, it was a mysterious injunction. But she'd worked it out soon enough, with the help of television. Legally, you were allowed to do whatever you liked in a car, including have sex – as long as the vehicle wasn't moving at the time.

Isserley put her left-hand blinker on as she approached a turn-off. *Bumf*, said the hitcher's head against the passenger window.

It was past six o'clock when she got back to the farm. Ensel and a couple of the other men helped her remove the hitcher from the car.

'Best one yet,' Ensel complimented her.

She nodded wearily. He always said that.

As they were loading the vodsel's limp body onto the pallet, she ducked back into her car and drove off into the unlit dark, aching and ready for bed.

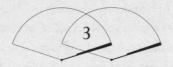

3

ISSERLEY WAS WOKEN next morning by an unusual thing: sunshine.

Normally, she would sleep only a few hours during the night, and then discover herself lying wide-eyed in the claustrophobic dark, her contorted back muscles keeping her hostage in her bed with the threat of needle-sharp pains.

Now she lay blinking in the golden glow of a sun which must have risen quite a while ago. Her attic bedroom, tucked under the steepled roof of the Victorian cottage, had walls which were vertical only half-way up to the ceiling, sloping sharply the rest of the way in line with the roof. From where Isserley lay, her bedroom looked like a hexagonal cubby, lit up like a cell in an irradiated honeycomb. Through one open window, she could see cloudless blue sky; through the other, the complex architecture of oak branches laden with fresh snow. The air was still; the spiderless cobwebs hanging loose from the blistered wooden window-frames hardly stirred.

Only after a minute or two could she detect the almost subsonic hum of the farm's activity.

She stretched, grunting in discomfort, and threw the bedclothes aside with her legs. The angle of the sunlight was such that her bed was in line for the warmest rays, so she lay exposed for a while, limbs spread in an X-shape, basking her naked skin.

The walls of her bedroom were bare, too. The floor was uncarpeted, an unvarnished lamina of ancient timber boards which would not have passed a spirit-level test. Just under one of the windows, a patch of frost glittered on the floor. Out of curiosity, Isserley reached down to the glass of water next to her bed and lifted it up to the light. The water in it was still liquid – just.

Isserley drank it, even though it crackled slightly in the pouring. After a whole night of lying still and letting nature take its course, her body had attained a simmering circulation that would persist until she'd exercised herself into diurnal metabolism.

In the meantime, she was as warm as a snow goose.

Drinking the water reminded her she had eaten nothing since yesterday's breakfast. She really must fuel up properly today before going out on the road. *If* she went out on the road, that is.

After all, who said she had to go out every day of her life? She wasn't a slave.

The cheap plastic alarm clock on the mantelpiece said it was 9:03. There was no other mechanical apparatus in the room except for the scuffed and grubby portable television wedged in the hearth. Its power cord was plugged into a long extension cable which snaked along the skirting-boards and out the door. Downstairs, somewhere, there was an electrical connection.

Isserley heaved herself out of bed and tested out what it felt like to stand up. It wasn't too bad. She had grown lax about her exercises, and that made her more stiff and sore than she need be. She could definitely do better.

She walked over to the fireplace and switched on the television. She didn't need her glasses to watch it. In fact, she didn't need her glasses at all; the lenses were bits of thick window-pane, pretending to be optical. They gave her nothing but headaches and eyestrain, but she needed them for her job.

On the television, a vodsel chef was instructing an inept female how to fry slivers of kidney. The female giggled in embarrassment as the smoke began to rise. On another channel, multi-coloured furry creatures unlike any Isserley ever saw in real life cavorted and sang songs about the letters of the alphabet. On another channel, a shivering food blender was being demonstrated by hands whose nails were painted peach. On another channel, an animated pig and an animated chicken were flying through space in a rocket-powered jalopy. Clearly, Isserley had missed the news.

She switched off the television, straightened up and took up her position in the centre of the room, to do her back exercises. Doing them properly took time and effort, but she'd been lazy lately, and her body was punishing her for it. She *must* get back into shape. Pain such as she'd suffered the last few days was simply not necessary. Allowing herself to get unfit proved no point, unless, for some perverse reason, she actually meant to make herself miserable. To make herself regret what she had done.

She didn't regret what she had done. No.

So, she arched her spine, swivelled her arms, stood on each leg in turn, then on tiptoe, with her arms upstretched and trembling. She held this stance for as long as she possibly could. The tips of her fingers brushed the dangling dead light bulb. Even extended to her full length like this, in a child-sized bedroom, she was well short of touching the ceiling.

Fifteen minutes later, perspiring, shivering a little, she padded over to the wardrobe and selected her clothes for the day, the same clothes as yesterday. The choice, in any case, was from among six identical low-cut tops in different colours, and two pairs of flared trousers, both green velvet. She possessed only one pair of shoes, a custom-made pair which she'd had to return to the shoemaker eight times before she could walk in them. She did not wear underwear, or a bra. Her breasts stayed up by themselves. One less problem to worry about, or two.

Isserley walked out of the back door of her cottage and sniffed the air. The sea breeze was especially spicy today; she would definitely go to the firth as soon as she'd had breakfast.

And afterwards, she must remember to wash and change her clothes, in case she came across another clever guesser like the vodsel with the mollusc in his pocket.

The fields all around her house were shrouded in snow, with patches of dark earth poking through here and there as if the world were a rich fruit cake under cream. In the western field, tiny golden sheep stood marooned in the whiteness, shoving their faces into the snow in search of buried sweet-ness. In the northern field, a giant mound of turnips on a raft of hay shone like frosted cherries in the sun. To the south, behind the farm steadings and silos, loomed the dense

Christmas firs of Carboll Forest. To the east, beyond the farmhouses, churned the North Sea.

There were no farm vehicles anywhere to be seen, and no workers.

The fields were all rented out to various local landowners, who would bring along what was needed at ploughing time, harvesting time, lambing time and so on. In between times, the land lay silent and untouched, and the farm buildings rotted, rusted and grew moss.

In Harry Baillie's time, several of the steadings had housed cattle through the winters, but that was in the days when there was money in it. The only cattle now were a few of Mackenzie's bullocks in the field near Rabbit Hill. On the cliffs at the sea-bound rim of Ablach, a hundred or so black-faced sheep grazed their cheap and salty forage. They were lucky there was a small stream flowing out to sea, as the old cast-iron water troughs were overflowing with the dark spinach of algae, or rusted nutmeg-brown.

No, Ablach's current owner certainly wasn't the pillar of the community Harry Baillie had been. He was some sort of Scandinavian, the natives thought, and a mad hermit besides. Isserley knew he had this reputation because, despite her policy of never giving lifts to locals, she'd had hitchers twenty miles up the A9 suddenly start talking about Ablach Farm. The odds against such a thing coming up in conversation with a stranger, even allowing for the sparse population of the Highlands, must be phenomenal, especially since Isserley was careful always to lie about where she lived.

But it must be a smaller world than she thought, because once or twice a year, a talkative hitcher would get onto the subject of incomers and how they were ruining Scotland's traditional existence, and, sure enough, Ablach would be mentioned. Isserley would play dumb while she heard the story of how a mad Scandinavian had gobbled up Baillie's farm and then, instead of turning it into one of these European money-spinning ventures, had just let it fall into decay, renting out the fields to the same farmers he'd outbid.

'It just goes to show,' one hitcher had told her. 'Foreigners' minds don't work the same as ours. No offence.'

'No offence taken,' she'd said, trying to decide if she should dispatch this vodsel back to the place he claimed to know so much about.

'So where are *you* from, then?' he'd asked her.

She couldn't remember now what she'd replied. Depending on how well-travelled the hitcher seemed to be, she had a number of places she might claim to be from. The former Soviet Union, Australia, Bosnia . . . even Scandinavia, unless the hitcher was saying nasty things about the mad bastard who'd bought Ablach Farm.

Over the years, though, it was Isserley's impression that the man she knew as Esswis was slowly winning the grudging respect of the community. To the other farmers he was known as *Mr* Esswis, and it was accepted that he would conduct all his affairs from inside 'the Big House', a cottage twice the size of Isserley's in the centre of the farm. Unlike her cottage, it had electric power in all its rooms, heating, furniture, carpets, curtains, appliances, bric-a-brac. Isserley didn't know what Esswis did with these things, but they probably impressed visitors – few though these were.

Isserley didn't actually know Esswis very well at all, despite the fact that he was the only person in the world who'd been through what *she* had been through. In theory, then, they had lots to talk about, but in practice they avoided each other.

Shared suffering, she'd found, was no guarantee of intimacy.

The fact that she was a woman and he was a man had nothing to do with it; Esswis rarely socialized with the other men either. He just stayed holed up in his big house, waiting to be useful.

He was, to be honest, virtually a prisoner in there. It was absolutely crucial that he be available twenty-four hours a day in the event of any emergency which might collide Ablach Farm with the outside world. Last year, for example, a carelessly driven pesticide sprayer had killed a stray sheep, not with pesticide or even under the wheels, but in a freak accident, braining the animal with the tip of one of its winglike booms. Mr Esswis had promptly negotiated an arrangement between himself, the owner of the sprayer and the owner of the sheep, nonplussing the other two farmers by accepting full blame for the straying of the animal, as long as unpleasantness and paperwork could be avoided.

That was the sort of thing that earned him his measure of respect in the area, foreign incomer though he was. He would never show his face at a ploughing championship or a ceilidh, everyone knew that now, but maybe it wasn't because he couldn't be bothered; there were sympathetic rumours of arthritis, a wooden leg, cancer. He also understood better than most wealthy incomers that times were tough for local farmers, and regularly asked for straw or surplus produce in lieu of rent. Pillar of the community Harry Baillie may have been, but he was a bugger when it came to contracts. With Esswis, a word muttered over the telephone was as good as his signature. And as for the way he tried to discourage tourists from trespassing, confronting them with barbed wire and threats, well, more strength to his arm. The Highlands were not a public park.

Isserley walked to the main path and, sighing with relief at being rid of her glasses for a while, peered across at Esswis's house. The lights were on in all the rooms. The windows were all shut and opaque with condensation. Esswis could be anywhere in there.

The sensation of fresh snow crunching underfoot was deeply satisfying to Isserley. Just the idea of all that water vapour solidifying by the cloudful and fluttering to earth was miraculous. She couldn't quite believe it, even after all these years. It was a phenomenon of stupendous and unjustifiably useless extravagance. Yet here it lay, soft and powdery, edibly pure. Isserley scooped a handful off the ground and ate some. It was delicious.

She walked to the largest of the steadings, the one that was in the best, or least shabby, condition. A dilapidated tile roof had been replaced by sheet metal. Whenever stones crumbled out of the walls, the cavities were promptly filled in with cement. The total effect was less like a house and more like a giant box, but these aesthetic sacrifices were necessary. This building must be protected from the elements and from the prying eyes of outsiders. It was the entrance to a much larger secret just below the ground.

Isserley stood in front of the aluminium door and pressed the buzzer underneath the metal signs saying DANGEROUS CHEMICALS and AUTHORIZED PERSONNEL ONLY. Yet another warning sign hung on the door itself, a stylized picture of a skull and two crossed bones.

The intercom crackled abstractly, and she leaned close to it, her lips almost brushing the grille.

'Isserley,' she whispered.

The door rolled open and she stepped inside.

*   *   *

Impatient to get out to the firth, Isserley didn't linger over breakfast. She was back at her cottage within twenty minutes, comfortably full of stodge and carrying a small plastic doggie bag of the German hitcher's personal effects.

The men down below had seemed pleased to see her, and had expressed concern about her having missed dinner the previous evening.

'It was a real treat,' Ensel told her, in a thick provincial dialect of her own language. 'Shanks of voddissin in serslida sauce. With fresh wild berries for dessert.'

'Well, never mind,' Isserley had said, spreading slice after slice of bread with mussanta paste. She never knew what to say to these men, these labourers and process workers she would certainly never even have met in the course of ordinary life back home. Of course it didn't help that they looked so different from her, and stared at her breasts and her chiselled face whenever they thought she couldn't see.

They were busy today, and had left her to her meal. But not before passing on an important bit of news: Amlis Vess was coming. Amlis Vess! Coming to Ablach Farm! Tomorrow! He'd sent a message, he was already on his way, they were not to go to any special bother, he wanted to see everything just as it was. Who would have thought it?

Isserley had murmured something noncommittal, and the men hurried off to make more preparations for the big event. Excitement was rare in their lives now that Ablach Farm was well established and they had time on their hands. No doubt this visit from the boss's son was an almighty thrill compared to spending yet another afternoon gambling with bits of straw or whatever men of their sort did. Left alone in the dining hall, Isserley had served herself a bowl of gushu, but it tasted strangely sour. It was then that she'd noticed that the whole subterranean complex, as well as smelling faintly of male sweat and crap food as always, smelled pungently of cleaning agents and paint. It made her even more determined to get back up into the fresh air as soon as possible.

The walk back to the cottage through the snow cleared her sinuses and helped the food settle. Clasping the doggie bag between her legs, she unlocked the front door of her house and let herself in to the living room, which was vacant and bare apart from some large piles of twigs and branches scattered over the floor.

She gathered an armful of the best ones and carried them out to the back yard, letting them fall along with the doggie bag onto the snowy earth. Those twigs that were the correct shape she arranged into a little pyre, the rest she kept in reserve.

Next she unlocked and swung open the rusty doors of the small cast-iron shed adjacent to her cottage. She laid the palms of her hands on the bonnet of her car, feeling how icy-cold it was; she hoped it would start when the time came. For the moment, however, this wasn't her concern. She opened the boot and fetched out the German hitcher's rucksack. It, too, was affected by the overnight freeze: not frosty exactly, but damp and chilled, as if from a refrigerator.

Isserley carried the rucksack out into the yard, having first checked that there was no-one around. There wasn't a soul. She lit the bottom twigs of the pyre. The wood was bone-dry, having been gathered months ago and kept indoors ever since: it crackled into flame immediately.

When upended, the backpack proved to be an unexpected cornucopia. More had been fitted into it than seemed concordant with the laws of physics. The most extraordinary variety of things, too, all tucked away in dozens of plastic boxes and bottles and pouches and slits and zip pockets, arranged and interleaved with great ingenuity. Isserley threw them, one by one, onto the fire. Multicoloured food containers squirmed and collapsed in a bubbling petroleum stink. T-shirts and underpants, thrown unfolded onto the flames, yawned black holes to let smoke exhale. Socks sizzled. A small cardboard box of prescription medicine exploded with a pop. A transparent cylindrical canister containing a little plastic figurine wearing Scottish national costume went through several stages, the last of which was the collapse of the naked pink doll, its limbs fusing, face-first into the flames.

The dearth of highly flammable items was putting a strain on the fire and, once a pair of trousers was added, it threatened to die. Isserley selected some dry twigs and laid them on in strategic places. The foldout maps of England, Wales and Scotland were useful too; loosely screwed up to facilitate aeration, they burned excitably.

Hidden near the bottom of the rucksack was a pink toiletries bag which contained not toiletries but a passport. Isserley hesitated over this item, wondering whether she could use a passport herself: she'd never seen one before, at least not in the flesh, so to speak. She flipped through its pages, examining it curiously.

The hitcher's picture was in there, as well as his name, age, date of birth and so on. These things meant nothing to Isserley, but she was intrigued by how, in the photograph, he looked chubbier and pinker than he had been in reality, and yet also queerly less substantial. His expression was one of crestfallen stoicism. Strange how a specimen like him, well cared for, healthy, free to roam the world, and blessed with a perfection of form which would surely have allowed him to breed with a greater selection of females than average, could still be so miserable. By contrast, other males, scarred by neglect, riddled with diseases, spurned by their kind, were occasionally known to radiate a contentment that seemed to arise from something more enigmatic than mere stupidity.

This inability of some of the most superbly fit and well-adapted vodsels to be happy while they were alive was, for Isserley, one of the great mysteries she encountered in her job, and one which her years of experience had only made more puzzling. There was no point discussing this with Esswis, much less with the other men on the farm. Well-intentioned though they were, she'd long ago discovered they lacked a spiritual side.

Isserley looked up and noticed she'd let the fire burn low, and rummaged around for something highly combustible. The hitcher's plastic pouch of signs was the first thing to hand, and she shook the sheaf of papers out onto the snow. She tossed them on the fire one by one: THURSO, GLASGOW, CARLISLE and half a dozen others, right down to SCHOTTLAND. They burned brightly enough, but were consumed in moments. The pyre was rapidly congealing into a smouldering porridge of ash and molten plastic unlikely to make much impact on the biggest item left, the rucksack itself.

Isserley hurried back to the shed and fetched out a can of petrol. She sloshed the gleaming fuel liberally all over the backpack and tossed it gingerly onto the flickering mound. The blaze revived with an intoxicating vomp.

Isserley had one last look at the passport. She decided that if she was going to risk holding onto documents, a driver's licence might come in handier. In any case, she noticed belatedly that the gender of the passport's owner was specified and that his height was officially certified to be

1 metre 90 centimetres. Isserley smiled and threw the little
red book onto the fire.

From the doggie bag, the wallet went onto the pyre too,
once she had removed the paper money. Some of the money
was not legal tender in the United Kingdom; this she
discarded. The sterling she could add to her supply for buying
petrol. It was just as well she never bought anything else, for
her hands stank of petrol now and she'd passed this smell onto
the banknotes.

A visit to the seashore and a shower afterwards seemed like
a better idea than ever. Then she would go out for a drive. *If*
she felt like it. Hitchers would be thin on the ground anyway,
on a snowy day. Amlis Vess would just have to understand
that.

Isserley walked along the pebbled shore of the Moray Firth,
drinking in the beauty of the great uncovered world.

To her right, trillions of litres of water surged between
Ablach's beach and an invisible Norway beyond the horizon.
To her left, steep gorse-encrusted hills led up to the farm.
Stretching endlessly behind and ahead of her was the penin-
sula's edge, whose marshy pasture, used for grazing sheep,
ended abruptly at the brink of the tide in a narrow verge of
rock, curdled and sculpted by prehistoric fire and ice. It was
along this verge that Isserley most loved to walk.

The variety of shapes, colours and textures under her feet
was, she believed, literally infinite. It must be. Each shell,
each pebble, each stone had been made what it was by aeons
of submarine or subglacial massage. The indiscriminate,
eternal devotion of nature to its numberless particles had
an emotional importance for Isserley; it put the unfairness of
human life into perspective.

Cast ashore, perhaps only briefly before being fetched back for another million years of polishing and re-shaping, the stones lay so serene beneath her naked feet. She would have liked to collect each of them for an infinitely complex display, a rockery for which she was personally responsible but which was so vast that she could never walk from one end of it to the other. In a sense, the Ablach shore was already such a rockery, except that she'd had no hand in preparing it, and she wished keenly to play some part in the design.

She picked up a pebble now, a smooth bell with a silky hole right through it. Its colours were stripes of orange, silver and grey. Another stone at her feet was spherical, pure black. She dropped the bell-shaped one and picked up the black globe instead. Even as she was lifting it, a bright pink and white crystal egg caught her eye. The challenge was exquisitely hopeless.

She dropped the black globe and straightened up, peering out across the ocean, across the dematerializing furrows of the waves. Then she looked the other way, to find the boulder on top of which she'd left her shoes. They were still there, the laces trembling in the breeze.

She was taking a risk in baring her feet to the world, but in the unlikely event that anyone else were to stray onto the beach, she'd see them coming for hundreds of metres or more. By the time they were close enough to see her feet, she could easily retrieve her shoes, or even wade into the water if need be. The relief she felt in allowing her long toes to splay over the rocky shore, curling round the stones, was inexpressible. Whose business but her own, anyway, were the risks she took? She was doing a job no-one else could do, and coming up with the goods year after year. Amlis Vess, if he had the audacity to find fault with her, would do well to remember that.

She walked on, veering nearer to the lapping of the tide. The shallow pools between the larger rocks were crammed with what she now knew were called whelks, though they appeared to be the 'piddly wee ones' the market did not require. She took one out of the glacial brine and lifted it up to her mouth, venturing the tip of her tongue into its glaireous hole. Its flavour was acrid; an acquired taste no doubt.

She put the whelk back into its pool, gently so as not to make a noise. She had a visitor of sorts.

A sheep had strayed onto the pebbled shore not far from her, and was sniffing boulders as large as itself, licking them experimentally. Isserley was intrigued: she hadn't thought sheep could walk on such a surface, had thought their hooves wouldn't permit it. But here it was, stepping across the treacherous morass of stones and shells with apparent ease.

Isserley approached stealthily, balancing gingerly on the fingers of her feet. She barely breathed, for fear of startling her fellow-traveller.

It was so hard to believe the creature couldn't speak. It looked so much as if it should be able to. Despite its bizarre features, there was something deceptively human about it, which tempted her, not for the first time, to reach across the species divide and communicate.

'Hello,' she said.

'Ahl,' she said.

'Wiin,' she said.

These three greetings, which had no effect on the sheep except to make it scramble away, exhausted all the languages Isserley knew.

She wasn't exactly a linguist, admittedly.

But then no linguist would ever have applied for her job, *that* was for sure. Only desperate people with no prospects except being dumped in the New Estates would have considered it.

And even then, only if they were out of their minds.

She had been totally crazy, looking back on it. Deliriously insane. But it had all turned out for the best, after all. The best decision she'd ever made. A very small personal sacrifice, really, if it avoided a lifetime buried in the Estates – a brutishly short lifetime, by all accounts.

In fact, whenever she found herself grieving over what had been done to her once-beautiful body in order for her to be sent here, she reminded herself what people who'd lived in the New Estates for any length of time looked like. Decay and disfigurement were obviously par for the course down there. Maybe it was the overcrowding, or the bad food or the bad air or the lack of medical care, or just the inevitable result of living underground. But there was an unmistakable ugliness about Estate trash, an almost subhuman taint.

When *she*'d got the news that she was going to be sent there, Isserley had made a fierce and solemn vow to stay healthy and beautiful against the odds. Refusing point-blank to be changed physically would be her revenge on the powers that be, her recoiling kick of defiance. But would she have had a hope, really? No doubt *everybody* vowed at first that *they* wouldn't allow themselves to be transformed into a beast, with hunched back, scarred flesh, crumbling teeth, missing fingers, cropped hair. But that's how they all ended up, didn't they? Would *she* have been any different, if she'd gone there rather than here?

Of course not. Of course not. And now, the way things had turned out, she didn't look any worse now than the worst Estate trash, did she? . . . or not *much* worse, anyway. And look what she'd got in exchange!

She looked at the whole wide world, from her rocky vantage point on the shore of Ablach Farm. It was unbelievably marvellous. She felt like running about in it forever — except that she couldn't run anymore.

Not that she'd have been doing any running in the Estates. She'd have been shambling around spiritlessly, along with all the other losers and low-lifes, in underground corridors of bauxite and compacted ash. She'd have been working her guts out in a moisture filtration plant or an oxygen factory, toiling in filth like a maggot among other maggots.

Instead, here she was, free to wander in an unbounded wilderness swirling with awesome surpluses of air and water.

And all she had to do in return, when it came right down to essentials, was walk on two legs.

Of course that wasn't all she'd had to do.

To stop herself thinking about the more embittering specifics of her sacrifice, Isserley abruptly decided to get back to work. There was only so much freedom she could wallow in before she began to grow uneasy. Work was the cure.

She'd already thrown the German hitcher's keys and wristwatch into the sea, where they would be re-shaped and re-textured along with all the other jetsam of the millennia. The empty plastic bag she had tucked into the waistband of her trousers, to avoid littering the beach. It was littered enough already with ugly plastic flotsam from passing ships and oil rigs; one day she would light a giant bonfire on the shore and burn all the rubbish on it. She kept forgetting to bring the equipment, that's all.

Now she retrieved her shoes and pulled them on, with some difficulty, over her icy and somewhat swollen feet.

She'd overdone the exposure to the cold, perhaps. A few hours in her little overheated car would put her to rights.

She strode over the shore towards the grassy fringe of pasture. Her sheep had rejoined its flock, far away now on the upper reaches of the hill. Trying to discern which sheep was the one she'd spoken to, Isserley stumbled and almost fell, made clumsy by the shoes; she must keep her eyes on where she was stepping. Intricate tangles of bleached and sundried seaweed lay scattered at the very edge of the living vegetation, resembling the skeletons, or parts of skeletons, of non-existent creatures. In amongst these deceptive simulacra, authentic husks of cannibalized seagulls fluttered in the wind. Sometimes, but not today, there was a dead seal, its back flippers tangled in an offcut of fishing net, its body hollowed out by other citizens of the sea.

Isserley walked along the path the generations of sheep-flocks had made, up the tiers of the hill. In her mind, she was already behind the wheel.

When she got back to the cottage, the bonfire had died. There was a halo melted around it, a dark circle of ash and scorched grass in the snow. On the pyre itself, some of the rucksack still lay unconsumed. She pulled the sooty metal support struts out of the ashes and cast them aside, for disposal later. Tomorrow, perhaps, if she was ready for the sea again by then.

She let herself into the house and walked straight to the bathroom.

It, like all the rooms in the house, had a bare and uninhabited appearance, tainted by mildew and the chaff of insects. Dim light leaked in through a tiny window of filthy frosted glass. A jagged shard of mirror slumped crookedly in the alcove behind the sink, reflecting nothing but peeling paintwork. The bathtub was clean but a little rusty, as was the sink. The yawning interior of the lidless toilet bowl, by contrast, was the colour and texture of bark; it had not been used for at least as long as Isserley had lived here.

Pausing only to remove her shoes, Isserley stepped into the ochre-streaked bathtub. Screwed into the wall above her head, there was a shower nozzle which she instructed by means of a Bakelite dial to spurt pressurized water down over her. Even as the torrent sputtered out, she was taking off her clothes and letting them fall into the tub around her feet.

On the rust-mottled ledge of the bath, three different bottles of shampoo stood ready. Together, they had cost exactly five pounds at the Arabella Service Station. Isserley picked up her favourite and squirted the pale green syrup over her hair. Then she squirted more of the stuff over her naked body and, lavishly, down into the sodden heap of clothing at her feet. With one foot she pushed the squelching pile over the plughole to allow the water level in the tub to rise.

She washed her hair carefully, rinsing it over and over. Her hair had always been her best feature, back home. A member of the Elite had once told her that with hair like hers it was out of the question she could possibly be destined for the New Estates: a cheap and fatuous compliment, in retrospect, but thrillingly encouraging at the time. She'd felt as if her passage into a bright future was a matter of physical inevitability, a lush and glossy birthright everyone could see at a glance, and a lucky few could stroke admiringly.

So little of it was left now that she couldn't bear to cherish it anymore. Most of it would never grow back again, the rest was just a nuisance.

She stroked the skin of her shoulders and arms, checking if

she needed to shave again just yet. Her palms, slippery with lather, detected the soft stubble, but she decided she could get away with leaving it for one more day. Lots of females had a bit of hair on them, she'd discovered. Real life wasn't at all like the smooth images celebrated by magazines and television. Anyway, nobody would see it.

She lathered up her breasts and rinsed them, with distaste. The only good thing about them was that they prevented her seeing what had been done to her down below.

Redirecting the shower nozzle, she turned her attention to the clothes, which now swirled in a shallow pool of sudsy grey water. She trampled them, rinsed them, trampled them some more, then wrung them out in her powerful claws. They would dry out, eventually, in a square of sunlight shining through her bedroom window, or, if that failed, on the back seat of her car.

It was after midday when Isserley finally drove out of the farm. The sun which had been so golden in the morning was barely visible now; the sky had turned slate-grey and hung swollen with undischarged snow. The likelihood of finding any hitch-hikers on the roads, let alone suitable ones, was slim. Yet she was in the mood to do some work, or at least get away from all the fuss she knew was still going on below ground.

On her way past the main steading, she noticed a most unusual sight: Esswis perched on a large wooden stepladder, a tin in one hand and a brush in the other, painting the stone walls white.

Isserley slowed the car to a stop near the foot of the ladder and looked up at Esswis. She was already wearing her glasses and so he wasn't all that clear, distorted by the glare of the sun. It occurred to her to take her glasses off for a moment, but that seemed impolite, given that Esswis was wearing his.

'Ahl,' she said, squinting up, not knowing if she'd done the right thing in stopping.

'Ahl,' he replied, as taciturn as the farmer he was supposed to be. Perhaps he was wary of their native language being spoken out in the open, even though there was no-one else around to hear it. Paint dribbled off the end of the brush he was holding, but, apart from frowning, he did nothing about it, as if Isserley's greeting were some sort of mishap which must be stoically endured. He was wearing overalls and a cap, and paint-spattered green wellingtons whose secret interiors had taken almost as long to design as Isserley's shoes.

All things considered, he'd got off more lightly than she had, Isserley felt. He had no breasts, for a start, and more hair on his face.

She waved at the task he was busy with. Only a fraction of the building had been whitened.

'Is this in honour of Amlis Vess?' she asked superfluously.

Esswis grunted.

'Quite a fuss,' ventured Isserley. 'Not your idea, surely?'

Esswis scowled and looked down at her in disgust.

'Fuck Amlis Vess,' he pronounced, very distinctly, in English, and then turned to continue painting.

Isserley wound up her window and drove on. One by one, feathery snowflakes started spiralling down from the sky.

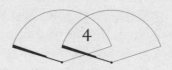

4

IT WAS AS SHE was crossing a concrete tightrope, high up in the air, that Isserley admitted to herself that she absolutely did not want to meet Amlis Vess.

She was driving towards the midpoint of the Kessock Bridge, gripping the steering wheel in anticipation of fierce side-winds trying to sweep her little red car into space. She was acutely conscious of the weight of the cast-iron under-carriage beneath her, the purchase of the tyres on the bitumen – paradoxical reminders of solidity. The car might have been protesting how heavy and immovable it was, in its fear of being moved.

You-ou-ou-ou-ou-ou-ou! jeered the atmosphere.

At intervals along the bridge were trembling metal signs depicting a stylized net inflated by the thrust of a gale. This, like all traffic symbols, had been a meaningless hieroglyphic to Isserley when she'd first studied it, long ago. Now it appealed directly to her second nature, and made her seize hold of the wheel as if it were an animal desperate to break free. Her hands were locked tight; she imagined she could see a heartbeat pulsing between the knuckles.

And yet, when she muttered under her breath that she would not let herself be pushed off course, no, not by anything, it wasn't the side-winds she was thinking of, but Amlis Vess. He was blowing in from somewhere much more dangerous than the North Sea, and she could not predict the effect he'd have. Whatever it turned out to be, she certainly wouldn't be able to negate it just by keeping a tight grip on her car's steering wheel.

She was past the mid-point now, minutes away from the Inverness end. Burring slowly forwards in the outer lane, she flinched every time a faster vehicle roared past her; the wind pressure would drop away suddenly, then swing back with a vengeance. To her left, the air was swirling with seagulls, a chaos of white birds endlessly falling towards the water, then hovering just above the firth, sinking gradually, as if caught in sediment. Isserley returned her attention to the distant out-skirts of Inverness, and tried to force herself to tread harder on the accelerator. Judging by her speedometer, she wasn't succeeding. *You-ou-ou-ou-ou-ou!* cried the wind all the rest of the way.

Cruising safely off the bridge at the far end, she hugged the slow lane, tried her best to breathe deeply and unclench her hands. The pressure had died down almost at once; she could drive normally, function normally. She was on terra firma now, in control, blending in perfectly, and doing a job only she could do. Nothing Amlis Vess thought or said could change that: nothing. She was indispensable.

The word troubled her, though. *Indispensable*. It was a

word people tended to resort to when dispensability was in
the air.

She tried to imagine herself being dispensed with; tried to
imagine it honestly and unflinchingly. Perhaps some other
person would be prepared to make the same sacrifices she and
Esswis had made, and take her place. She and Esswis had been
desperate, in their different ways; might not other people be
equally desperate? It was hard to imagine. No-one could be as
desperate as she had been. And then, anyone new to the job
would be inexperienced, untested. With mind-boggling
amounts of money at stake, would Vess Incorporated take
such a risk?

Probably not. But it was difficult for Isserley to draw much
comfort from this, because the thought of being genuinely
indispensable was troubling too.

It meant that Vess Incorporated would never let her go.

It meant that she would have to do this job forever. It
meant that a day would never come when she could enjoy the
world without worrying about the creatures crawling on its
surface.

All of which, Isserley reminded herself irritably, should
have nothing whatsoever to do with Amlis Vess. How could
it? Whatever the reason for young Amlis's visit, it must be a
purely personal one, unconnected to Vess Incorporated. Just
hearing the name Amlis Vess was no reason to get all excited.

OK, granted, Amlis was the big man's son, but there was
no sign of him inheriting the big man's empire. Amlis didn't
even have a *job* at Vess Incorporated – he'd never had a job of
any kind – and he couldn't possibly have any power to make
decisions on the Corporation's behalf. In fact, to the best of
Isserley's knowledge, Amlis actually felt disdain for the world
of business and was a big failure in his father's eyes. He was

trouble, but not for Isserley. There was nothing to fear from him dropping in, however inexplicably, on Ablach Farm.

So why did she want to avoid him so badly?

She had nothing against the boy himself (or the man? – how old would he be by now?); he hadn't asked to be the sole heir of the world's biggest corporation. He'd done nothing to offend her personally, and in the past she'd followed his exploits with amusement. He was always in the news, for the usual rich-young-pretender reasons. One time, he shaved all his hair off, as an initiation rite into a bizarre religious sect which he joined in a blitz of publicity and left, weeks later, with no comment to the press. Another time, he and his father were reported to be bitterly estranged over Amlis's support of extremists in the Middle East. Another time, he made a public statement that icpathua, when used in small enough doses, was a harmless euphoric that should not be against the law. Countless times, some girl or other made a fuss, claiming to be pregnant with his baby.

All in all, he was just another typical rich kid with a colossal fortune hanging over his head.

Isserley's second nature, alert while she'd been busy brooding, fetched her back into the driver's seat to notice something important: a hitch-hiker standing in the distance, opposite the first of the many garish roadside diners between Inverness and the South. She listened to her own breathing, assessing whether she'd calmed down enough to take the challenge on. She felt she had.

At closer quarters, though, the figure at the roadside proved to be a female, harried-looking, grey-haired, shabbily dressed. Isserley drove straight past, ignoring the appeal to shared gender in the eyes. A single instant was enough to communicate injury and dejection, then the figure was a dwindling fleck in the rear-view mirror.

Isserley was all geared up now, grateful to have had her mind on something other than Amlis Vess. Fortuitously, another hitcher was standing only a couple of miles further on. This one was a male, and fairly impressive on first sight, but unfortunately positioned in a spot where only the most foolhardy motorist would consider stopping. Isserley flashed her headlights, hoping to let him know that she might have picked him up had he not made it so dangerous for her to do so. She doubted that a simple flash of lights could communicate this; more likely he would simply assume she was beaming out ill-will, a jab of mockery.

All was not necessarily lost, though – perhaps she would see him again later on the way back, by which time he might have walked to a safer spot. Over the years, Isserley had learned that life often offered a second chance: she had even picked up hitchers who, many hours and miles before, she'd observed climbing gratefully into someone else's car.

So, optimistic, Isserley drove on.

She drove all day, backwards and forwards between Inverness and Dunkeld, over and over. The sun set. The snow, which had retreated during the morning, returned. One of the windscreen wipers developed an annoying squeal. Fuel had to be bought. Through it all, nobody suitable reached out to her.

By six o'clock, she had just about decided why she was dreading meeting Amlis Vess so much.

It had nothing to do with his status really; *she* was an invaluable part of the business, *he* a thorn in its side, so he probably had more to fear from Vess Incorporated than she did. No, the main reason why she was dreading him was simpler than that.

It was because Amlis Vess was from home.

When he set eyes on her, he would see her the way any normal person from home would see her, and he would be shocked, and she would helplessly have to watch him being shocked. She knew from experience what this felt like; would do anything to avoid feeling it again. The men she worked with on the farm had been shocked too, at first, but they were used to her now, more or less; they could go about their business without gawping (though if there was a lull in activities she always felt their eyes on her). No wonder she tended to keep to her cottage – and why Esswis did too, she guessed. Being a freak was so wearying.

Amlis Vess, never having seen her before, would recoil. He'd be expecting to see a human being, and he would see a hideous animal instead. It was that moment of . . . of the sickening opposite of recognition that she just couldn't cope with.

She decided to return to the farm immediately, lock herself in her cottage, and wait until Amlis Vess had come and gone.

In the mountainous desolation of Aviemore she caught a hitcher in her headlights. A little gargoyle gesturing in a flare of illumination, registering almost as an after-image on the retina; a little gargoyle foolishly attached to a spot where cars would be whizzing by him at maximum speed. Isserley's maximum speed being about fifty, however, she had time to notice him. He seemed awfully keen to be picked up.

Passing him, Isserley thought seriously about whether she wanted a hitcher just now. She waited for clues from the universe.

The snow had died down again, the windscreen wipers lay still, the motor was purring nicely, she was perhaps in slight danger of dozing off. Isserley slowed, cruised to a stop in a bus bay, and let the car idle, headlights dimmed. The Monadhliath Mountains loomed on one side of her, the Cairngorms on the other. She was alone with them. She closed her eyes, slid her fingertips under the rims of her glasses and rubbed her big satiny eyelids. A massive tanker roared into view, flooding the cabin of Isserley's car with light. She waited until it had gone, then revved her engine and flicked on the indicator.

On the second approach, passing by on the other side of the road, she noted that the hitcher was small and barrel-chested, with lots of exposed flesh so darkly tanned it resisted being bleached by the full beam of headlights. This time she observed that he was standing not far from a car which was parked, or possibly stuck, in a ditch off the road. It was a shabby blue Nissan estate, scratched and battered all over but not in such a conspicuously fresh way as to suggest an accident. Both hitcher and car seemed upright and in one piece, although the one was making exaggerated gestures to draw attention to the other.

Isserley drove on for a couple of miles, reluctant to involve herself in anything that might already be of interest to the police or a vehicle rescue service. Eventually, however, she reasoned that if a stranded motorist had any expectation of being found by such authorities, he surely wouldn't be trying to hitch. She turned around then, and drove back.

The final approach revealed the hitcher to be an odd creature, even by Scottish standards. Though not much taller than Isserley, with a wizened, wispy-haired little head and spindly legs, he had improbably massive arms, shoulders and torso, as if these had been transplanted onto him from a much beefier creature. He was wearing a frayed and faded flannel-ette shirt, sleeves rolled up, and seemed impervious to the cold, thumbing the bitter air with almost clownish enthu-siasm, making elaborate gestures towards his decrepit Nissan. Isserley wondered momentarily whether she had seen him somewhere before, then realized she was confusing him with certain cartoon characters on early-morning television. His kind weren't the title characters, though; they were the ones who got squashed flat by giant mallets or burnt to a crisp by exploding cigars.

She decided to stop for him. He had more muscle mass packed in between his neck and hips, after all, than many vodsels twice his size had on their entire bodies.

Seeing her slow down and veer towards him, he nodded idiotically and held two stiff-thumbed fists aloft in an expres-sion of triumph, as if awarding her two points for her decision. Above the crunch of gravel, Isserley thought she could hear a throaty whoop.

She parked as close as she could to the stranger's own car without snaring her wheels in the ditch, and trusted that her flashing rear lights would warn any motorists coming up behind her. This really was a very awkward spot, and she was curious to find out if the hitcher would acknowledge it. That would already tell her something worth knowing about him.

She wound down the passenger window as soon as she'd pulled on the handbrake, and the hitcher immediately poked his tiny head into the car. He was smiling broadly, a mouthful of crooked brown-edged teeth inside two leathery crescents of lip. His brown face was bristly, wrinkled and scarred, with a mottled snout of a nose and two spectacularly bloodshot chimpanzee eyes.

'She's gonna skelp my bot, I tell ya,' he leered, breathing alcohol into the car.

'I beg your pardon?'

'My girlfriend. She's gonna skelp my bot,' he repeated, his grin deepening to a grimace. 'I shoulda been at her place by tea-time. That's *always* when I'm supposed to be there. And it *never* happens, can you believe it, eh?' He slumped a little in the window-frame and his eyes closed slowly, as if the power that was keeping his eyelids up had abruptly run out. With effort he roused himself, and continued, 'Every week this same thing.'

'What same thing?' asked Isserley, trying not to pull a face at the beer fumes.

He winked, laboriously. 'She's got a temper.' Eyes falling shut again, he sniggered, like a cartoon tomcat in the shadow of a falling bomb.

Isserley found him actually quite good-looking compared to other vodsels, but his mannerisms were distinctly odd and made her wonder if he was mentally defective. Would an imbecile be given a licence to drive? Why was he just hanging in her window-frame, simpering, when both their cars were liable to get annihilated by a passing lorry? Nervously she glanced in her rear-view mirror to confirm no speeding vehicles were coming up behind.

'What happened to your car?' she asked, hoping to shift his attention to the heart of the matter.

'It won't go no more,' he explained dolefully, his eyes crusty slits. 'No more. That's the truth. No use arguin', eh? Eh?'

He grinned fiercely, as if hoping to charm her into dropping some opposing point of view.

'Engine trouble?' prompted Isserley.

'Nah. I ran out of petrol, like,' he said, snorting with embarrassment. 'On account of my girlfriend, y'understand. Every minute counts, with her. But I shoulda put in more petrol, seemin'ly.'

He squinted into Isserley's giant eyes, and she could tell he saw nothing more exotic there than the imagined reproach of a fellow motorist.

'The fuel gauge is a piece a'shite, you see,' he elaborated, stepping back from Isserley's car to display his own. 'Says empty when it's near full. Says full when it's near empty. Can't listen to a word it tells ya. Ya just have to rely on your memory, y'understand?' He yanked the door of his car open, as if intending to give Isserley a guided tour of its frailties. The light went on in the cabin – a pale and flickering light, attesting to the vehicle's dodgy reputation. Beer cans and crisps packets littered the passenger seats.

'I been up since five this morning,' the snout-nosed hitcher declared, banging his car's door shut. 'Worked ten days straight. Four – five hours sleep a night. Wicked. Wicked. No use complainin', though, eh? Eh?'

'Well . . . can I give you a lift, perhaps?' suggested Isserley, waving her thin arm in the empty space over her passenger seat, to capture and hold his attention.

'It's a can of petrol I'm needin',' he said, lurching into the window-frame of Isserley's car again.

'I haven't got any,' said Isserley, 'But get into the car anyway. I'll drive you to a garage, or maybe further. Where were you heading?'

'To my girlfriend's place,' he leered, winching his eyelids up off his eyeballs again. 'She's got a temper. She'll skelp my bot.'

'Yes, but where is that exactly?'

'Edderton,' he said.

'Get in, then,' she urged. Edderton was only five miles out of Tain, thirteen miles or so from Ablach Farm. How could she lose? If she had to give him up, she could soothe her disappointment by retreating instantly to the farm; if she took him, so much the better. Either way she'd be safe in her cottage by the time Amlis Vess arrived, and might even sleep through all the brouhaha – as long as nobody came knocking on her door.

Hitcher safely strapped in, Isserley pulled away from the gutter and accelerated up the A9 towards home. She regretted that this stretch of the road was unlit and that she couldn't legally turn on the cabin light; she would have liked this guy to have the opportunity to examine her properly. She sensed he was dim-witted, and likely just now to be fixated on solving his immediate problems; he might well need extra enticement to talk about himself. The darkness of the road, however, made her too nervous to drive with only her right hand on the steering wheel; he would just have to strain his eyes a bit, that's all, if he wanted to see her breasts. Admittedly, his eyes looked pretty strained already. She faced front, drove carefully, and left him to it.

She would throw him out on his arse, for sure, the hitcher was thinking, but maybe she'd let him sleep a bitty first.

Ha! No chance! She'd make him look at an oven dish full of dried-out supper, and say it couldn't be et now even though he'd be desperate to get stuck into it, but she wouldn't let him of course. That's what he drove like a maniac up the A9 for, every week, week after week. His girl. His Catriona. He could lift her up and toss her through the window like a vase if he wanted to, and *she* was the one who pushed *him* around. What was that all about, eh? Eh?

This girl who'd picked him up, now. *She*'d probably be all right. As a girlfriend, like. She'd let him sleep when he was dying for it, he could tell. She wouldn't poke him just when he was drifting off and say, 'You're not falling asleep are you?' Kind eyes, she had. Bloody big knockers, too. Pity she didn't have any big containers of petrol tucked away somewhere. Still, he couldn't complain, could he? No use complaining. Face the future with a smile, as the old man always used to say. Mind you, the old man never met Catriona.

Where was this girl going to drive him? Would she be willing to drive him back to his car again if he could get some petrol? He hated to leave his car in a ditch like that. A thief could steal it. Thief'd need petrol, though. But there were probably car thieves driving all around the countryside, with big petrol containers in the boot, just looking for a car like his. How low could some people go, eh? Dog eat dog, that's what it all boiled down to.

Catriona would murder him if he turned up any later than he already was. That wasn't so bad in itself, but she wouldn't let him sleep, this was the thing. If he could get some petrol into his car he could sleep in that, and maybe visit Catriona in the morning. Or sleep in the car all weekend even, sit around in Little Chefs during the day and drive back down to work on Monday morning. Fucking great, eh? Eh?

This girl here wouldn't mind if he rested his head back on the seat for just a few minutes, would she? He wasn't much of a talker anyway. 'Thick as two planks,' Catriona always said.

But how thick exactly was a plank, eh? It just depended on the plank, didn't it, eh?

Isserley coughed, to summon him back to consciousness. Coughing didn't come easily to her, but she tried every so often, just to see if she could pull it off convincingly.

'Eh? Eh?' he yapped, his bloodshot eyes and snot-shiny snout leaping out of the dimness like startled wildlife.

'What do you work at?' said Isserley. She'd been quiet for a minute, assuming the hitcher was ogling her, but a strangled snort from his direction had let her know he was falling asleep.

'Woodcutting,' he said. 'Timber. Eighteen years in the business, eighteen years behind a chainsaw. Still got two arms and two legs! Heh! Heh! Heh! Not bad, eh? Eh?'

He held his fingers up above the dashboard and wiggled them, presumably to demonstrate that he had all ten.

'That's a lot of experience,' complimented Isserley. 'You must be well known to all the timber companies.'

'Yeah.' He nodded emphatically, his chin almost bouncing off his barrel chest each time. 'They run when they see me coming. Heh! Heh! Heh! Ya got to keep smiling, eh?'

'You mean, they're not satisfied with your work?'

'They say I'm not a good time-keeper,' he slurred. 'I keep the trees waiting too long, y'understand? Late, late, late, that's me. La-a-a-a-ate . . .' His head was slumping, the attenuated vowel describing a slow lapse into oblivion.

'That's very unfair,' Isserley remarked loudly. 'It's how well you do your job that matters, not the hours you keep, surely.'

'Kind words, kind words,' simpered the woodcutter, staring ever deeper into his lap, his tufty hair slowly rearranging itself on his compact skull.

'So,' exclaimed Isserley, 'you live in Edderton, do you?'

Again he snorted to the surface.

'Eh? Edderton? My girlfriend lives there. She's gonna skelp my bot.'

'So where do *you* live?'

'Sleep in the car through the week, or bed and breakfast. Work ten days straight, thirteen sometimes. Start five in the morning summertime, seven in winter. Or I'm suppo-o-o-o-sed to . . .'

She was just about to rouse him from his slump when he roused himself, shifted around in his seat and actually laid his cheek against the headrest, pillow-style. He winked again, and, with a weary obsequious smile, mumbled across to her,

'Five minutes. Just five minutes.'

Amused, Isserley drove in silence while he slept.

She was mildly surprised when, more or less exactly five minutes later, he jerked awake and stared at her dazedly. While she was thinking of something to say to him, however, he relaxed again, and laid his cheek back against the headrest.

''Nother five minutes,' he pouted placatingly. 'Five minutes.'

And once more he was gone.

Isserley drove on, this time keeping one eye on the digital clock on the dashboard. Sure enough, some three hundred seconds later, the woodcutter jerked awake again.

'Five minutes,' he groaned, turning his other cheek to the headrest.

This went on for twenty minutes. Isserley was in no hurry at first, but then a road sign alerted her to the fact that they would soon be driving past a services turn-off, and she felt she'd better get down to business.

'This girlfriend of yours,' she said, the next time he woke. 'She doesn't understand you, is that right?'

'She's got a temper,' he admitted, as if he'd been spurred to articulate this for the first time ever. 'She'll skelp my bot.'

'Have you ever thought of leaving her?'

He grinned so broadly it was like an incision slicing his head in two.

'A good girl is hard to find,' he chided her, barely moving his lips.

'Still, if she doesn't care for you . . .' persisted Isserley. 'For example, would she be worried about you if you didn't turn up tonight? Would she try to find you?'

He sighed, a long wheezy exhalation of infinite weariness.

'My money's good enough for her,' he said. 'And, *plus*, I got cancer in the lungs. Lung cancer, in other words. Can't feel it, but the doctors say it's there. I might not have long, y'understand? No use giving up a bird in the hand, y'understand? Eh?'

'Mmm,' replied Isserley vaguely. 'I see what you mean.'

Another sign reminding motorists that services were not far ahead flashed by, but the woodcutter was nuzzling into the seat again, mumbling, 'Five minutes. Just another five minutes.'

And again, he was gone, his boozy breath snortling gently.

Isserley glanced at him. He sat slumped, his head lolling against the headrest, his rubbery mouth open, his red-lidded eyes closed. He might as well have been pricked by the icpathua needles already.

Isserley thought about him as she drove through the soundproof night, weighing up his pros and cons.

On the pro side, the woodcutter's drunkenness and sleepless excesses were no doubt well understood by all who knew him; nothing would surprise them less than if he failed to turn up wherever he was supposed to be. The car would be found, full of empty alcohol containers, on a windswept ribbon of road through two mountain ranges; there would be no doubt that the driver had stumbled away, drunk, into a frozen expanse of bog and precipice. Police would dutifully search for the body, but be resigned from the outset that it might never be found.

On the con side, the woodcutter was not a healthy specimen: his lungs, by his own admission, were full of cancer. Isserley tried to visualize this; imagined someone slicing him open and being squirted in the face by a stream of malodorous black muck made of burnt cigarette tar and fermented phlegm. However, she suspected this was a lurid fantasy based on her own distaste at the thought of inhaling burning punk into her lungs. It probably bore no relation to what cancer really was.

She frowned, straining to recall her studies. She knew cancer had something to do with runaway cell reproduction . . . mutant growth. Did that mean that this vodsel had huge abnormal lungs crammed into his chest? She didn't want to cause any problems for the men back at the farm.

On the other hand, who cared if the lungs were too big? They could surely be discarded whatever size they were.

On the *other* hand, she felt squeamish about bringing a vodsel onto the farm which she knew to be diseased. Not that anyone had ever told her in so many words that it was wrong, but . . . well, she had her own internal moral sense.

The woodcutter was murmuring in his sleep, a slack-lipped crooning sound like 'moosh'n, moosh'n, moosh'n', as if he were trying to placate an animal.

Isserley checked the clock on the dashboard. More than five minutes had elapsed; quite a bit more. She took a deep breath, settled back in her seat, and drove.

An hour or so later, she had bypassed Tain and was approaching the Dornoch Bridge roundabout. It struck her that the weather conditions were so different from what she had experienced earlier that day on the Kessock Bridge that they could have been on a different planet. Lit up against the pitch-black environs by strips of neon on long stalks, the roundabout glowed eerily in the windless, trafficless stillness. Isserley drove onto its steeply ascending spiral, glancing at the woodcutter to see if the blaze of light would wake him. He didn't stir.

Pootling gently along, high up off the ground, Isserley's car described an arc on the surreal concrete labyrinth. So monstrously ugly was this structure that it could have been mistaken for something from inside the New Estates, were it not for the open sky above. Isserley veered to the left to avoid crossing Dornoch Firth, and started a steep descent into leafy gloom. Her headlights, on full beam, picked out the flank of the Jehovah's Witnesses' Kingdom Hall nestled below, then tunnelled into Tarlogie forest.

Remarkably, it was now that the woodcutter squirmed in his sleep; having failed to react to the merciless lights of the roundabout, he seemed to sense, despite the darkness, the forest pressing in on the narrow road.

'Moosh'n, moosh'n, moosh'n,' he crooned wearily.

Isserley leaned forward as she drove, peering into the almost subterranean blackness. She felt fine. The forest's underground effect was an illusion, after all, and so it could not exert the nauseous claustrophobic power of the New Estates. She knew the barrier keeping out the light overhead was nothing more than a feathery canopy of twigs, beyond which lay a comforting eternity of sky.

Minutes later, the car emerged from the forest into the pastured surrounds of Edderton. The dismal caravan sales-yard welcomed her to this minuscule village. Street lights illuminated the defunct post office and the thatched bus shelter. There was no sign of life.

Isserley flipped the toggle for the indicator, even though

there was no vehicle to see it, and brought the car to a stop in a spot where the light was brightest.

She nudged the woodcutter gently with her strong fingers. 'You're here,' she said.

He jerked violently awake, his eyes wild as if he was in immediate danger of being brained with a blunt instrument.

'Wha-wha-where?' he waffled.

'Edderton,' she said. 'Where you wanted to be.'

He blinked several times, struggling to believe her, then squinted through the windscreen and the passenger window.

'Zaddafact?' he marvelled, orienting himself in the oasis of familiar aridity outside. Clearly, he was having to concede that nowhere else could look quite like this.

'Gee, this is . . . I dunno . . .' he wheezed, grinning with embarrassment and anxiety and self-satisfaction. 'I must of fell asleep, eh?'

'I guess you must have,' said Isserley.

The woodcutter blinked again, then tensed up, peering nervously through the windscreen at the deserted street.

'I hope my girlfriend's not out,' he grimaced. 'I hope she don't see you.' He looked at Isserley, his brow wrinkling as he considered the possibility that this might offend her. 'What I mean to say is,' he added, even as he was fumbling to unclasp his seatbelt, 'she's got a temper. She's what-would-you-say . . . jealous. Aye: jealous.'

Already out of the car, he hesitated to slam the door before he had found the right words to leave her with.

'And you're' – he drew a deep, rasping breath – '*beauti*-ful,' he beamed.

Isserley smiled back, bone-weary all of a sudden.

'Bye for now,' she said.

*   *   *

Isserley sat in her car for a long time, engine off, in the pool of light near the thatched bus stop in Edderton village. Whatever was needed to enable her to leave, she lacked it just now.

While waiting for whatever it was to be granted her, she rested her arms on the steering wheel, and her chin on her arms. She didn't have much of a chin, and what little she did have was the result of much suffering and surgical ingenuity. Being able to rest it on her arms was a small triumph, or maybe a humiliation, she could never decide which.

Eventually, she removed her glasses. A stupid risk to take, even in this somnolent village, but the sensation of tears collecting inside the plastic rims and leaking through onto her cheeks was unbearable in the end. She wept and wept, keening softly in her own language, watching the street carefully in case any vodsels strayed out. Nothing happened, and time stubbornly refused to pass.

She looked up into the rear-view mirror, adjusting the angle of her head until what she saw reflected was just her moss-green eyes and the fringe of her hair. This little sliver of face, poorly illumined, was the only bit she could look at nowadays without self-loathing, the only bit which had been left alone. This little sliver was a window into her sanity. She had sat in her car like this many times over the years, staring through that window.

A pair of headlights glimmered on the horizon, and Isserley put her glasses back on. By the time the vehicle arrived in Edderton, quite some time later, she had pulled herself together.

The vehicle was a plum-coloured Mercedes with tinted windows, and it winked its lights at Isserley as it passed through the village. It was a friendly gesture, nothing to do with warning or the codes of traffic. Just one vehicle saluting another of a vaguely similar shape and colour, in ignorance of the contents inside.

Isserley started her own car and turned it round, following her unknown well-wisher out of Edderton and into the forest.

All the way back to Ablach, she thought about Amlis Vess and what he might think when he learned she had come back empty-handed. Would he assume that the reason why she was hidden away in her cottage was embarrassment at her lack of success? Well, let him. Perhaps her failure, if that's how he chose to see it, would make clear to him that her job was not an easy one. Pampered dilettante that he was, he probably imagined it was like picking wildflowers from the side of the road, or . . . or whelks from the sea-shore, if he had the faintest notion what whelks were, or what a sea-shore looked like. Esswis was right: fuck him!

Maybe she should have taken the woodcutter after all. How massive his arms had been! – such massive chumps, bigger than any she'd ever encountered. He would have been good for something, surely. Ah, but the cancer . . . She really would have to find out whether cancer made any difference, for future reference. It was no use asking the men on the farm, though. They were thick; typical Estates types.

Ablach Farm was snowy pale and as quiet as ever when she drove up its overgrown private road. There were actually two roads leading into the farm, one nominally for heavy machinery, but both were cracked and bumpy and wild with weeds, and Isserley used either depending on her mood. Tonight she turned into the one supposedly for cars, though no cars except hers ever drove on it. Already at the mouth of Ablach, a cluster of signs warned of death, poison, and the full penalty of law. Just passing these signs, Isserley knew, triggered alarms in the farm buildings a quarter of a mile ahead.

She liked this road, especially one gorse-infested stretch of it which she called Rabbit Hill, where colonies of rabbits lived and could be depended on to hop across at any time of day or night. Isserley always drove very slowly here, taking great care not to run over these winsome little creatures.

Through the camouflage of trees at the top of the road she glimpsed the lights of Esswis's farmhouse, remembered their awkward conversation that morning. Hazily though she knew him, she could well imagine his back would be torturing him by now, and she felt pity, contempt (he could have said no, couldn't he?), and a queasy pang of kinship.

She drove past the stable, illuminating its blistered door in a flash of orange and black. There were no horses in there, only a pet project of Ensel's.

'It'll work, I know it will,' he'd told her, just days before abandoning it and letting Esswis tow it away. She'd shown no interest, of course. Men of his sort could bore you to death if you encouraged them.

The main steading, when she pulled up to it, was ridiculously white, its fresh paint glowing in the moonshine. As soon as she'd switched off her engine, the great metal door rolled open and several men hurried out. Ensel, first as always, peered into the passenger window.

'I couldn't get anything,' said Isserley.

Ensel poked his snout inside the cabin, much as the woodcutter had done, and sniffed the alcoholic upholstery. 'I can smell it wasn't for want of trying,' he said.

'Yes, well,' responded Isserley, hating herself for what she was about to say, but saying it anyway, 'Amlis Vess will just have to appreciate it isn't as easy as all that.'

Ensel noted her discomposure, smiled. His teeth weren't so good, and he knew it; for her sake, he lowered his head.

'You got a big one yesterday, anyway,' he said. 'One of the best ever.'

Isserley stared into his eyes, yearning to be sure whether, just for once, the compliment was sincere. As soon as she caught herself yearning, she yanked this contemptible little shoot of sentimentality out by the root. Estate trash, she thought, looking away, determined to get herself locked up safely in her cottage as soon as possible. She'd had far too long a day.

'You look exhausted,' said Ensel. The other men had already gone back inside; he was attempting a private moment with her, the way he sometimes did, always at lamentably inopportune times.

'Yes,' she sighed. 'It would be fair to say that.'

She recalled another occasion, a year or two ago, when he'd had her trapped like this – him leaning into the car, her foolish enough to have turned off the motor. He'd told her conspiratorially, almost tenderly, that he'd got her a present. 'Thanks,' she'd said, taking the mysterious little parcel from him and tossing it onto the seat beside her. Unwrapping it later, she'd found an almost transparently thin fillet of braised voddissin – a delicacy which Ensel must surely have stolen. Nestled in greaseproof paper, it winked at her, still moist and warm, irresistible and disgusting at the same time. She'd eaten it, even licked the juices from the creases in the paper, but she never mentioned it to Ensel afterwards, and that was the end of that. Still he tried, in other ways, to impress her.

'Amlis Vess will probably arrive in the early hours,' he was saying now, leaning further into the car. His hands were dirty and gnarled with scabs. 'Tonight,' he added, in case there was some misunderstanding.

'I'll be asleep,' said Isserley.

'Nobody knows how long he's coming for. He might leave again, on the same ship, as soon as the cargo is loaded.' Ensel used one hand to mime a ship departing, a precious opportunity swallowed up into the void.

'Well, I guess all will be revealed when the time comes,' said Isserley brightly, wishing she hadn't switched off the ignition.

'So . . . shall I let you know?' suggested Ensel.

'No,' said Isserley, striving to keep her voice level. 'No, I don't think so. You can say Isserley says hello and goodbye, how's that? Now, I really must get to my bed.'

'Of course,' said Ensel, bowing out of the window-frame.

Bastard, thought Isserley as she drove off. Tired and vulnerable, she'd lost concentration and let slip that little detail about going to her bed. No doubt Ensel would relish that, share it with the other men, this titillating proof of her subhumanity. Had she shaken him off sooner, he would never have been any the wiser; he and the other men would have carried on assuming that when Isserley slept, in that secretive cottage of hers, she slept like a human being, on the ground.

Instead, in one humiliating instant, she'd thoughtlessly given him the gift of the tawdry truth, a vision of an ugly freak sleeping on a strange oblong structure of iron and cloth-wrapped kapok, her body wreathed in sheets of old linen, just like a vodsel.

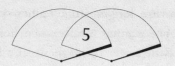

5

ISSERLEY, HAVING VOWED to be uncaringly asleep when the ship came in, lay in bed, in the midnight dark, listening for its arrival.

She hadn't changed her attitude; it was sheer anxiety keeping her awake, anxiety that she'd be roused out of her bed by the men, or, worse, by Amlis Vess.

More than anything she was afraid of not hearing them knocking at the front door, of sleeping right through the noise. They might just let themselves in then, come up to her bedroom, and have a good look at the denuded freak, the gargoyle girl, snoring on the pallet. Ensel was Estate trash, after all; his idea of privacy bore no relation to hers. He'd seemed to have trouble hearing her when she told him she didn't want to be disturbed; it wouldn't take much to make him forget. And wouldn't he just love to see what the surgeons had done to her below the waist! Well, he could go fuck himself.

Hours eroded by. Isserley's eyes swelled and itched with the imaginary grit of sleeplessness. She squirmed in slow motion on her stained and ancient mattress, listening.

The ship's berthing, shortly after 2 a.m., was almost noiseless: she could barely distinguish it from the sound of the waves on the Moray Firth. But she knew it had come. It came every month at the same time, and she was intimately acquainted with its smell, its great, secretive groan of docking, and the metallic sigh of its insertion into the steading.

Isserley lay awake longer still, waiting for the clouds to uncover the moon, waiting for the men, for Amlis Vess, to just *dare*, to have the *nerve*. 'Well then, let's see this Isserley,' she imagined Amlis Vess saying, and the men scurrying off to fetch her. 'Fuck off,' she would call out to them.

She lay for another hour or so, coiled ready with her 'Fuck off' sizzling on the tip of her tongue. Nervous moonlight hesitated into her bedroom, drawing a spectral line around the meagre contents, stopping well short of the bed. Outside, a screech owl began its performance of wails and shrieks, one calm and unruffled bird sounding deceptively like a horde of much larger creatures in terror and agony.

Serenaded thus, Isserley fell asleep.

It seemed she had only slept a few minutes when she was shocked awake by urgent hammering at the front door of her cottage.

Frantic, she reared up on her bed, clutching the rumpled sheet to her breasts, pressing her legs together. The knocking continued, echoing around the bare trees like phantom knocks on dozens of phantom houses.

Isserley's bedroom was still shut tight and snug, but through the window she could see the darkness of the world starting to go a pre-dawn blue. She squinted at the clock on the mantelpiece: it was half past five.

Isserley wound the bedsheet around her body and hurried out to the landing, where there was a tiny four-paned casement. She unlatched it, poked her head out into the night and looked straight down.

Still hammering energetically at her front door was Esswis, all dressed up in his best farmer gear, complete with deerstalker and shotgun. He looked ridiculous and terrifying, lit up luridly by the headlights of his Land-rover parked nearby.

'Stop banging, Esswis!' Isserley warned, her voice half hysterical. 'Can't anyone understand I'm not interested in Amlis Vess!'

Esswis stepped back from the door and lifted his face to get her in his sights.

'Fine with me,' he said brusquely. 'But you'd better get your clothes on and come out.' He adjusted the shotgun on its strap, as if he was authorized to shoot her if she refused.

'I told you——' she began.

'Forget Amlis Vess,' barked Esswis. 'He'll keep. There are four vodsels loose.'

Sleep made Isserley stupid. 'Loose?' she repeated. 'What do you mean, loose?'

Esswis waved his arms around irritably, indicating a random sweep of Ablach Farm and everything beyond.

'What do you *think* I mean?'

Isserley jerked her head back inside the casement and stumbled back into her bedroom to dress. The full implications of Esswis's announcement were well on the way to sinking in by the time she was struggling to get her feet into her shoes.

In less than a minute she was outside, accompanying Esswis across the frosty ground to his car. He swung into the driver's seat; she bounced into the passenger side and slammed the door. The car was cold as a stone, its windscreen an opalescent swirl of mud and frost. Warm and sweaty from the metabolism of sleep, Isserley wound her window down and leaned one arm out onto the car's freezing flank, ready to scan the dark.

'How did they get out?' she demanded as Esswis revved the engine.

'Our distinguished visitor *let* them out,' growled Esswis as the car pulled away with a crunch of ice and gravel.

For Isserley, it feld odd, even frightening, to be in the passenger seat. She was fumbling in the clefts of the upholstery, but if Esswis's vehicle had seat-belts, they must be well hidden. She didn't want to reach too far down; there was dirt and grease everywhere.

Esswis made no attempt to swerve when they reached the morass of pot-holes near the old stable. Isserley's spine was jolted repeatedly, as if furious assailants were kicking her through the seat; she looked aside at Esswis, wondering how he could stand such punishment. Obviously, he hadn't taught himself to drive the way she had, puttering round and round the farm at ten miles an hour. His teeth were bared as he leaned over the steering wheel, and despite the treacherous surface, the dark, and the semi-opaque windscreen, his speedometer needle reeled between thirty and forty. Twigs and leaves slapped Isserley's left elbow, and she pulled it in.

'But why didn't anyone *stop* him?' she called over the engine's noise. All she could imagine was Amlis Vess ceremonially granting vodsels their freedom while the workers stood by, nervously applauding.

'Vess got a guided tour of the factory,' growled Esswis. 'Seemed impressed. Then he said he was tired, he was going to have a sleep. Next thing anyone knew, the steading door was open and four vodsels were gone.'

The car slewed through the main entrance to the farm and sharp left onto the public road without even slowing down. Indicators and brakes were an alien concept to Esswis, it seemed, and gears were fortunately automatic.

'Left side of the road, Esswis,' Isserley reminded him as they hurtled into the darkness.

'Just look out for the vodsels,' he said.

Swallowing hard on retaliation, Isserley peered into the fields and scrub, straining for a glimpse of hairless pink animals.

'What grade am I looking for?' she asked.

'Monthlings,' Esswis replied. 'Almost ready. Would have gone on this shipload for sure.'

'Oh *no*,' said Isserley. The thought of a shaved, castrated, fattened, intestinally modified, chemically purified vodsel turning up at a police station or a hospital was a nightmare made flesh.

Grim with worry, they drove all around the inland borders of the farm, a massive pie-slice some three miles in perimeter. They saw nothing unusual. The public road and both the roads leading in and out of Ablach were deserted, at least by anything larger than rabbits and feral cats. That meant either the vodsels had already escaped, or they were still on the farm somewhere.

The most likely hiding places were the derelict cattle sheds, the stable, and the old granary. Esswis drove to each of these in turn, shining the Land-rover's powerful headlights into filthy black cavities and echoing spaces, hoping that four vodsels would stand luridly revealed. But the cattle sheds were eerie with emptiness, their floors moated with a slurry of rainwater and the compost of cows long gone. The stable, too, was the same as usual. Its contents were all inanimate. Cluttering up the rear lay bits and pieces of Isserley's previous cars (the doors of the Lada, the chassis and wheels of the Nissan). The rest of the space was mainly taken up by Ensel's attempted hybrid of a Fahr Centipede hay-turner and a Ripovator fork-lift. With its farrago of welded appendages it had looked grotesquely comical when Esswis was towing it out of the steading; in the spotlit gloom of the stable, its rusty claws and gleaming spines seemed more sinister. Isserley peered into the greasy, solder-spattered cabin, to make sure there were no vodsels inside.

The old granary was labyrinthine, full of nooks and compartments to hide in, but access to these crannies was only for creatures that could fly, jump, or climb ladders. Monthling vodsels, with their quarter-tonne of stiff flesh, were not so sprightly. They would either be on the granary floor, or not there at all. They weren't there at all.

Back at the main steading, Esswis screeched the car to a standstill and elbowed his way out of the door, taking his shotgun with him. He and Isserley didn't need to confer about what should happen next. They climbed over a stile and began to stump across the frosty stubble of the field leading to Carboll Forest.

Esswis handed Isserley a torch the size of a thermos flask. She shone it back and forth across the fields as they hurried towards the trees.

'A fall of snow would have helped,' she panted, detecting no tracks in the dark expanse of muddy earth and prickly harvest debris.

'Look for blood,' said Esswis irritably. 'Red,' he elabo-rated, as if she might be at a loss without this extra guidance.

Isserley stumbled along beside him in silence, humiliated. Did he think a big shining trail of crimson was going to blaze out of acres of field? Just because he played at being a farmer and landowner didn't mean he had any more of a clue than she did. Men! Armchair heroes the lot of them, while women were sent out to do the dirty work.

They reached the forest, and Isserley shone the torch to and fro across the dense jostle of trees. The very idea of the search seemed hopeless: a narrow beam of battery-generated light flickering around an acre of arboreal gloom.

Nevertheless, before very long, she caught a fleeting glimpse of pink amongst the dark boughs.

'There,' she said.

'Where?' said Esswis, squinting grotesquely.

'Trust me,' said Isserley, savouring the delicious realization that he was less sharp-sighted than she.

Together they loped through the thicket, Isserley leading. Within moments they could hear more snapping and rustling of bracken than they themselves were causing; another second, and they had the creature exposed in their sights. Eyes met across the forest floor: four large and human, two small and bestial.

'Just the one, eh?' grimaced Esswis, disguising his relief behind a bluff of disappointment.

Isserley was breathing hard, panting embarrassingly, her heart slamming in her chest. She wished there were a big icpathua toggle growing out of the ground that she could flip like a sapling, causing needles to spring up from the earth. She was aware, all of a sudden, that she had no idea what Esswis actually expected her to do.

The vodsel had lumbered to a standstill, and now stood cowering in the torchlight, naked and sluggish. Clouds of bright steam swirled around its head as it wheezed for breath. Removed from the warmth of its pen, it was pathetically unfit for the environment, bleeding from a hundred scratches, pinky-blue with cold. It had the typical look of a monthling, its shaved nub of a head nestled like a bud atop the disproportionately massive body. Its empty scrotal sac dangled like a pale oak leaf under its dark acorn of a penis. A thin stream of blueish-black diarrhoea clattered onto the ground between its legs. Its fists swept the air jerkily. Its mouth opened wide to show its cored molars and the docked stub of its tongue.

'Ng-ng-ng-ng-gh!' it cried.

Esswis shot the creature in the forehead. It flew backwards and bounced off a tree trunk. A cacophonous chuckling erupted nearby, making Esswis and Isserley jump; a pair of pheasants catapulting themselves out of hiding.

'Well, that's *one* down,' muttered Esswis superfluously, striding forwards.

Isserley helped him lift the carcass off the ground. She grabbed the ankle end, and her hands were instantly slippery with blood and half-frozen shreds of flesh. Amlis Vess had done this poor animal no favours in letting it go.

Even as they prepared to carry the carcass, figuring out how best to tackle its joints to distribute the weight manageably, Esswis and Isserley were coming to the same conclusion. A pale frosting of light was building up on the horizon, diffusing upwards into the cyanose sky. They were running out of time.

Having dumped the vodsel under a bush for collection later, they hurried back across the fields to where they'd left the Land-rover. Barely pausing for Isserley to get in next to him, Esswis started the car up with a hideous cough of ignition and a stink of choked petrol. He drove off at high speed, seemed dissatisfied with the vehicle's progress, and belatedly released the handbrake.

Once again, they drove all the way around Ablach Farm; once again, the open road and both farm tracks were deserted. The outlines of the mountains beyond Dornoch could be made out plainly now, and something which looked worryingly like another vehicle's headlights was winking somewhere on the road to Tain. On the way back into the farm, a misty impression of the open sea was starting to luminesce out of the murk.

'What if they've gone to the firth?' suggested Isserley when the car stood idling in front of the steading again.

'There's nowhere to go,' retorted Esswis dismissively. 'What are they going to do: swim to Norway?'

'They wouldn't know the sea was there until they got to it.'

'We'll check there last. The roads are more important.'

'If one of the vodsels drowns, it could get washed up anywhere.'

'Yes, but they'll stay away from the water if they've got any brains.'

Isserley clenched her fists in her lap, struggling to keep her temper. Then suddenly she was distracted, frowning, trying to hear something above the puttling of the motor.

'Switch the engine off for a second,' she said. Esswis complied, his hand first hesitating around the steering wheel for a while as if he was unfamiliar with its physiognomy. Then the car shuddered into silence.

'Listen,' whispered Isserley.

Flurrying through the chill air came the distant but unmistakeable rumble of large beasts, running en masse.

'The field near Geanies,' said Esswis.

'Rabbit Hill,' confirmed Isserley at the same instant.

They drove there immediately, and found two vodsels trying to climb out of the western field, to get away from a scrum of bullocks snorting and pawing the ground behind them.

The vodsels' eyes were wild with fear, and the barbed-wire fence was only waist-high, but their frozen and lacerated legs, weighed down by the added fat and muscle of a month's regime in the pens, refused to be lifted very far off the frigid ground, and the vodsels looked as if they were engaging in desultory callisthenics against the wire, or ballet warm-ups.

When they saw the Land-rover pull up, they stood transfixed. At the sight of Esswis's unfamiliar whiskery face poking out of the driver window, however, they got very excited, and began waving and ululating loudly. The cattle, startled by the headlights, were already cantering off into the gloom.

Isserley got out of the car first, and the vodsels stopped their noise abruptly. One of them began to stumble away into the field, the other stooped to pick up a clod of soil, which it threw straight at Isserley. There was so much meat and muscle on the vodsel's arms and chest by now though, that the swing of its arm was comically impeded, and the clod of earth landed with an impotent *ploff* on the concrete path.

Esswis took aim and shot first one vodsel and then the other. Obviously what he lacked in driving skills he made up for in marksmanship.

Isserley climbed into the field and found the carcasses. She dragged the nearest one back to the fence and lifted its limbs onto the barbed wire so that Esswis could grab hold of something. The creature that had thrown the clod of earth was distinctively tattooed all over its chest and arms; as she heaved the flesh over the wire to Esswis, she remembered something oddly specific about these tattoos – they were done in Seattle, by a 'fucking genius', the vodsel had told her. Isserley had been struck by the word 'Seattle'. A beautiful word, she'd thought then, and she thought so again now.

Despite their best efforts, the flesh of the vodsel's back became snarled on the barbed wire, and they grunted with effort as they tried to free it with minimum damage. All the while, blood was leaking copiously onto the concrete path from the blasted head, whose shattered jaw dangled loose like a glibbery hinge of gore.

'They'll clean up fine,' muttered Esswis stoically.

The other vodsel was lighter, and Isserley almost did herself an injury in her effort to lift its torso over the fence without touching the wire.

'Don't be stupid,' said Esswis. 'You may regret it.' But he strained himself too, reluctant to be shown up by a woman.

It was only when both vodsels were safely in the back of the Land-rover that Isserley and Esswis looked at each other and laughed. Retrieving these animals was a spectacularly messier business than either of them had imagined. A glutinous soup of cow shit was dripping down their clothes and arms, mingled with blood and earth. They even had smears of it on their faces, like military camouflage.

'Three down,' said Esswis, opening the passenger door for Isserley with a hint of new respect.

They did another circuit of the farm, finding nothing on the roads. Everything looked unrecognizably different from the previous time, because somewhere on the shore-side of

Ablach, unseen below the cliffs, the sun was coming up from the sea. Darkness was evaporating minute by minute, revealing a sky promising to be clear and benign, as if to invite other motorists to take to the roads as early as possible. Sheep and cattle which had moved numberless and invisible all night were materializing into view; some beasts could be seen from a quarter of a mile away.

The last vodsel could easily be such a beast, if it only managed to get to the right place at the right time.

Driving back up the Ablach path, Esswis glanced beyond the fields, and noticed a fishing boat on the firth, drifting close to land. His fists tightened in mortification on the steering wheel; Isserley could guess he was imagining exactly the same thing she'd imagined before: a naked two-legged creature standing on the shore, frantically waving.

'Maybe we should give you your trip to the seaside now,' quipped Esswis awkwardly, trying to make light of his concession. And of course, his about-face was less humble than it seemed: if there was nothing to be found at the firth, he could act as if he'd merely indulged her in a waste of valuable time.

'No,' said Isserley. 'I've got a feeling. Let's do one more round of the perimeter.'

'Your choice,' he grunted, infuriatingly. The fault was already hers, then, for newspaper headlines that might read MONSTER FOUND BY FISHERMEN.

They drove in silence over Rabbit Hill. The passage of the car's tyres back and forth over the concrete had dispersed the blood somewhat, diluting it with dirt, scuffing it into the cracks. Still it would need a good rinse, later.

If there was a later.

On the public road between the two Ablach tracks, Isserley

leaned forward in her seat, her back crawling with sweat and the prickle of instinct.

'There!' she cried, as they crested the hill and barrelled down towards the junction.

In truth, no special powers of observation were needed. The junction was an exposed crucifix of roads, and in the very centre of it stood the vodsel. Its meaty body shone golden-blue in the sunrise, like a garish fibreglass tourist attraction, and, on hearing the vehicle's approach from behind, it turned stiffly and lifted one arm, pointing sideways towards Tain.

Isserley reared up in her seat in a paroxysm of anticipation, but incredibly, when Esswis reached the junction, he didn't stop. He just drove straight on, following the border of farmland towards the village of Portmahomack.

'What are you *doing*?' shrieked Isserley.

Esswis shied violently, as if she were clawing at him or trying to wrest his hands from the wheel.

'There were headlights coming up the road from Tain,' he growled.

Isserley tried to see, but the junction was already past and the Tain road hidden behind trees.

'*I* didn't see any headlights,' she protested.

'They were there.'

'For God's sake – how far away?'

'Close! Close!' shouted Esswis, bashing the steering wheel with one hand, immediately causing a dangerous swerve.

'Well, don't just keep driving,' Isserley hissed. 'Go back and have a look!'

Esswis pulled the car in beside Petley's Farm and executed a three-point turn, except in half a dozen points or more. Isserley sat helpless and frantic in the passenger seat, unable to believe what was happening to her.

'Hurry *up!*' she whined, shaking her inward-turned fists under her chin.

But Esswis seemed to have discovered caution all of a sudden, and drove slowly and carefully back to the junction, stopping just short of it, behind the cover of trees. Through the foliage, they could both clearly see the vodsel, still standing upright and expectant on the asphalt. No evidence of any other vehicle was visible anywhere.

'There was definitely a car coming,' insisted Esswis, grimly pedantic. 'As close as Easter Farm.'

'Maybe it turned *in* to Easter Farm,' suggested Isserley, trying not to scream. 'It *is* inhabited, you know.'

'Still, the odds against—'

'For God's sake, Esswis,' squealed Isserley. 'What's wrong with you? He's right there! Let's get moving!'

'How are we going to get him in the car?'

'Just *shoot* him.'

'It's daylight now, on a crossroads. A car could come along any moment.'

'So shoot him before a car comes.'

'Anyone sees us shooting him, or chucking him into the car, and we're finished. Even a pool of blood would do it.'

'Anyone picks him up, we're finished, too.'

They were locked in a grotesque impasse for several seconds, as the sun shone in on them through the filthy windscreen and an almost unbearable stink of shit began to steam off both their bodies. Then Esswis revved the car, launched it with a lurch, and drove up to the crossroads.

The vodsel took a couple of shambling steps forward to greet their arrival. It lifted one of its arms and again pointed towards Tain, straining to erect a blueish thumb on its swollen paw. At close range they could see it was nearly dead with cold, swaying on pulpy feet in a vegetative trance of determination.

Still, the sight of a vehicle slowing to a stop brought a glimmer of sentience back to its eyes. Its mouth twitched, too stiff with cold and overfeeding to smile, but still the thought was there.

Esswis reached over to the back seats, groping for the shotgun, which had slipped onto the floor. The vodsel stumbled painfully to the car.

'Forget the shotgun,' said Isserley, and she twisted around, opening one of the back doors.

The vodsel bowed its head, heaved its body into the car, and collapsed in exhaustion across the seats. Isserley, grunting with effort, pulled the door shut with one hooked finger.

'Four,' she said.

Back at the steading, Esswis barely had time to speak his name into the intercom before the aluminium door rolled open. Four men jostled in the widening gap, their snouts straining out anxiously, their legs pawing the concrete.

'Did you get them? Did you get them?' they cried.

'Yes, yes,' growled Esswis exhaustedly, and motioned to the Land-rover.

The men piled out into the bright air, breathing a locomotive row of steam on their way to help with the cargo. Esswis and Isserley didn't go with them, but remained standing in the doorway, as if to block the view of any trespassers who might stray by. There was, after all, a foreign cargo ship nestled inside the building. It wasn't the sort of thing that could be mistaken for a tractor.

Isserley watched the men wrench open a side door of the Land-rover, and saw the swollen, bloody legs of the last vodsel flop out like a pair of giant salmon. She looked away. The barn walls were brilliant white in the sun, making the yellow tungsten light inside look dim and sickly.

Suddenly Esswis slumped slightly where he stood, as if something had come loose inside his shoulders, and he leaned against the steading wall, his hairy hand trembling under the skull-and-crossbones sign.

'I'm going home,' he sighed.

Isserley couldn't tell, from his hunched back, how far-reaching a statement this was supposed to be. But evidently Esswis meant his farmhouse, and he shambled off towards it.

'What about your vehicle?' Isserley called after him.

'I'll come and fetch it later,' he groaned without turning.

'I'll drive it to your place, if you like,' she offered.

Still walking, still not turning, he raised one arm and let it drop wearily. Isserley couldn't tell if this was a gesture of thanks or discouragement.

A shocked expletive in her native language came from near the Land-rover: the men had found the messier specimens jammed into the back. Isserley wasn't interested in their qualms; she and Esswis had done their best to retrieve the animals in one piece – what did they expect?

To spare herself the men's complaints, and to avoid offering to help them carry the carcasses in, she slipped inside the steading to search out the true cause of all the trouble: Amlis Vess.

The barn's echoing ground level was empty of movable things, apart from the great black oblong of the transport ship parked directly under the roof hatch. Even the token farm equipment that was usually littered about in case of government inspection had been removed for unimpeded loading. At this time of the month – all things being well – the men would already be busy packing the goods into the ship, but Isserley could smell that nothing had been done today.

In one corner of the barn stood a massive steel drum, seven feet tall and at least five in diameter, embossed with a rusted and faded image of a cow and a sheep. A brass tap beckoned out of its side; Isserley twisted the handle and the drum opened up for her, a concealed seam parting smoothly like a vertical eyelid.

She stepped inside, the metal enclosed her, and she was on her way underground.

The lift opened its door automatically when it reached the shallowest level, the workers' kitchen and recreation hall. Low-ceilinged and harshly lit like a motorway service station, it was a utilitarian eyesore that always, always smelled of fried potatoes, unwashed men, and mussanta paste.

Nobody was there, so Isserley let herself be taken down further. She hoped Amlis Vess wasn't hiding in the deepest levels, where the killing and processing was done; she had never been there and didn't wish to see it now. It was no place for a claustrophobic.

The lift stopped again, this time at the men's living quarters – the most likely place (now that she thought about it) for Amlis Vess to be. Isserley had only once visited here, when she'd first arrived at Ablach Farm. She'd never found a reason to revisit its musty warren of clammy maleness: it reminded her of the Estates. She had a reason now, though. As the door parted its metal veils, Isserley braced herself for an angry confrontation.

The first thing she saw was Amlis Vess himself, standing

startlingly close to the lift. She hadn't expected him to be so close; it was as if he was about to step inside with her. But he kept perfectly still. In fact, *everything* seemed to keep perfectly still: time appeared to have stopped, without a qualm, for Isserley to take Amlis in, her mouth open to spit abuse. Her mouth stayed open.

He was the most beautiful man she had ever seen.

Unsettlingly familiar in the way that famous people are, he was also utterly strange, as if she had never seen him before; the half-remembered images from the media had conveyed nothing of his attraction.

Like all of Isserley's race (except Isserley and Esswis, of course) he stood naked on all fours, his limbs exactly equal in length, all of them equally nimble. He also had a prehensile tail, which, if he needed his front hands free, he could use as another limb to balance on, tripod-style. His breast tapered seamlessly into a long neck, on which his head was positioned like a trophy. It came to three points: his long spearhead ears and his vulpine snout. His large eyes were perfectly round, positioned on the front of his face, which was covered in soft fur, like the rest of his body.

In all these things he was a normal, standard-issue human being, no different from the workman standing behind him, watching him nervously.

But he *was* different.

He was almost freakishly tall, for one thing. His head was at the level of her breast; were he to be surgically made vertical, as she had been, he would tower over her. Wealth and privilege must have excused him from the typically stunted growth of Estate males like the one who was guarding him now; he was like a giant, but slender with it, not massive or lumpish. His colouring was unusually varied (gossips sometimes suggested it wasn't natural): dark brown on his back, shoulders and flanks, pure black on his face and legs, pure white on his breast. The fur was impossibly lustrous, too, especially on his chest, where it was thicker, almost straggly. In musculature he was lean, with just enough bulk to carry his large frame; his shoulder-blades were startlingly prominent under their satiny layer of fur. But it was his face that was most remarkable: of the males Isserley worked with, there was not one who didn't have coarse hair, bald patches, discolorations and unsightly scarring on the face. Amlis Vess had a soft down of flawless black from the tips of his ears to the curve of his throat, as if lovingly tooled in black suede by an idealistic craftsman. Deeply set in this perfection of blackness, his tawny eyes shone like illuminated amber. He breathed, preparing to speak.

Suddenly, the metal door slid shut between them, as if drawing curtains on the spectacle. Only now did Isserley realize that several seconds had passed, and that she had failed to step out of the lift. The door sealed itself and Amlis was gone; the floor moved gently underneath her.

The lift was descending further, towards the Processing Hall and the vodsel pens – exactly where Isserley didn't want to go. Peevishly, she banged on the UP button with the palm of her hand.

The lift came to a stop, and its doors twitched, as if about to open, but they managed no more than a centimetre or two before the cabin lurched back upwards towards the surface. A whiff of dank animal smell had entered; nothing more.

Back on the men's level, the lift opened again.

Amlis Vess had moved back a little from the door, closer to the workman guarding him. He was still beautiful, but the few moments' separation from him had given Isserley a chance to regain her grip on her anger. Good-looking or not, Vess was responsible for a juvenile feat of sabotage which had just put her through hell. His appearance had startled her, that's all: it meant nothing. She'd expected him to have no presence except as the perpetrator of a wickedly foolish act; he wasn't quite so anonymous, and she had to adjust.

'Oh good; I thought you'd decided against us,' Amlis Vess said. His voice was warm and musical, and terribly terribly upper-class. Isserley seized hold of the frisson of resentment it caused in her, and hung onto it resolutely.

'Spare me the witty comments, Mr Vess,' she said, stepping out of the lift. 'I'm *very* tired.'

Deliberately, pointedly, she turned her attention to the other man, whom she belatedly recognized as Yns, the engineer.

'What do you think, Yns?' she said, happy to have remembered his name in time to use it. 'Is it safe to take Mr Vess back up to ground level?'

Yns, a swarthy old salt of heroic ugliness, bared his stained teeth awkwardly and made fleeting eye contact with Amlis. Plainly the two men had had ample opportunity to talk during the vodsels' adventure outside, and had come to appreciate the artificial absurdity of their captor–captive relationship.

'Um . . . yeah,' grimaced Yns. 'Nothing else he can do now, is there?'

'I think Mr Vess should come up to ground level,' Isserley said, 'and have a look at what the men are carrying in.'

Without taking her eyes off Amlis Vess, she twisted one arm backwards and pressed the button summoning the lift. In doing so, she winced in unexpected pain, and could tell he saw her wince – damn him. So rare were her opportunities to exploit her natural multi-jointedness, so careful was she always to move with the crude hinge-like motions of the vodsels, that she was seizing up. Wouldn't he just love to know what her body could and couldn't do!

The lift arrived, and Amlis Vess obediently walked inside. His bones and muscles moved subtly under his soft hide, without swagger, like a dancer. He was probably bisexual, like all rich and famous people.

Noting that the cabin wasn't big enough for three, Amlis Vess looked to Isserley, but she made it clear that he and Yns should go first, and she would follow. She tried to convey, in her stance, a wary, fastidious disgust, as though Amlis Vess were some huge animal that might soil her, just now when she was too tired to clean herself.

As soon as the lift ascended, she felt sick, as if the earth had closed over her and she was inhaling a miasma of spent breath. It was how she expected to feel, though, and she counselled herself to hang on. Being underground was always a nightmare for her, especially a place like this. You'd almost need to be a lower life form not to go insane.

'Come *on*,' she whispered, longing to be rescued.

When at last they were all standing together in the steading – Isserley, Amlis Vess, and five of the farm workers – a solemn and surreal sight had been arranged before them. The vodsels had been carried into the barn; first the live one, then the three gory carcasses. Actually, the live one wasn't alive anymore; Ensel had given it a cautionary dose of icpathua on the way in, which seemed unfortunately to have stopped the creature's overtaxed heart.

The bodies were laid in a row on the concrete in the middle of the barn. The legs of the most complete one were still seeping grume; the heads of the shot ones had more or less stopped bleeding. Pale and glistening with frost, the foursome looked like massive effigies made of candlefat, unevenly melted from their hairy wicks.

Isserley looked at them, then at Amlis Vess, then at the bodies again, as if drawing a direct line for his attention.

'Well?' she challenged. 'Proud of yourself?'

Amlis Vess stared at her, his teeth bared in pity and disgust.

'You know, it's very strange,' he said. 'I don't recall shooting these poor animals' heads off.'

'You might as well have done,' snapped Isserley, mortified to hear Yns snorting inappropriately behind her.

'If you say so,' Amlis Vess said, in a tone (if not an accent) she herself might have used to humour an alarmingly deranged hitcher.

Isserley was rigid with fury. Fucking elite bastard! He was behaving as if his actions didn't need defending. Typical rich kid, typical pampered little tycoon. None of their actions ever needed defending, did they?

'Why did you do it?' she demanded bluntly.

'I don't believe in killing animals,' he replied without raising his voice. 'That's all.'

Isserley gaped at him for a moment in disbelief; then, incensed, she drew his attention to the toes of the dead vodsels, an untidy row of approximately forty swollen digits splayed on the concrete before them.

'You see these parts here?' she fumed, singling out the worst affected ones with her pointing finger. 'See the way the toes are grey and mushy? It's called frostbite. The cold does it. These bits are *dead*, Mr Vess. This creature would certainly have died, *just* from being outside.'

Amlis Vess fidgeted uncomfortably, his first sign of weakness.

'I find that hard to believe,' he frowned. 'It's their world out there, after all.'

'Out *there*?' Isserley yelled. 'Are you kidding? Does *this*' — she jabbed her finger at the frostbitten toes, unintentionally slashing an additional perforation in one of them — 'look like they've been running around in their natural element to you? Does it look like they've been having a little . . . *frolic*?'

Amlis Vess opened his mouth to speak, then apparently thought better of it. He sighed. And when he sighed, the white fur on his chest expanded.

'It looks like I've made you angry,' he said gravely. 'Very angry. And the strange thing is, I don't think it's because I caused these animals to come to harm. I mean, you were just about to kill them yourself, were you not?'

With unconscious cruelty, all the men joined Vess in looking to Isserley for an answer. Isserley went quiet, her fists clenched. She was aware all of a sudden of why she should never clench her fists: the ineradicable pain in each hand where her sixth finger had been removed. And this, in turn, reminded her of all her other differences from the men who stood in a semicircle before her, across a divide of corpses. She cringed instinctively, dropping her posture as if to brace herself for all fours, then folded her arms across her breasts.

'I suggest you keep Mr Vess out of trouble until he can be shipped back where he came from,' she said icily, directing the instruction to no-one in particular. Then, one slow and painfully dignified step at a time, she walked out of the steading.

Those left behind stood in silence for a while.

'She likes you,' said Yns to Amlis Vess at last. 'I can tell.'

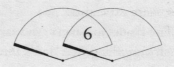

6

ON THE WINDSWEPT A9 an hour later and forty miles away, a bleary-eyed Isserley squinted up at a vast electronic traffic sign that said TIREDNESS CAN KILL: TAKE A BREAK. It was a self-confessedly 'experimental' sign, inviting comment from motorists by means of a telephone number on its bottom rim.

Isserley had passed under this sign hundreds of times on her way to Inverness, always wondering if it might one day display important traffic information: news of an accident or tailback up ahead, perhaps, or of severe weather conditions on the Kessock Bridge. There was never any message of that kind. Only generic homilies about speed, courtesy and tiredness.

Today, she smiled ruefully at the sign's advice. It was true: she *was* tired, and she ought to take a break. To be reminded of this by a soulless machine was funny, in a way – but easier to obey. She'd never been very good at listening to advice when it came from her fellow human beings.

She pulled the car in at a layby and switched off its engine. A belligerent sun was staring her right in the eyes and she considered darkening the windows, but thought better of it, in case she fell asleep and was wakened by police banging on her opaquely amber windows. That had never happened yet, but if it did, it would be the end of her. There were quite a few things police might ask to see which she didn't have – including a pair of vodsel-sized eyes behind those big thick glasses of hers.

Isserley's eyes were sore right now, irritated by lack of sleep and the strain of looking through two layers of glass. She blinked, then blinked again, slower and slower, until the lids stayed shut. She would rest her eyes for just a little while, then drive back north for a proper sleep. Not on the farm, somewhere else. The farm might well be in an uproar again, with that idiot Amlis Vess at large.

There was a spot she knew off the main road, on the B9166 to Balintore, where she sometimes pulled in at the ruins of a medieval abbey to doze. Nobody ever went there, despite it being an official tourist attraction; its far-flung web of promotional signs was too sparse to draw motorists in. It was just the place for Isserley when she'd had almost no sleep and been forced to chase lost vodsels for hours before dawn.

Imagining herself in Fearn Abbey already, Isserley fell asleep, her head and one arm cradled inside the padded steering wheel.

She dreamed, at first, of the abbey's roofless ruins as if she were sleeping inside them, with the ocean of sky above, azure and cirrus-striped. But then, as so often happened, she slipped down into a deeper level of dream, as if through a treacherous crust of pulverulent earth, and landed in the subterranean hell of the Estates.

'This is a mistake,' she told the overseer as he led her deeper into labyrinths of compacted bauxite. 'I have powerful friends in high places. They're absolutely shocked that I was sent here. Even now they're working on my reclassification.'

'Good, good,' murmured the overseer as he pulled her deeper. 'Now, I'll show you what your job will be.'

They had arrived at the dark centre of the factory, the smooth cervix of a giant concrete crater filled with a luminous stew of decomposing plant matter. Huge roots and tubers turned lazily in the albumescent gleet, obese leaves convulsed on its silvery surface like beached manta rays, and billows of blueish gas ejaculated from sudden interruptions in the surface tension. All around and above this great churning cavity, the stifling air swirled with green vapour and particles of sphagnum.

Peering closer despite her revulsion, Isserley noticed the hundreds of tubes, thick as industrial hose, draped over the rim all round, disappearing into the glutinous murk at intervals of a few metres. One of these tubes was being reeled in by an indistinct mechanical agent, the sheer glistening length of it a clue to how deep the crater really was. After some time, at the very end of the tube, attached to it by an artificial umbilicus, emerged a baggy diver's suit enslimed in black muck. Still clutching a spade-like implement in its gloves, the diver's suit slithered clumsily onto the concrete rim and struggled to raise itself to its knees.

'This,' the overseer explained, 'is where we make oxygen for those above.'

Isserley screamed herself awake.

She found herself sitting inside a vehicle by the side of a road stretching from eternity to eternity, in a strange and far-off land. Outside, the sky was blue, transparent and without upper limits. Millions, billions, maybe trillions of trees were making oxygen without human intervention. A newly mature sun was shining, and only a few minutes had passed since she had fallen asleep.

Isserley stretched, rotating her thin arms through 360 degrees with a grunt of discomfort. She was still exhausted, but the dream had put her off sleep for the time being, and she felt she was no longer in immediate danger of dozing off at the wheel. She would do some work, then assess how she was feeling by sundown. Obviously, the pressure she'd felt herself under yesterday to deliver the goods for the boss's son, the distinguished visitor, to admire, had vanished now. Bringing home a vodsel for Amlis Vess was plainly not the way to his heart, or whatever part of him she'd been hoping to impress. However, visiting crackpots aside, she did have her own expectations to live up to.

Still driving south, just beyond Inverness, she spotted a big hitcher holding up a cardboard sign saying GLASGOW.

She drove past him out of habit, out of adherence to procedure, but she had no doubt that she would pick him up on the second approach: he was powerfully built and in the prime of life. It would be criminal to leave a specimen like that standing there.

Despite his bulk, he ran quite nimbly to meet her when she stopped the car near him; always a good sign, since drunk or disabled vodsels could only stumble.

'Pitlochry all right?' she offered, judging from his open, eager-to-please expression that this would be more than enough.

'Brilliant!' he enthused, jumping in.

He had a big meaty face, a bit like a monthling already,

with tight blond curls at the top. The curls were sparse, though, and the skin rough and blotchy, as if the vodsel's head had been lost at sea at some stage in its life, then cast ashore and weathered for years in the sun before finally being reunited with the body.

'Mah name's Dave.' He reached one hand over to her, and she awkwardly allowed one of hers to be grasped, trying not to wince as he pressed on the place where her sixth finger had been. It was so unusual for a hitcher to introduce himself, she was slow to think of a reply.

'Louise,' she said, after a few moments.

'Pleased tae meet you,' he beamed, busily buckling himself in as if they were about to embark on a professional adventure together, like breaking the sound barrier in a racing vehicle, or test-driving a jeep in rocky terrain.

'You seem to be in a good mood,' observed Isserley as she pulled away from the kerb.

'Too right, hen, Ah'm well pleased,' affirmed Dave.

'Is it something to do with what's waiting for you in Glasgow?' she pursued.

'Right again, hen,' he grinned. 'Ah goat tickets tae see John Martyn.'

Isserley mentally scrolled through the entertainers she'd seen on television during her morning exercises, or who'd figured in the evening news for some reason. John Martyn was not a name she remembered, so quite possibly he did not bend spoons by psychic power or break laws against inhaling vegetable smoke.

'I don't know him,' she said.

'You'll ken some ae his songs for sure,' promised Dave, his brow crinkled with incredulity. ' "May You Never" is a big yin.' All of a sudden, without warning, he began singing loudly. '*Ah-M-A-A-AY YOU never lay your head down, without a hand to hold . . .* No?'

Isserley was hastily correcting the startled swerve her car had taken towards the middle of the road.

'Whit aboot "Over the Hill"?' Dave persisted. Strumming one beefy hand against his ribcage, the other fingering the neck of an invisible guitar, he sang, '*Been worried about my babies, I been worried about my wife; there's just one place for a man to be when he's worried about his life; I'm goin' home, HEY HEY HEY over the hill!*'

'Are you worried about your wife, Dave?' enquired Isserley evenly, keeping her eyes on the road.

'Yeah, Ah'm worrit she might find oot whir Ah stay, hyuh hyuh.'

'Any babies?' She was being audacious, she knew, but she felt in no mood to waste time today.

'Nae babies, hen,' said Dave, sobering his tone abruptly and bringing his hands to rest in his lap.

Isserley wondered if she'd overstepped the mark. She shut up, pushed her breasts out, and drove.

It was a pity, Dave reflected, that this Louise was only taking him as far as Pitlochry. At this rate he'd get to Glasgow about four hours earlier than he needed to, and this girl wouldn't be a bad way to spend that time. Not that he was a sexist, mind, but she had that upfront way of speaking that easy girls had, and she'd picked him up, him a big beefy guy, which let's face it females almost never did. She had fantastic bosoms, and bigger eyes than Sinéad O'Connor even, and nice hair too, although it was a bit of a mess really, sticking out like a mop so he couldn't see her face from the side. Maybe this was what women meant when they talked about having a bad hair day.

Maybe he should mention something about bad hair days, to show her he had some idea about these things. Women liked to think there wasn't a hopeless divide between the sexes; it was a real leg-opener, he'd found.

Maybe something would happen between them on the way to Pitlochry! Beds weren't essential, after all. Louise could pull in at a layby and show him what she was made of.

Dream on, dream on, Dave. This is what would really happen: at Pitlochry she'd set him down at the roadside and drive off with a wink of her tail-lights. End of story.

But he'd get to see John Martyn, just remember that. Trying to get off with a woman was always a bit of an embarrassment when you looked back on it later, but a great musical performance was a warm buzz forever.

Thinking of which: what did this girl have in the way of music? There was a car cassette player just above his knee: plenty of time for a C-90 before Pitlochry!

'Goat any tapes, hen?' he said, pointing at the machine. Isserley glanced at the metal slit, trying to recall what had or had not been inside it when she'd first acquired this car, years ago.

'Yes, I think there's one in there,' she replied, vaguely remembering being startled by unwelcome music when she'd been familiarizing herself with the dashboard controls.

'Brilliant: put it oan then,' he urged, smacking the thighs of his jeans as if to kick-start the drums.

'Feel free to do it yourself,' Isserley said. 'I'm driving.'

She felt his gaze on her, incredulous at her carefulness, but there were cars overtaking hers constantly and she was too nervous to look down. Being driven around at high speeds by that maniac Esswis had rattled her and she was in no mood to exceed forty-five.

Dave switched on the tape player and sound issued forth obediently. At first Isserley was relieved that he'd got what he wanted, but she soon sensed that all was not well, and made herself focus on the music. It seemed to be submerging itself every few seconds, as if passing through watery obstacles.

'Oh dear,' she fretted. 'Perhaps my machine is malfunctioning?'

'Nah, it's yir tape, hen,' he said. 'It's loast its tension.'

'Oh dear,' repeated Isserley, frowning in concentration as a car behind her hooted its horn in apparent chagrin at her refusal to pass a tourist coach. 'Does it need . . . uh . . . disposing of?'

'Nah!' Dave assured her, happily fiddling with the cassette controls while she endured the sound of beeping. 'It's just needin' windin' backwards an' forwards a few times. Daes wonders. You'll see. Folk throw tapes oot thinkin' they're deid. Nae need for it.'

For a few minutes more he busied himself with the tape player, then switched it on afresh. The song rang out of the speakers, clear and harsh as television. A twangy male voice was singing about driving a truck all night long, to put a hundred miles between him and a town called Heartache. The tone was one of jovial dolefulness.

Isserley trusted that Dave would be satisfied now, but instead he radiated puzzlement.

'Ah goat tae say, Louise,' he said after a while. 'It's funny you huvin' Coontry and Western music.'

'Funny?'

'Well . . . unusual, fur a wumman. At least a *young*

wumman, y'ken. You'd be the furst young wumman Ah've met that's goat a Coontry and Western tape in her motor.'

'What kind of music would you have expected?' Isserley enquired. (Some of the larger service stations sold cassettes; perhaps she could buy the correct ones there.)

'Oh, dance stuff,' he shrugged, beating the air rhythmically with his fist. 'Eternal. Dubstar. M Pipple. Or mebbe Björk, Pulp, Portishead . . .' These last three names sounded to Isserley like varieties of animal feed.

'I suppose I have strange tastes,' she conceded. 'Do you think I'd like John Martyn? What does his music sound like? Can you describe it to me perhaps?'

Her question lit up the hitcher's face with a glow of serene and yet intense concentration, as if his whole life had been leading up to this moment and he knew he was equal to the challenge.

'He daes a loaty stuff wi' echoplex – foot pedals, y'ken? It's acoustic, but it soonds electric – spacey, even.'

'Mm,' said Isserley.

'One second he'll be playin' this ril soaft acoustic guitar, next second it's like WHAAANG! WAKKA WAKKA WAK-KA WAKKA, birlin' all roond yir heid.'

'Mm,' said Isserley. 'Sounds . . . effective.'

'An' his singin'! That manny sings like naebody oan earth! It's like . . .' Dave began to sing again, in a melismatic convulsion of slurring and growling which made him sound alarmingly drunk. For years now it had been Isserley's policy never to allow a very drunk hitcher into her car, in case he fell asleep before she could make an informed decision about the icpathua. Had Dave greeted her with this extraordinary performance, she would definitely not have taken him. But, he assured her: 'It's deliberate. Like jazz, y'ken?'

'Mm,' she said. 'So, have you seen John Martyn many times?'

'Oh, six or seven, over the yirs. But he's well intae the drink, y'ken. Y'canny be sure someboady like that isnae gauny pop off any day noo. Then you'd be tellin' y'self, Ah couldy went and seen John Martyn, an' now he's deid! An' whit did Ah dae instead, eh? Watched telly mebbe!'

'Is that what you do with most of your time, Dave?'

'Right, hen. Too right,' he confessed emphatically.

'During the daytime too?'

'No, hen,' he laughed. 'Ah'm at work, then.'

Isserley digested this, rather disappointed. She'd had such a strong hunch that he was unemployed.

'So,' she persisted, hoping to uncover a reputation for poor attendance at his place of work, 'you took the day off today to see the concert.'

He looked at her a little pityingly.

'It's Saturday, hen,' he informed her gently.

Isserley winced. 'Of course, of course,' she said. All this, she was sure, was Amlis Vess's fault somehow. His stupid act of sabotage had achieved nothing except to ruin her concentration for the rest of the day.

'You all right, Louise?' asked the vodsel next to her. 'Fell oot the wrong side ae bed the day?'

She nodded. 'Working too hard,' she sighed.

'Ah thoat so,' he affirmed sympathetically. 'Well, cheer up: you goat the weekend, mind!'

Isserley smiled. She did indeed have the weekend — and so did he. His workmates would not be expecting to see him until Monday, and even then, if he failed to turn up, they would assume he was having trouble getting back from Glasgow. She would take him after all. He would do fine.

'So, where will you stay when you get to Glasgow?' she said, her finger hovering over the icpathua toggle in anticipation of the usual mumbles about mates and hotels.

'Mah mam,' he replied promptly.

'Your mam?'

'Mah mam,' he confirmed. 'She's greht. A raver at hert, y'ken? She wouldy went tae see John Martyn wi' me, if it wisnae for the cold wither.'

'How nice,' said Isserley, curling her fingers away from the icpathua toggle and wrapping them around the blistered steering wheel.

Conversation was minimal for the remainder of the journey. The Country and Western tape played until it ended, and Dave turned it over, making the most of what was on offer. The jovially doleful singer yodelled on and on about sweet memories, long highways and lost chances.

'You know, I think I've outgrown this music,' Isserley told Dave at last. 'I liked it years ago, but now I'm ready to move on. Maybe I'll get some John Martyn next.'

'Brilliant,' he said encouragingly.

At Pitlochry, she set him down at the roadside and drove off with a wink of her tail-lights.

He was still waiting there, holding his little GLASGOW sign, when she drove past him on the other side of the road five minutes later. If he saw her (which she was almost sure he did) he must have wondered what had gone wrong.

By two o'clock the sun had been lured deep into a slate-grey sea of cloud: more snow on the way. If it came sooner rather than later, dark would fall almost immediately rather than waiting another hour and a half; only the seriously deranged and the desperate would be venturing out to hitch then.

Isserley doubted she had the energy to deal with the seriously deranged today, or the good luck to find the desperate. As far as her day's work went, it was probably realistic to regard it as being over as soon as the first snowflake fell.

And then? Where would she go then? Not back to Ablach Farm, if there was any alternative – somewhere more private, where no-one was subjecting her to surveillance or speculation. Somewhere only she knew about.

Maybe she could try sleeping at Fearn Abbey – sleeping there all night long, that is, not just for a doze. Was a bed really so essential? She could manage without one and sleep like a normal human being for just one night, surely! Let Ensel and his cronies rack their brains over what had become of her, while she slept under the stars, in utter privacy.

A stupid idea, she knew. Her spine would never let her get away with it. You couldn't expect to be able to lie down on an unyielding surface and curl snugly into yourself, when you'd had half your backbone amputated and metal pins inserted into what was left. Inescapably, there was a price to be paid for sitting upright at the wheel of a motor car.

Driving north again now, Isserley was functioning on autopilot, watching for hitchers and, further off the road, for seals on the Moray Firth. Much more vivid on the screen of her attention, though, was a mental picture of her own soft bed on the farm: how she yearned to be lying in it! How wonderful it would feel to stretch out in her usual X-shape, passing on to the mattress the burden of keeping her back in order. The old bed, broken in by generations of vodsels, had just the right amount of 'give': sagging enough to allow her spine to relax and curve a little, but not so much that the metal clamps stabbed into her tendons the way they mercilessly did whenever she slumped too much at the wheel. Pathetic, but there it was.

She wished the men wouldn't always come rushing out of the steading whenever she returned, whether she had a vodsel for them or not. How had this stupid habit arisen in the first place? Couldn't they just wait, until she gave them some sort of signal? Why couldn't she just drive into the farm unobserved and unnoticed sometimes, slip into her cottage and go to sleep? Was there some good reason why she had never been given the power to switch off the farm's alarm systems as she approached? Could it be that the fuss that always surrounded her return was someone's bright idea, to make sure she felt the pressure to deliver? Who would think of such a thing? They could go fuck themselves, whoever they were. Old man Vess probably set up these little schemes to keep his workers in line; he was probably just as twisted and crazy as his son, but in a different direction . . .

Suddenly, with a sickening lurch, she found herself transported, as if through space and time, into a strange and terrifying emergency: while electronic horns screamed all around her, she was lost in a darkening nowhere, mesmerized by the dazzling approach of a dilating light. She had no sense of herself as moving; she might have been a pedestrian staring up at a falling meteorite or a firebomb. Frozen, she waited for death to blaze her into extinction.

Only when the first vehicle had screeched past her, detonating her side mirror with a loud bang and a shower of glass, did Isserley appreciate where she was and what was going on. Still dazzled by headlights, she wrenched the steering wheel counterclockwise as several more vehicles slewed narrowly past her, whumping the side of her car with scuds of displaced air.

Then, as abruptly as it had flared, the danger was whisked

into the past, and Isserley's was just one of a line of cars driving on a twilit road, neatly on course for Thurso.

At the first opportunity, Isserley pulled over into a layby and sat there for a while, quaking and sweating, as the night and the snow silently let themselves fall.

She hadn't died, but was bewildered at the thought that she might have. How terrifyingly fragile human life was, that it could be forfeited in an unnoticed instant, during a few degrees' deviation in direction. Survival was something that couldn't be taken for granted: it depended on concentration and luck.

It made you think.

This incident was the closest call she'd ever had on the roads, even including her first anxious days behind the wheel. And whose fault was it? Isserley had no doubt: Amlis Vess again. Four long years she had been driving, and in all that time she had never caused any problem. She must be the most careful driver in the world, so what had been so different about today? Amlis Vess, that's what. He and his infantile act of sabotage had managed to send her very nearly into the jaws of death.

What the fuck was he *doing* here anyway? He couldn't tell the difference between a vodsel and his own arse! Who was responsible for letting him get onto that cargo ship? Didn't old man Vess know his own son was dangerous? With so much at stake, wasn't *anybody* in control?

It took another few minutes for Isserley to calm down enough to realize she was raving. Raving inside herself, that is. Even now that she was aware of it, it was still almost impossible to think clearly. All day there had been waves of irrationality rising towards her, threatening to pull her under. She must force herself to take stock of her more urgent practical needs. Anger at Amlis Vess, paranoia about Ensel and his dimwitted cronies – these things would keep until she was safely off the road. (Still: wasn't it striking how *not one* of the men had come to her defence when Vess had been attacking her! – they were all boys together, no fucking doubt – *or was there something more to it than that?*) Never mind, never mind: check the fuel gauge.

Her car's tank was almost empty. She would have to fix that.

And her own stomach, now that she thought of it, had run out of fuel hours ago: she was absolutely ravenous, just about ready to faint! God, how long had it been since she'd eaten anything? Yesterday morning! And today she'd been running around like a maniac since before dawn, on top of almost no sleep.

In all honesty, she had to face facts: from the moment she'd driven onto the roads today, she'd been a tragedy waiting to happen.

Bone-tired and dizzy, Isserley stopped at Donny's Garage in Kildary for petrol. She wished she could buy fuel for her own body as easily. Skulking inside the shop while a queue of other motorists were paying, she peered longingly at the snacks displayed in the sickly fluorescent light. There was nothing fit for human consumption, as far as she could tell.

And yet, there surely must be. It was just a matter of making the correct choice. Which was not easy. The last time she had been adventurous and eaten something meant for vodsels she had ended up in bed for three days.

Sluggish with indecision, she glanced around the shop in case there were any cassettes, by John Martyn or musicians with names like animal feeds, for sale at £5 or £10 exactly. There were no cassettes at all.

But to return to her unfortunate experience with vodsel food: perhaps her mistake had been to select something that looked exactly like serslida husks baked into a bar shape. Perhaps this time she could select something not according to how it looked, but according to what it claimed to be. In fact, she really *should* select something while she had the chance. Any risk of getting sick later was surely outweighed by the risks of pushing herself any further when she was so empty.

The queue was dispersing: she would have to pay for her petrol soon, or risk attracting attention. She picked up a packet of potato crisps from a little metal cage and with some effort read the microscopic list of ingredients on its shiny packaging. It seemed to contain nothing exotic, just potato and oil and salt; the men on the farm were routinely served a potato dish very like this from their canteen, albeit prepared in a different kind of oil.

Calculating prices hastily, Isserley selected three packets of the crisps, a gift box of chocolates and a copy of the *Ross-shire Journal*, bringing the cost to £5 exactly. She handed two banknotes to the bored youth behind the counter and hurried out to her car.

Fifteen minutes later, Isserley's car stood idling in another layby, and she was leaning over its purring engine, scraping fluffy snow off the windscreen with the edge of her hand. She collected some of it in her palms and sucked it gratefully into her mouth. There was no feeling in her lips – there never was – but the soft flesh of the insides of her mouth and throat thrilled to the melting purity and the heavenly taste of the frozen moisture. Three packetfuls of scorched potato slivers had made her extraordinarily thirsty.

When she'd swallowed enough snow, she returned to the driver's seat.

Only ten miles from home, she passed a hitcher, signalling forlornly in the dark.

Forget it, she thought, as she crested a hill and left him behind.

But then, as if photographic chemicals in her mind had been activated, an image of him began forming. He really was rather impressive. Worth a second look, anyway. It was only five o'clock, virtually daytime, if this had been summer. Lots of hitchers who weren't necessarily deranged might be out on the road. She mustn't be so dismissive.

Isserley doubled back, executing her turns carefully and safely. Nobody hooted at her or flashed warning lights; she was an ordinary capable motorist as far as the other traffic was concerned. Inside herself, she felt less exhausted than before, and the food had done her good.

The hitcher, when she passed him on the other side of the road, looked glum but unaggressive in the fleeting periphery of her headlights. He carried no sign, and was perhaps a little under-dressed for the weather, but not bizarrely so. He *was* wearing leather gloves, and his leather jacket was zipped up to the neck. Snow twinkled on his dark-haired head, his moustache, and the shoulders of his jacket. He was tall by Scottish standards, and powerfully built. And, in the glimpse she caught of his expression, Isserley thought she detected an impatience, a nearness to some self-imposed limit, which would make him abandon his attempt to hitch if someone didn't stop for him bloody soon.

So she turned again, drove back, and stopped for him.

He leaned his face to the passenger window, which she had wound half down.

'Bad time to be out,' she remarked cautiously, challenging him to explain.

'Job interview,' he replied, melted snow dripping from his moustache. 'Finished later than they said it would. There's another bus in an hour, but I thought I'd try and thumb it.'

She opened the door for him, clearing the empty crisps packets off his seat.

'Thanks,' he said, not smiling, but with a deep cloudy sigh, presumably of appreciation. He removed his gloves to fasten his seatbelt; on both of his big hands, a tattooed swallow flew in the web of flesh between thumb and forefinger.

As they were pulling away from the kerb together, Isserley remembered something.

'It's Saturday,' she said.

'Yeah,' he acknowledged. 'This interview wasn't at the Job Centre or anything, it was a private arrangement.' He eyed her momentarily as if assessing whether she could be trusted, then added, 'I told them I had a car parked not far away.'

'Work can be hard to find,' Isserley reassured him. 'Sometimes you have to be crafty to get it.'

He did not reply, as if loath to surrender too much of his dignity all at once. After a few moments, though, he said, 'I *do* have a car, actually. Needs road tax, MOT. Nothing a couple of weeks' wages wouldn't sort.'

'So, do you think these people you've just seen will give you a job?' said Isserley, nodding backwards at the mysterious interviewers they were leaving behind.

His reply was instant and bitter. 'Time-wasters. Just trying on the *idea* of employing somebody, yunderstandwhatI'm-saying?'

'Yes, I think so,' said Isserley, sitting up straighter in her seat.

*   *   *

Observing his rescuer, the hitcher was not impressed. What *was* this obsession women had with showing cleavage these days? he thought. You saw it all the time on TV, all those greasy-haired young females in London, going to nightclubs wearing little black vests not even big enough to cover a dachshund. They'd get the shock of their lives if they had to survive in the wild, that's all he could say. No wonder the army wasn't happy about women soldiers. Would you trust your life to someone who went out in the snow with an acre of tit showing?

Christ, could this girl not drive a little faster! This was barely faster than walking. He should just suggest they switch seats, he could get this thing moving at twice the speed, even if it was Japanese crap. Oh, to have that Wolseley he'd owned in the eighties back again! He could still remember the feel of the gearstick. Quality leather on the knob. Soft as pigskin. Probably *was* pigskin. Where was his Wolseley now? Some idiot with a mobile phone would be driving it. Or crashing it. Not everyone could handle a Wolseley.

There had been no bloody point in even bothering to go and see these people today. Typical two-income poncy show-offs. Lights that came on automatically when you stepped close to the house. Choice of coffees. Computer in every room. Maple bookcases full of bloody *Feng Shui and Gardening* and *The Joy of* bloody *Sex*, and a pedigree Samoyed they didn't have a bloody clue how to care for properly. 'Don't chew our nice sheepskin rug, darling.' Jesus, how he would have liked to take the rug out of that dog's mouth and teach her the first few rules of obedience.

Maybe starting a dog obedience school was the answer. Except you'd have an even harder job convincing these dipshits that they needed to sort out their dogs' behaviour than that they needed to spend some serious money on a gardener. That was yuppies for you. He'd never had this sort of trouble with the aristocracy, in the good old days. They understood that you only get what you pay for. *And* they knew how to bring up a dog.

Good days, good days. Would they ever come again? Not bloody likely. Class, *real* class, was getting the chop everywhere you looked. The queen would be out on her arse next. The new millennium cleared for spotty little queers in oversized suits, and clueless foreign females with too much cleavage.

Forty-five miles an hour! Lord love a duck!

Isserley glanced surreptitiously at her passenger, trying to figure him out, for he had lapsed into silence and sat with his arms folded over his chest. He looked exactly like a hitcher she'd given a lift to about a year ago, who'd talked non-stop about the Territorial Army all the way from Alness to Aviemore. In fact, for a few moments she was sure it *was* him, until she remembered this wasn't possible: she'd stung that particular vodsel shortly after he'd got around to telling her how his devotion to 'the TA' had cost him his marriage and taught him who his true friends were.

Of course she knew that these creatures were all exactly the same fundamentally. A few weeks of intensive farming and standardized feeds made that clear enough. But when they wore clothes, styled their hair into odd patterns, and ate strange things to distort themselves into unnatural shapes, they could look quite individual – so much so that you sometimes felt, as with human beings, that you'd seen a particular one somewhere before. Whatever the vodsel from the Territorial Army had done to make himself look the way he'd looked, this one here must have done something very similar.

He had a thick moustache which was curtailed severely in line with the outer limits of his great red mouth. His eyes were bloodshot and full of stoically endured pain which only tsunamic revenge and the grovelling apologies of world leaders could hope to cure. Hard wrinkles added a sculptur-esque emphasis to a frowning forehead, under a symmetrical haircut combed back like a rinsed paintbrush. He was well-muscled, but with a thickening around the waist and a fawn-coloured leather jacket that had started to flake, and jeans that had fluffy fray-holes where keys and the hard edges of wallets had worn through.

Isserley bit back on the temptation to come right out and ask him about the Territorial Army, and found it surprisingly difficult. Again she blamed Amlis Vess; his ethical posturings and phony courage had annoyed her so deeply that she was finding any hint of it in another creature hard to tolerate. She wanted to ferret out this vodsel's hare-brained passions, rudely yank them out into the light, before he had the chance to bore her with preambles.

She longed to sting him, to get it over with, which she knew was a very bad sign. It showed she was in danger of blundering towards an act of resolute foolishness not so very different, perhaps, from what might be expected from some-one like Amlis Vess. As a matter of professional and personal pride, she must not sink to his level.

So, 'Tell me,' she said brightly, 'What job were you hoping to get back there?'

'I'm doing a bit of landscape design, just to tide me over,' he replied. 'My real profession is whatyou'dcall on hold just now.'

'What *is* your real profession, then?'

'I breed dogs.'

'Dogs?'

'Pedigrees. Sighthounds and scenthounds mainly, though I was getting into mastiffs and terriers towards the . . . the last few years. But *crème-de-la-crème* animals, yunderstand-whatI'msaying? Prize winners.'

'Fascinating,' said Isserley, letting her forearms droop forward at last. 'I suppose you've supplied dogs to some well-known and influential people?'

'Tiggy Legge-Burke's had one of my dogs,' the hitcher affirmed. 'Princess Michael of Kent's had one. Lots of people from show business. Mick McNeill out of Simple Minds. The other bloke from Wham. They've all had one.'

Isserley had no idea who these people were. She'd only ever watched television to learn the language, and to check if there were any police investigations being mounted into lost hitchhikers.

'I suppose it must be difficult to train a dog and then let it go,' she commented, trying not to let her loss of interest in him show. 'It would get attached to you, wouldn't it.'

'Not a problem,' he said pugnaciously. 'Train them, hand them over. One master to another. Dogs have no problem with that. Dogs are pack animals. They need a leader, not a bosom buddy – well, not a two-legged one, anyway. People get too sentimental about dogs. Comes from not understanding the first thing about them.'

'I'm sure I don't understand the first thing about dogs,' conceded Isserley, wondering if she had missed the right moment to ask him where he wanted to be dropped off.

'First thing to understand,' said the hitcher, coming to life, 'is that to a dog, you're pack leader. But only if you remind them who's boss, same as a pack leader does. In a dog pack, there's no such thing as a soft boss, yunderstandwhatI'msaying? Take my Shepherd bitch, Gertie. I'll go up to her when she's sleeping on my bed, and just push her off, wham! onto the floor, just like *that*.' He shoved his massive hands forward violently, and accidentally triggered the clasp of the glovebox, which sprang open and discharged something furry into his lap.

'Jesus, what's this?' he muttered. Fortunately he picked the wig up himself, saving Isserley from having to grope for it in his crotch. Taking her eyes off the road for an anxious second, she snatched the clump of hair gently out of his hand and tossed it backwards into the darkness of the car's rear.

'It's nothing,' she said, removing the gift box of chocolates from the overcrammed glovebox and snapping it shut. 'Help yourself to one of these.'

She was proud of herself for handling so many challenges while driving, and couldn't help breaking into a smile.

'You were saying?' she enquired as he fumbled with the cellophane. 'You push your dog off the bed . . .'

'Yeah,' he rejoined. 'That's to remind her, this bed is mine. YunderstandwhatI'msaying? Dogs *need* that. A dog with a weak leader is an unhappy dog. That's when they start to chew carpet, piss on your sofa, steal food off your table – like kids, desperate for a bit of discipline. No such thing as a bad dog. Clueless owners, that's what it is.'

'You seem to know such a lot about dogs, you must have been a very good breeder. Why are you designing landscapes just now?'

'The bottom fell out of the dog-breeding business in the early nineties, that's why,' he said, his tone suddenly sour.

'What caused that?' she said.

'Brussels,' he declared darkly.

'Oh,' said Isserley. She struggled to see the connection between dogs and the small green spherical vegetables. She was almost certain that dogs were wholly carnivorous. Perhaps this breeder had fed his dogs on sprouts; if so, it was no wonder his business had ultimately failed.

'Frogs, Sprouts, Clogs and Krauts,' he elaborated meaningfully.

'Oh,' said Isserley.

She should, she felt, have listened to her own misgivings before night fell: only the deranged would be hitching afterwards. Never mind: the turn-off for the seaboard villages was only a few minutes away, and she could get rid of this character then, unless he was heading for her neck of the woods himself, of course. She hoped not. She was feeling ghastly again, exhaustion and an inexplicable misery throbbing in her system like poison.

'Those bastards are sitting in judgement over there,' the dog breeder blustered, stabbing his fingers clumsily into the chocolate selection, 'far away from this fucking country – excuse my French – and they don't have a fucking clue. YunderstandwhatI'msaying?'

'Mm. I'm turning off in a minute,' she said, frowning and weaving her head from side to side as she searched the gloom for the familiar B9175 sign.

His reaction to her being momentarily preoccupied like this was sudden and vehement.

'Jesus Christ!' he groaned. 'You're not even listening. A bunch of foreigners from over your way fucked up my whole life, yunderstand? One year I've got eighty grand in the bank, a Wolseley, a wife, more dogs than I can shake a stick at. Five years later, I've got sweet FA! Living alone in a prefab in fucking Bonar Bridge, with a fucking Mondeo rusting in the back yard! Looking for work as a fucking gardener! Where's the sense in that, eh? You tell me!'

The indicator was already ticking, flashing in the dimness of the cabin. Isserley slowed the car down in anticipation of the turn, checked the surviving mirrors for traffic. Then she turned to face him, meeting his glazed little eyes with her own enormous ones.

'No sense at all,' she assured him, flipping the icpathua toggle.

Back on the farm, Ensel was first out of the steading as always, bounding up to the car with an almost grotesque eagerness. His two companions were still silhouetted in the light, slow to follow, as if bowing to some ritual privilege of Ensel's.

'I wish you wouldn't do that,' said Isserley irritably as he poked his snout through the passenger window to admire the paralysed vodsel.

'Do what?' he retorted, blinking.

Isserley leaned across the dog-breeder's lap to unlock the door.

'Rush out to see what I've got,' she grunted, half blinded by a stab of pain in her spine. The door opened and the vodsel's body tipped out into Ensel's arms. The other men crowded around to help him.

'Couldn't I come and let you know,' persisted Isserley, straightening up gingerly, 'if I've got anything, and otherwise just go straight to my cottage without any fuss?'

Ensel was fumbling about, trying to find a secure grip on the vodsel's torso. The cow leather of the creature's jacket, alarmingly, had just unzipped itself with a heavy lurch of unrelated flesh.

'But we don't mind if you haven't managed to get anything,' protested Ensel in a wounded tone. 'Nobody blames you.'

Isserley gripped the steering wheel and fought back tears of rage and exhaustion.

'It's not about whether I've managed to get anything or not,' she sighed. 'Sometimes I'm . . . tired, that's all. I want to be alone.'

Ensel backed away from the car, dragging his bit of the vodsel onto the waiting trolley, frowning with effort as he and his companions wheeled their burden backwards towards the light. Frowning too, perhaps, at the way she'd just attacked him.

'I just . . . we're just trying to help, that's all,' he called to her miserably.

Isserley laid her head on her arms, slumping over the steering wheel.

'Oh God,' she moaned under her breath. This really was too much on top of a hard day's work in impossible circumstances and a narrow escape from death: having to juggle the fragile complexities of human emotions.

'Forget it!' she yelled, peering straight down into the darkness at her feet, an oily confusion of foot pedals, filthy rubber matting, leather gloves and spilled chocolates. 'We'll talk about it in the morning!'

By the time the steading door had rolled shut and silence had returned to Ablach Farm, Isserley was weeping again, so that her glasses, when she finally removed them, almost slipped out of her fingers.

Men, she thought.

7

WHEN ISSERLEY FINALLY clawed her way back to the surface
from a black hole of sleep, she opened her eyes to find that it
was still dark. Floating in a void, her little clock's digital
numbers were feeble and flickering, and said zero, zero, zero,
zero. The internal power source needed replacing. She should
have anticipated this, she thought, instead of . . . instead of
what? Instead of wasting money on a box of chocolates she had
no intention of eating.

She lay tangled in the bedclothes, confused, disoriented and
mildly anxious. Though she could see nothing in the blackness
except the flickering clock, she suddenly had a vivid mental
picture of the floor of her car, the last thing she could recall
seeing before plummeting into sleep. She must remember to
clear out the spilled chocolates before driving off again, or else
they would get squashed underfoot. She'd seen the dog
breeder bite into one. They had some sort of goo inside

them that would make a sticky mess and no doubt decompose in time.

She'd let things veer a little out of control lately; she must restore some order at the earliest opportunity.

Isserley had no idea how many hours she had slept; whether the long winter night was still young or would soon be ending. It was even possible she'd slept through the brief pale hours of daylight, and that it was now already the dark afternoon of the following day.

She tried to gauge from how she was feeling how long she had been unconscious. She was as warm as an overheated engine, sweat simmering out of those parts of her that could still sweat. That meant, assuming she could still trust her cycles, that she had slept either a very short or a very long time.

She stretched her limbs cautiously; the pain was no worse than usual, but usual was bad. She would have to get up and do her exercises, regardless of what time it was, or she would end up unable to get up at all, trapped in a cage of her own bone and muscle.

Moonlight was sketching some detail into her bedroom now as the pupils of her eyes at last began to dilate. Because her room was bare, though, the details were things like cracks in the walls, shards of peeled paint, functionless light switches, and, in the hearth, the dull pearly gleam of the sleeping television. Parched, Isserley fumbled for the glass of water beside the bed, but it was empty. She raised it to her lips and tipped it upside down just to make sure. Empty. Never mind: she could wait. She was strong. Needs could not bully her.

She sat up, clumsily disentangled herself from the bed-sheets, and launched herself off the mattress onto the floor, landing crookedly, almost pitching sideways. A long needle of pain stabbed through the base of her spine, the amputation site; she'd tried to steady her balance with her tail again. She swayed back and forth, finding her new centre of gravity; the palms of her feet, damp with perspiration, adhered slightly to the frigid floorboards.

The moonlight was not enough to do her exercises by. She didn't know why she should need to *see* her limbs in order to exercise them, but she did. It was as if, in too profound a darkness, she could not be sure what sort of creature she was. She needed to verify what remained of her body.

Perhaps the television, as well as providing some illumination, would serve to orient her. Unreality was swirling all around her like the delirious miasmas above the oxygen pits at the heart of the Estates; she had been dreaming again.

After dreams of the pits, it would have been comforting to wake up in the sunlight of a safe world. Failing that, it would have been reassuring to see the clock glowing promisingly at her. But if she could have neither, she could do without.

Isserley stumbled over to the hearth and switched on the television. Its tarnished screen revived sluggishly, like embers fanned by a breeze; then a bright image materialized like a psychedelic fire in the hearth, as Isserley prepared to contort herself into shape.

Two male vodsels dressed in mauve tights, ruched blouses and bizarre green hats like stuffed Loch Ness Monster toys were standing next to a hole in the ground, out of which loose earth was being jettisoned like little puffs of brown breath. One of the vodsels was holding a small white sculpture in the palm of his hand, a three-dimensional version of the danger symbol displayed on Ablach's main steading.

'. . . and now my lady worms,' he was saying, addressing

the sculpture in an outlandish accent stranger still than Glaswegian. 'Chapless, and knocked about the muzzard with a sexed unspayed.'

Isserley pondered this for a few seconds, grunting with effort as she tipped her stiff torso repeatedly against her right hip.

The television camera took her (*ugh!*) inside the hole in the ground, where there was an ugly old vodsel digging in the earth. He was singing as he laboured, in a slurry voice like John Martyn.

'A pee cacks and a spayed, a spayed friend, a shrouding sheet, oh, a pit of clay for to be made . . .'

It was all a bit depressing, so Isserley changed channels with the fingers of her foot.

A large crowd of vodsels was advancing down a wide sunlit street paved with stones. Each member of the procession was shrouded in a bedsheet, with a narrow slit cut out for eyes. One held aloft a placard on which was affixed an enlarged and indistinct newspaper photograph of a bedsheet-shrouded creature just like them. A reporter's voice was saying that with the whole world watching, the big question was just how far these women would be allowed to go.

Isserley watched the procession for another couple of seconds, curious how far the vodsels would be allowed to go, but the camera didn't show her; it switched to something entirely different, a large crowd of male vodsels in a sports stadium. Many of them resembled the dog breeder, and some were punching and wrestling each other while police tried to shepherd them away from the others.

The camera switched to a close-up of an impressively beefy vodsel bulging out of a colourful football shirt. He was pushing his upper lip over his nose with his thumbs, revealing the word BRITISH branded on the wet pink flesh squirming above his yellow teeth. Then he pulled his lower lip down over his chin, revealing the word BULLDOG.

Isserley changed the channel. A female vodsel with breasts almost as big as Isserley's was screaming hysterically, clutching her cheeks with her hands, at the sight of a creature Isserley could not identify. It resembled a giant insect and waved pincers like a crab, but advanced clumsily on two legs. A male vodsel ran into the picture and shot the insect creature with what looked like a beam of torchlight from a plastic pistol.

'I thought I told you to stay with the others,' barked the male to the female, while the poor insect creature writhed in agony. Its dying cries, barely audible above the din of animal orchestrations, were alarmingly human-sounding, as sibilant as sexual passion.

Isserley switched the television off. More awake now, she'd remembered something she should have known from the beginning, which was that there was no point trying to orient yourself to reality with television. It only made things worse.

Years ago, television had been a wonderful teacher, offering her titbits of information constantly, which she could consume if she was ready, leave alone if she wasn't. Unlike the books Esswis had gathered together for her to study, the luminous box in the hearth chattered indefatigably whether she was listening or not, never getting stuck on a word or a page. In all those early months of reading and re-reading, Isserley never managed to get through more than a few paragraphs of *History of the World* by W.N. Weech, JP, FSA, MA (even the fearsomely detailed farming pamphlet *Which Rotovator?* was less daunting) but the basics of vodsel psychology had been made crystal clear by the television within a couple of weeks.

Strangely, however, she seemed to have reached a point, years ago already, when there wasn't room for any more titbits from the television. It had passed its prime of usefulness, and was reverting to babble.

She still wanted to know what day of the week it was, and whether the sun was near or far. She would, she decided, go outside as soon as she was limber, and interpret the night for herself. In fact, why wait? She could finish her exercises at the beach, under cover of darkness; she suspected strongly it was the small hours of the morning. Monday morning.

She was regaining her grip.

Feeling her way down the banister, she descended the stairs to the bathroom. The bedroom and the bathroom were the only rooms in her cottage that she knew well; the other rooms were a bit of a mystery. But the bathroom was not a problem. She had gone there countless times in the dark – virtually every morning during the winter months.

Isserley walked in, blind. The palms of her feet sensed the change from wood to mouldering linoleum. She had little difficulty finding the things she needed. The tub, the taps, the shampoo, the sudden pressurized torrent of water: all these things were in their usual places, waiting for her. No-one ever tampered with them.

Isserley showered with care and patience, giving special attention to the scar-lines and alien clefts in which she had a dangerous lack of sensation: places where infections could grow and where wounds that had never quite healed could slyly venture open. Her hands smoothed great foams of lather back and forth across her body, spongy slathers of creamy detergent which she imagined as more copious than they probably were. She pictured herself wreathed and haloed in foam, little clouds of it like the frothy spume of pollution carried on the waves sometimes at Ablach Beach.

Abstracted, she drifted away from consciousness, slowly revolving under the warm cascade of water. Her hands and arms continued to slither around on her flesh, slick with lather, settling into a regular rhythm, a regular route. She closed her eyes.

Only when she realized that some of her fingers had strayed between her legs, searching blindly for what was no longer to be found there, did she come back to her senses and rinse herself with businesslike efficiency.

Fully dressed as if for work, Isserley walked through a tunnel of trees towards the sea. Her boots made soft crackling sounds in the frozen mud; her wet hair steamed in the chill air. She moved carefully, measuring her steps in the dimness, her hands hovering away from her hips, ready to break a fall. At one point she turned, waiting a moment for her cloud of breath to clear so she could see how far she had come. Her cottage was a vague silhouette hunched against the night sky, with two upstairs windows reflecting moonlight like the eyes of an owl. She turned back to the firth and kept walking.

After the avenue of trees, the land was opened up to the atmosphere; the size of Ablach Farm became obvious, and Isserley walked a long grassy path snaking between great fields of dormant barley and potatoes. The sea was already visible from here, and the sound of waves seemed all around her.

The moon hung low over the firth, and countless tiny stars shone clearly from the darkest, furthest reaches of the universe; the time must be about two or three in the morning.

Back in the steading, the men would most likely be loading

the ship at last. That was a good thing. The sooner they finished, the sooner it could leave. The moment would arrive when Amlis Vess was sent back where he had come from. What a wonderful release of tension that would be!

She breathed deeply, anticipating it, visualizing him being bundled off. The men would usher him into the hold of the ship, and he would saunter in arrogantly, showing off his pampered, glossy body, holding his head high in an attitude of adolescent disdain. He would probably turn, just at the moment before entering, and cast a piercing glance at whoever was in range, his amber eyes burning in the exquisite blackness of his fur. Then he would be gone. Gone.

Isserley had reached the boundary of Ablach's farmland, fenced off from the cliffs and the steep paths down to the water. The gate was a massive construction of cast iron, half-petrified planks and wire mesh, hingeing on a couple of posts as thick as tree-trunks. The locks and hinges resembled, especially in the moonlight, unwieldy chunks of car engine welded to the wood. Fortunately, the farm's previous owners had built a little wooden stepladder on either side of the gate, to save trouble for two-legged passers-by. Isserley scaled these little steps, three on either side of the gate, with clownish difficulty, thankful no-one could see her struggling. Any normal human could have leapt over.

On the other side of the fence, not far from the gate, a small herd of cows was camped on the narrow fringe of grassy earth between Ablach's boundary and the cliff rim. They snorted nervously at Isserley's approach, the paler-coloured ones luminescing faintly in the gloom. A calf started to its feet, the glints in its eyes swirling like sparks off a fire. Then the entire herd roused itself, and retreated further along the boundary, making the utterly distinctive sound of cluntering hoofs and the heavy *ploff* of faeces.

Isserley turned to look back at the farm. Her own cottage was hidden behind trees, but the farmhouse stood exposed. Its lights were off.

Esswis was asleep, probably. Yesterday morning's gruelling adventures had, she was sure, taken more out of him than he could have admitted to a woman. She pictured him stretched out on a bed just like hers, still wearing his ridiculous farmer clothes, snoring noisily. Tough man or not, he was much older than she was, and had toiled in the Estates for years before Vess Industries had fished him out; Isserley had been offered rescue after only three days. Also, he'd been operated on a whole year before her. Quite possibly the surgeons had done a worse job on him, experimenting with techniques they didn't perfect until Isserley came under the knife. If so, she pitied Esswis. His nights could not be easy.

Isserley walked down the cattle path towards the beach, choosing her footing carefully on the steep slope. She got half-way, almost to the point where the gradient became gentler, then she paused. Sheep were grazing at the bottom, and she didn't want to scare them off. She liked sheep more than any other animal; they had an innocence and a serene intentness about them that was worlds away from the brutish cunning and manic excitability of, say, vodsels. Seen in poor light, they could almost be human children.

So, Isserley stopped, half-way down the cliff, and finished her exercises there. With the cows dawdling uneasily somewhere above her head and the sheep grazing unperturbed below her, she assumed the correct positions, extending her arms towards the silvery horizon, then bending down to the shore of the Moray Firth, then tipping sideways, north towards Rockfield and the lighthouse, south towards Balintore and the denser populations beyond, then, finally, reaching up towards the stars.

After a long time repeating these actions over and over, she achieved a state of half-consciousness, mesmerized by the moon and the monotony, and persisted far longer than usual, becoming so limber in the end that her movements became graceful and fluid.

She might have been dancing.

Back in her cottage, still hours before dawn, Isserley found her mood darkening again. She loitered in her bedroom, bored and irritable.

She really would have to ask the men to fix up the wiring in this house, so she could have electric light. The steading had electric light, Esswis's farmhouse had electric light; there was no reason why her cottage shouldn't. In fact, come to think of it, it was quite amazing that her cottage *didn't* – outrageous, even.

She tried to recall the circumstances of her coming to live here. Not the journey, certainly not what had happened in the Estates, but what had happened immediately upon arrival at Ablach Farm. What arrangements had been made? Had the men expected her to live under the steading with them, in their fetid burrows? If so, she would have knocked that idea on the head pretty smartly.

So where had she slept the first night? Her memories were as indistinct as the fused and blackened contents of an exhausted bonfire.

Perhaps she'd chosen this cottage herself, or maybe it had been suggested by Esswis, who'd had a whole year, after all, to become familiar with what was on the farm. All Isserley knew was that, unlike Esswis's farmhouse, her cottage had been derelict when she'd moved into it, and of course it was still more or less derelict now.

But the electrical extension cord that snaked all the way through her house, connecting the television, the water heater and the outside lamp to a generator: who had organized that, and how grudgingly? Was this another example of her being exploited, used like a piece of brute equipment?

She strained to remember, then was embarrassed and slightly bewildered when she did.

The men – mainly Ensel, most likely, though she couldn't recall any individuals – had fussed around her from the moment she arrived, offering to perform all kinds of miracles just for her. Ogling her in fascinated pity, they had ganged up to douche her with reassurance. Yes, they appreciated that what had been done to her by Vess Industries couldn't be helped now, but it wasn't the end of the world. They would make it up to her. They would make this cottage, this draughty near-ruin, a real home for her, a cosy little nest; she was a poor little thing, she must be so upset at how she had been . . . messed about with, yes, they understood all about that, I mean, look at Esswis, poor old bastard; but she was brave, yes, she was a plucky girl, and they would treat her as if there was nothing odd or ugly about her at all, for she and they were all the same under the skin, weren't they?

She'd told them she wanted nothing from them, nothing. She would do *her* job, they would do theirs.

To do her job properly, she would need a bare minimum of things provided for her: a light in or near the shed where the car was kept, running hot water, and one electrical connection to power a radio or some similar apparatus. For the rest she would be fine. She would take care of herself.

In fact, she'd spelled it out more crudely still, in case they were too stupid to take the hint: what she needed most was privacy. They were to leave her alone.

But wouldn't she get lonely? they'd asked her. No, she wouldn't, she'd told them, she'd be too busy. She had to prepare for a job whose complications and subtleties they couldn't hope to understand. She had a lot of brain work to do. She would have to learn everything from first principles, or this whole thing would come falling down on all their heads. The challenges she was about to tackle couldn't be mastered quite so easily as carrying bales of straw into a barn or digging holes beneath the ground.

Isserley paced her bedroom now, aware of the clock radio's constant feeble flashing. Her footsteps rang loud and hollow against the bare floorboards; it was rare for her to be wearing shoes indoors unless she was on the point of leaving the house.

Irritably, she switched the television on again, even though she'd tried it once already since returning to the cottage and given up in annoyance.

Because it had been switched off so recently, the machine came back to life at once. The vodsel who, a few minutes ago, had been peering through binoculars at an assortment of brightly coloured underpants fluttering on a washing-line was now licking his lips and twitching his cheeks. Female vodsels had gathered under the line, reaching up to unpeg the garments. Inexplicably, the twine hung higher than they could easily reach, and they teetered on tiptoe, jumping like infants, their pink breasts quivering like jelly.

On another channel, several very serious-looking vodsels of mixed gender were sitting behind a desk, shoulder to shoulder. Above their heads, a long narrow electronic sign, like a toy

version of the one near Kessock Bridge, was displaying a
sequence of letters and spaces: I | I | u I | Y

'R?' ventured one of the vodsels.

'No-o-o, I'm afraid not,' purred an unseen voice.

Isserley's car stood idling next to the shed, lit up by the lone
tungsten lamp. She was cleaning out the car's cabin, slowly
and contemplatively, making each small action last. The sun
was still a long way from coming, hidden behind the curve of
the planet.

Isserley was kneeling beside her vehicle, leaning in through
the open door. She was using the *Ross-shire Journal* as a
groundsheet, to save the green velvety knees of her pants
getting muddy. With the tips of her fingers she felt for the
spilled chocolates and threw them one by one over her
shoulder. Birds would eat them by and by, she was sure.

Suddenly, reminded, she felt weak and sick with hunger.
She'd eaten nothing since the potato crisps yesterday afternoon, a little snow, and about a litre of warm water she'd
drunk this morning straight from the shower stream. It was
not nearly enough to keep a human being fuelled.

So strange, the way she never seemed to be aware she was
hungry until she was ravenous, almost collapsing. An unfortunate idiosyncrasy, and a potentially dangerous one: she
would have to be careful managing it. A routine was
important, like eating breakfast with the men every morning
before going out on the road – a routine which had been
disturbed by Amlis Vess.

Breathing deeply, as if a few good mouthfuls of air might
tide her over for a while longer, Isserley continued cleaning
out her car. There seemed no end to the spilled chocolates;
they had found hiding places in every cranny like rotund

beetles. She wondered if her body would let her get away with eating some of them.

She picked up the box, which, along with the dog breeder's gloves, she'd laid on the ground for burning later. Holding the cardboard rectangle up to the light, she squinted at its list of ingredients. 'Sugar', 'milk powder' and 'vegetable fats' sounded safe enough, but 'cocoa mass', 'emulsifier', 'lecithin' and 'artificial flavours' had a chancy ring to them. In fact, 'cocoa mass' sounded positively lethal. Her gut-reflex queasiness was probably Nature's way of telling her to stick to the foods that she knew.

But if she went into the steading to eat with the men, she might run into Amlis Vess. That was the last thing she needed. How long could she hang on? How soon might he go? She gazed at the horizon, yearning for that first glimmer of light.

Over the years, her reluctance to have more than the minimum necessary contact with men had made her very self-reliant, especially when it came to caring for her car. She'd already replaced the broken side-mirror, a job she would once have needed Ensel for. If she could just avoid trouble, she could keep this car forever without having to change it. It was made of steel and glass and plastic – why should it wear out? She put fuel in it whenever it needed it, oil, water, everything. She drove it slowly and gently, and kept it safe from police.

She'd got the new side-mirror from the already much cannibalized grey Nissan estate. A sad-looking carcass it was now, but there was no point being sentimental. The mirror fitted perfectly into her little red Corolla; all sign of the accident was expunged.

Isserley, still admiring the neatness of the surgery she'd performed, cleaned her little Corolla some more. Its engine was still idling, a well-oiled machine breathing aromatic gas into the raw air. She liked her car. It was a good car, really. If she took care of it, it wouldn't let her down. Meticulously, Isserley wiped mud and grease off the foot pedals, tidied the glovebox, topped up the icpathua reservoir under the passenger seat with a sharp-nozzled flask.

Perhaps she could drive out to find an all-night garage somewhere, and buy herself something to eat. Amlis Vess would be gone very soon, probably within a day or two. It wouldn't kill her, surely, to eat vodsel food for a day or two. Then he would be gone, and she could get herself back to normal.

She knew, however, that if she went out on the roads now there was a risk – remote but real – that some miserable lunatic of a hitcher would be out there too, thumbing a ride. And, knowing her, she would probably pick him up, and he would be totally unsuitable, and she would end up in the Cairngorms. She was like that.

The men always had a big breakfast, high in protein and starch. A dish piled high, steaming. Meat pies, sausages, gravy. Bread fresh out of the oven, cut in slices as thick as you liked. She always cut hers thin, and made sure the slices were neat and of even width, not like the deformed clumps the men hacked off for themselves. She usually had two of these, three at most, with gushu or mussanta paste. But today . . .

Isserley stood up and slammed the car's door shut. There was no way she was going underground to be harangued by some pompous troublemaker while a bunch of Estate trash looked on, wondering if she would crack. Hunger was one thing, principles another.

She walked round to the front of her car and opened the bonnet. Leaning in, she surveyed the warm, strong-smelling, gently trembling engine. She confirmed that she had replaced, in its correct groove, the slender antenna of stainless steel with which she'd recently penetrated the oil tank and checked the level. Now, with a canister of spray from Donny's Garage, she tended to the spark-plugs and the ignition cables. With her fingers she exposed the gleaming cylinder of liquid aviir, the one imported modification to this vehicle's indigenous motor. The metal of the cylinder was transparent, and Isserley could clearly see the aviir inside, its oily surface tension vibrating in sympathy with the engine. This, too, was as it should be, though with any luck she would never have to use it.

She closed the bonnet and, on an impulse, sat down on it. The warm, vibrating metal gave her a pleasant sensation through the thin fabric of her trousers, and distracted her from the insistent rumbling in her stomach. On the horizon, a glimmer of sunrise defined the contours of the mountains. Right in front of her nose, a single snowflake spiralled down.

'Isserley,' said Isserley into the intercom.

The door of the steading rolled open immediately, and she hurried into the light. A whirl of snow, sharp as pine needles, followed her inside, as if sucked by a vacuum. Then the door rolled shut again, and she was out of the weather.

As she had expected, work was well underway in the hangar; two men were busy loading the ship. One was perched inside the hull, waiting for more glistening cargo to be handed up. The other was with the trolleys, which were by now piled high with pinky-red packages. A fortune's worth of raw meat, all neatly parcelled into portions, swathed in transparent viscose, packed into plastic pallets.

'Hoi, Isserley!' The workman pushing the trolleys was

stopping to greet her. Hesitating on her way towards the lift, she waved back, as perfunctorily as she could manage. Encouraged, the man allowed his little wheeled tower of pallets to roll to a standstill and ambled over to her. Isserley had no idea who he was.

No doubt she'd been introduced to each one of the men personally when she'd first arrived at the farm, but this one's name escaped her now. He was stupid-looking, fat and squat — a full head shorter than Amlis Vess — and his fur reminded her of some dead thing drying out on the side of the A9, a wiry grey pelt made indistinct by car tyres and the elements. Into the bargain he had some sort of disgusting skin ailment that made half his face look like mouldy fruit. Isserley at first found it difficult to look at him directly, then, for fear of offending him and causing him to retaliate on her own disfigurement, she leaned closer to him and concentrated on his eyes.

'Hoi, Isserley,' he said again, as if the effort of coming up with this much of their shared language was too good to waste.

'I thought I'd better have a meal,' announced Isserley in a businesslike tone, 'before I start work. Is the coast clear?'

'The coast?' The mouldy man squinted at her in confusion. His head turned unconsciously in the direction of the firth.

'I mean, is Amlis Vess safely out of the way?'

'Oh yeah, he don't bother us,' drawled the mouldy man in an accent twice as thick as Ensel's. 'He just stays down in the food hall, or down in the vodsel pens, and we get on with the loading up here, no problem.'

Isserley opened her mouth to speak, couldn't think of anything to say.

'He won't do nothing now,' the mouldy man assured her. 'Yns and Ensel take it in turns to watch him. He basically just hangs around and talks crap. He don't care if nobody's got a clue what he's on about. Goes and talks to the animals when the humans get sick of him.'

Just for an instant Isserley forgot that the vodsels were tongueless, and was alarmed at the thought of them communicating with Amlis Vess, but she calmed down when the mouldy man laughed coarsely and added, 'We says to him, "Do the animals talk back to you, then?"'

He laughed again, a despicable whinny tainted by half a lifetime in the Estates. 'Funny bastard, good for killing the boredom,' he winked in summation. 'We'll want him back when he's gone.'

'Well, maybe . . . if you say so,' grimaced Isserley, making a break for the lift. 'Excuse me, I'm starving.'

And she was away.

Amlis Vess was not in the food and recreation hall.

Isserley verified this, by casting one more glance across the sterile, low-ceilinged barracks, then resumed breathing.

The hall, though large, was a simple rectangle, crudely excavated without nooks or recesses, and containing little except for the low dining tables; there was nothing big enough to hide a tall man with strikingly beautiful markings. He simply wasn't here.

Though the hall itself was empty, the long low bench outside the kitchen was already laid with bowls of condiments, tureens of cold vegetables, tubs of mussanta, loaves of newly baked bread, cakes, pitchers of water and ezziin, large plastic trays of cutlery. A divine smell of roasting was coming out of the kitchen.

Isserley pounced on the bread and cut herself two slices, which she spread liberally with mussanta paste. Pressing them into a sandwich, she started eating, pushing the food past her insensate lips into her yearning mouth. Mussanta had never tasted so delicious. She swallowed hard, chewing energetically, impatient to cut more bread, spread more paste.

The smell from the kitchen was intoxicating. Something much better than usual was cooking in there, something more adventurous than potato in fat. Admittedly Isserley was rarely here when the cooking was being done; she often took her meals cold after the cook had left and most of the men had already eaten. She'd pick at leftovers, trying to look inconspicuous, concealing her distaste at the smell of cooling fat. But this smell today was something else.

Still clutching her sandwich, Isserley edged up to the open door of the kitchen and peeked inside, catching a glimpse of the great brown back of Hilis, the cook. A notoriously sharp-sensed character, he was aware of her presence immediately.

'Fuck off!' he yelled cheerfully, before he'd even turned around. 'Not ready!'

Embarrassed, Isserley made to retreat, but as soon as Hilis swung round and saw who she was, he threw out a singed and sinewy arm in conciliation.

'Isserley!' he cried, smiling as broadly as his massive snout allowed. 'Why must you always eat that crap? You break my heart! Come in here and see what I'm about to serve!'

Awkwardly she ventured into the kitchen, leaving the offending sandwich on the bench outside. Ordinarily, no-one was permitted in here; Hilis was protective of his gleaming domain, beavering away in it alone like an obsessed scientist in a humid and luridly lit laboratory. Oversized silver utensils hung all over the walls like the tools in Donny's Garage, dozens of specialized implements and gadgets. Transparent jars of spices and bottles of sauce on the shelves and workbenches added some colour to the metallic surfaces, though most of the actual food was stashed away inside refrigerators and metal drums. Hilis himself was unarguably the most vividly organic thing in the kitchen, a thickly furred, powerfully built bundle of nervous energy. Isserley barely knew him; she and he had exchanged perhaps forty sentences over the years.

'Come on, come on!' he growled. 'But watch your step.'

The ovens were inside the floor, so that a human could tend to the food without overbalancing. Hilis hunched over the biggest of them, looking down through the thick glassy door into the glowing recess. Gesturing urgently, he invited Isserley to do the same.

She knelt next to him.

'Look at that,' he said with pride.

Inside the oven, shimmering in an orange halo, six spits rotated slowly, each loaded with four or five identical cuts of meat. They were as brown as freshly tilled earth, and smelled absolutely heavenly, sizzling and twinkling in their own juices.

'Looks good,' admitted Isserley.

'It *is* good,' affirmed Hilis, lowering his twitching nose as close to the glass as he could short of touching. 'Better than what I've usually got to work with, that's for sure.'

Everyone knew this was a sore point with Hilis: the best cuts of meat were always reserved for the cargo ship, and he was allotted the poorer-quality mince, the necks, offal and extremities.

'When I heard old man Vess's son was coming,' he said, basking in the oven's orange glow, 'I assumed I'd be free to put on something special for a change. I wasn't to know, was I?'

'But . . .' frowned Isserley, puzzling over the delay

between Amlis's arrival and these wonderful steaks revolving in the oven now. Hilis interrupted her, grinning.

'I had these steaks marinating for twenty-four hours already before the mad bastard even arrived! What was I going to do? Rinse 'em off under the tap? These little fuckers are perfection, I tell you, they are absolute bloody perfection on a skewer. They are going to taste fucking unbelievable!' Enthusiasm was making Hilis hyperactive.

Isserley stared down at the roasting meat. Its aroma was pushing through the glass and floating straight into her nostrils.

'You're smelling it, aren't you!' Hilis proclaimed in triumph, as if he was responsible for conjuring up something that had, against all odds, managed to penetrate her pathetically tiny, surgically mutilated nose. 'Isn't it glorious!'

Isserley nodded, dizzy with desire.

'Yes,' she whispered.

Hilis, unable to keep still, paced around his kitchen in tight circles, fidgeting and fussing.

'Isserley, please,' he implored her, transferring a prong and a carving knife back and forth from hand to hand. 'Please. You've *got* to have some of this. Make an old man happy. I *know* you can appreciate good food. You hung around with the Elite when you were a girl, that's what the men say. You didn't grow up eating garbage like these dumb goons from the Estates.'

In a state of exhibitionist excitement, he flipped open the lid of the oven, releasing a richly flavoursome blast of heat.

'Isserley,' he begged, '*Let* me cut you a slice of this. Let me, let me, let me.'

She laughed, embarrassed. 'Fine, OK!' she agreed hastily.

He was quick as a spark, his carving technique a performance that could be missed in an eye's blink.

'Yesyes*yes*,' he enthused, springing up. Isserley recoiled slightly as a steaming, sizzling morsel appeared inches from her mouth, impaled on the razor-sharp tip of the carving knife. Gingerly she took the meat between her teeth and tugged it free.

A soft voice sounded from the doorway of the kitchen.

'You just don't know what you're doing,' sighed Amlis Vess.

'No unauthorized fucking personnel in my kitchen!' retorted Hilis instantly.

Amlis Vess took a step backwards; to be fair, very little of him had been inside the room in the first place. Only his startling black face and perhaps the swell of his white breast. His retreat didn't even look like a retreat, more like a casual realignment of balance, a shifting of his muscles. He came to rest technically outside the room, but with the undiminished intensity of his gaze still taking up a great deal of space inside. And his gaze was directed not at Hilis, but at Isserley.

Isserley chewed what remained of her delicious morsel self-consciously, too unnerved to move. Luckily the meat was virtually melting in her mouth, it was so tender.

'What's your problem, Mr Vess?' she said at last.

Amlis's jaw tensed in anger and the muscles in his shoulders flexed as if he was considering attacking her, but instead he relaxed abruptly, as if he'd just given himself an injection of something calmative.

'That meat you're eating,' he said softly, 'is the body of a creature that lived and breathed just like you and me.'

Hilis groaned and rolled his eyes in despair and pity, for the pretensions and dopey confusions of the young. Then, to Isserley's dismay, he turned his back on it all, applying himself to the work at hand, seizing hold of the nearest cooking pot.

With Amlis's words still ringing in her ears, Isserley took courage, as she had done last time, by focusing on his upper-class accent, his velvety diction groomed by wealth and privilege. Deliberately, she recalled being petted and then discarded by the Elite; she pictured the authorities who'd decided she would be more suited to a life in the Estates, men with accents just like Amlis Vess's. She invited that accent in, listening to the sharp chord of resentment it struck deep inside her, letting it reverberate.

'Mr Vess,' she said icily, 'I hate to tell you this, but I really doubt there's much similarity between the way you and *I* live and breathe, let alone between me and' – she passed her tongue over her teeth for provocative effect – 'my breakfast.'

'We're all the same under the skin,' suggested Amlis, a little huffily she thought. She would have to aim for this weak spot of his, his filthy-rich idealist's need to deny social reality.

'Funny how you've managed to keep your looks, then,' she sneered, 'with all the hard backbreaking work you've had to do.'

A direct hit, Isserley noted. Amlis seemed poised to spring again, his eyes burning, but then once more he relaxed: another shot of the same drug.

'This is getting us nowhere,' he sighed. 'Come with me.'

Isserley's mouth fell open in disbelief.

'Come with you?'

'Yes,' said Amlis, as if confirming the finer details of a venture they'd already agreed on. 'Down below. Down where the vodsels are.'

'You . . . you must be joking,' she said, uttering a short laugh which she'd intended to be contemptuous, but which came out merely shaky.

'Why not?' he challenged innocently.

She almost choked on her reply; perhaps it was a tiny thread of meat lodged in her throat. Because I'm so scared of the depths, she was thinking. Because I don't want to be buried alive again.

'Because I have work to get on with,' she said.

He stared intently into her eyes, not aggressively, but as if he was judging the distance, the logistics for a leap into her soul.

'Please,' he said. 'There's something I've seen down there, that I need you to explain. Honestly. I've asked the men; none of them know. Please.'

There was a pause, during which she and Amlis stood motionless while Hilis kept the air generously stocked with banging and clashing. Then, astounded, Isserley heard her belated response as if from a great distance. She heard it only vaguely; couldn't even be sure of the exact wording. But whatever it was, it meant yes. In a dream, to the surreal accompaniment of clashing metal and the sizzle of meat, she was saying yes to him.

He turned, his lithe body flowing away. She followed him, out of Hilis's kitchen, towards the lift.

Several men were gathered in the dining hall by now, loitering, murmuring, chewing; watching Isserley and Amlis Vess pass among them.

No-one made a move to intervene.

No-one threatened Amlis with death if he dared take another step.

Alarms failed to scream into action when the lift opened for them, nor did the lift's doors refuse to close when they stepped inside together.

All in all, the universe seemed not to appreciate that anything was amiss.

Utterly bewildered, Isserley stood next to Amlis in the featureless confines of the lift, facing front, but aware of his long dark neck and head somewhere near her shoulder, his smooth flank breathing inches from her hip. The cabin descended noiselessly, arrived with a hiss.

The door slid open, and Isserley moaned softly in claustrophobic distress. Everything out there was steeped in almost complete darkness, as if they had been dropped into a narrow fissure between two strata of compacted rock with only a child's faltering flashlight to guide them. There was a stench of fermenting urine and faeces, a few spidery contours of wire mesh sketched in by feeble infra-red bulbs, and, swaying everywhere before them, the firefly glints of a swarm of eyes.

'Do you know where the light is?' said Amlis politely.

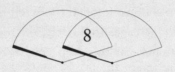

8

ISSERLEY FUMBLED, AND found the switch. A flood of harsh light rushed to fill the compound from floor to ceiling, like a tide of seawater into a crevice.

'Ugh,' she groaned squeamishly. To be so far inside the earth was a nightmare come true.

'A nightmare, yes?' said Amlis Vess.

Isserley looked to him, scared and in need of comfort, but he meant the livestock, of course, not the claustrophobia – she could tell from that infuriating grimace of pity on his face. Typical man: so obsessed with his own idealism he was incapable of feeling empathy for a human being suffering right under his nose.

Isserley stepped clear of the lift, determined not to humiliate herself in front of him. A few moments ago, she'd felt like burying her face in the soft black fur of his neck, clinging to his perfectly balanced body; now she felt like killing him.

'It's just the stink of animals,' she sniffed, eyes averted from him as he padded up to her side. The lift hissed shut behind them and disappeared.

In excavating this deepest of the levels, the men had burrowed out no more of the solid Triassic rock than they absolutely had to. The ceiling was less than seven feet high, and the accumulated steam of cattle breath hung in a haze around the fluorescent strips. The vodsel enclosures, a corona of linked pens all along the walls, took up almost the entire floor space; there was just enough room left down the middle for a walkway. In the cages to the left, the monthlings; to the right, the transitionals; at the deep end, against the far wall facing the lift, the new arrivals.

'This is your first time, isn't it?' came Amlis's voice.

'No,' she retorted irritably, unnerved by how closely he must be watching her body language.

She had, in point of fact, been here just once before, at the very beginning before there were any animals. The men had wanted to show her what they'd constructed in honour of her coming to the farm, all ready and waiting for her vital contribution.

'Very impressive,' she'd said, or words to that effect, and fled.

Now, years later, she had returned, with one of the world's wealthiest young men at her side, because he wanted to ask her a question. 'Surreal' did not begin to describe the situation.

The cages were grimier and more cramped than she remembered; the wooden beams pitted and discoloured, the wire mesh soiled, masked in places with the dark putty of faeces and other unidentifiable matter. And of course, the livestock added stench and the looming density of flesh, the humid ambience of recycled breath. In all, there were more than thirty vodsels impounded here, which came as rather a shock to Isserley: she hadn't realized how hard she must constantly be working.

The few remaining monthlings were huddled together in a mound of fast-panting flesh, the divisions between one muscle-bound body and the next difficult to distinguish, the limbs confused. Hands and feet spasmed at random, as if a co-ordinated response was struggling vainly to emerge from a befuddled collective organism. Their fat little heads were identical, swaying in a cluster like polyps of an anemone, blinking stupidly in the sudden light. You would never guess they'd have the cunning to run if released.

All around the monthlings, their thick spiky carpet of straw glistened with the dark diarrhoea of ripeness. Nothing which might cause the slightest harm to human digestion survived in their massive guts; every foreign microbe had been purged and replaced with only the best and most well-trusted bacteria. They clung to each other, as if to keep their number undiminished. There were four of them left; yesterday there had been five, the day before, six.

Across the neatly swept division, the transitionals in the cages opposite squatted torpidly, each on his own little patch of straw. By dividing the available floor space according to an unspoken, instinctual arithmetic, they managed to keep themselves to themselves, if only by inches. They glowered at Isserley and Amlis, some chewing warily on their unfamiliar new feed, others scratching at hair that was growing sparse and mossy, others clenching their fists in their castrated laps. Though still vaguely differentiated in physique and colouring, they saw their own future constantly before them. They were slowly maturing towards their destiny, towards a natural mean.

At the end of the walkway, the three most recent arrivals were on their feet, leaning against the wire mesh, waving and gesticulating.

'Ng! Ng! Ng!' they cried.

Amlis Vess hastened to respond, his luxuriant tail swinging between his powerful silky buttocks as he ran. Isserley followed, advancing slowly and cautiously. She hoped all the vodsels' tongues had been thoroughly seen to. What Amlis didn't know wouldn't hurt him.

As soon as Isserley had stepped within a body's length of the enclosure, she was frightened half to death by a large projectile hurtling against the wire from within, bulging the web of metal directly towards her with a juddering crash. For a nauseous moment she was convinced the barrier had been penetrated, but the bulge sprang back and the vodsel collapsed to the floor, bawling in pain and fury. The inside of his gaping mouth was roasted black where the stub of tongue had been cauterized; white spittle clung to his moustache. He struggled to his feet, clearly intending to lunge at Isserley again, but two of the other vodsels seized hold of him and dragged him back from the wire.

Held down by a tall and athletic individual much younger than himself, the excitable vodsel slumped impotently in his nest of straw, his knees jerking. The third creature scrambled forwards and fell to his knees on a patch of soil right near the wire mesh. He stared down into it, grunting and snuffling in distress as if he'd lost something.

'It's all right, boy,' encouraged Amlis earnestly. 'Do it again. You can do it. I know you can.'

The vodsel bent over the earth, erasing his wild

companion's scuffed footprints from it with the edge of one hand. His empty scrotal sac, still speckled with dried blood from his gelding, swung back and forth as he smoothed the soil and picked fragments of scattered straw out of it. Then he gathered a handful of long straws together, twisted and folded them to make a stiff wand, and began to draw in the dirt.

'Look!' Amlis urged.

Isserley watched, disturbed, as the vodsel scrawled a five-letter word with great deliberation, even going to the trouble of fashioning each letter upside down, so that it would appear right-way-up for those on the other side of the mesh.

'No-one told me they had a language,' marvelled Amlis, too impressed, it seemed, to be angry. 'My father always describes them as vegetables on legs.'

'It depends on what you classify as language, I guess,' said Isserley dismissively. The vodsel had slumped behind his handiwork, head bowed in submission, eyes wet and gleaming.

'But what does it *mean*?' persisted Amlis.

Isserley considered the message, which was M E R C Y. It was a word she'd rarely encountered in her reading, and never on television. For an instant she racked her brains for a translation, then realized that, by sheer chance, the word was untranslatable into her own tongue; it was a concept that just didn't exist.

Isserley stalled, mouth hidden behind one hand, as if finding the stench increasingly hard to take. Though her face was impassive, her mind was racing. How to discourage Amlis from making an unwarranted fuss?

She considered trying to pronounce the strange word with a contortion of her lips and a frown on her brow, as if she were being asked to reproduce a chicken's cackle or a cow's moo. Then, if Amlis asked her what it meant, she could honestly say that there was no word for it in the language of human beings. She opened her lips to speak, but realized just in time that this would be a very stupid mistake. For her to speak the word at all dignified it with the status of being a word in the first place; Amlis would no doubt go into ecstasy over the vodsels' ability to link a pattern of scrawled symbols with a specific sound, however guttural and unintelligible. At a stroke, she would be dignifying the vodsels, in his eyes, with both writing and speech.

But isn't it true, she asked herself, that they have that dignity?

Isserley pushed the thought away. Just look at these creatures! Their brute bulk, their stink, their look of idiocy, the way the shit oozed up between their fat toes. Had she been so badly butchered, brought so close to an animal state physically, that she was losing her hold on humanity and actually *identifying* with animals? If she wasn't careful, she would end up living among them, cackling and mooing in meaningless abandon like the cavorting oddities on television.

All this passed through her mind in a couple of seconds. In a second or two more, she had devised her response to Amlis.

'What do you *mean*, "What does it mean"?' she exclaimed testily. 'It's a scratch mark that means something to vodsels, obviously. I couldn't tell you what it means.'

She looked straight into Amlis's eyes, to add the power of conviction to her denial.

'Well, I can guess what it means,' he observed quietly.

'Yes, I'm sure you wouldn't let a little thing like ignorance stop you,' sneered Isserley, noticing for the first time that he had a few pure white hairs around his eyelids.

'All I'm trying to get across to you,' he persisted, nettled, 'is that the meat you were eating a few minutes ago is the same meat that is trying to communicate with us down here.'

Isserley sighed and folded her arms across her chest, feeling sick from the fluorescent glare, the laboured breathing of thirty beasts inside a fissure far beneath the ground.

'It doesn't communicate to *me*, Amlis,' she said, then blushed at having carelessly addressed him by his first name. 'Can we leave now?'

Amlis frowned, and looked down at the scratches in the dirt.

'Are you sure you don't know what these marks mean?' he asked, with a sharp edge of disbelief in his voice.

'I don't know what you expect of me,' Isserley burst out, suddenly near tears. 'I'm a human being, not a vodsel.'

Amlis looked her up and down, as if only now noticing her horrific disfigurements. He stood there in all his beauty, his black pelt glistening in the humid air, and stared at Isserley, and then at the vodsels and the marks in the dirt.

'I'm sorry,' he said at last, and turned his head towards the lift.

Hours later, as Isserley was driving on the open road, breathing in great mouthfuls of sky from her open window, she thought about how the encounter with Amlis Vess had gone.

She'd coped well, she thought. She had nothing to be ashamed of. He'd been out of line. He had apologized.

The thing about vodsels was, people who knew nothing whatsoever about them were apt to misunderstand them terribly. There was always the tendency to anthropomorphize. A vodsel might do something which resembled a human action; it might make a sound analogous with human distress, or make a

...nalogous with human supplication, and that made the ...ant observer jump to conclusions.

In the end, though, vodsels couldn't do any of the things that really defined a human being. They couldn't siuwil, they couldn't mesnishtil, they had no concept of slan. In their brutishness, they'd never evolved to use hunshur; their communities were so rudimentary that hississins did not exist; nor did these creatures seem to see any need for chail, or even chailsinn.

And, when you looked into their glazed little eyes, you could understand why.

If you were looking clearly, that is.

So, that's why it was better that Amlis Vess didn't know that the vodsels had a language.

She'd have to be careful, then, never to speak it in his earshot. It would only provoke him. It would achieve nothing. In a case like this, a little knowledge was more dangerous than none at all.

It was a good thing the vodsels were always unconscious when they were carried into the steading. Then by the time they were up and about again, they'd already been seen to, so they couldn't make any more noise. That nipped any problems in the bud.

If Amlis could just be kept out of trouble until the transport ship was ready to leave, he need never know any . . . anything else.

And then, once he was in the ship heading home, he could indulge his overdeveloped conscience, his sentimentality, to his heart's content. If he wanted to throw what remained of the vodsels overboard as a way of granting the creatures posthumous freedom, he could go right ahead, and it would be someone else's problem, not hers.

Her problem was more basic, and self-indulgence didn't come into it: she had a difficult job to do, and no-one but her could do it.

Driving past Dalmore Farm in Alness, she spotted a hitcher up ahead. He stood out like a beacon on the crest of a hill. She wound her window closed and turned up the heating. Work had begun.

Even from a distance of a hundred metres or more, she could tell that this one was built like a piece of heavy farm machinery, a creature who would put a strain on any set of wheels. His massive bulk was all the more conspicuous for being crammed into yellow reflective overalls. He might have been an experimental traffic fixture.

As Isserley drove closer, she noted that the yellow overalls were so old and tarnished that they were almost black: the colours of rotting banana peel. Overalls as filthy and decrepit as that couldn't belong to an employee of a company, surely; this fellow must be his own boss; perhaps he didn't work at all.

That was good. Unemployed vodsels were always a good risk. Although to Isserley they looked just as fit as vodsels who had jobs, she'd found that they were often cast out from their society, isolated and vulnerable. And, once exiled, they seemed to spend the rest of their lives skulking at the peripheries of the herd, straining for a glimpse of the high-ranking males and nubile females they yearned to befriend but could never approach for fear of a swift and savage punishment. In a way, the vodsel community itself seemed to be selecting those of its members it was content to have culled.

Isserley reached the hitcher and drove past him, at her usual leisurely speed. He registered her passing, her apparent snub of him, with a squint of indifference; he knew perfectly well that his rotting banana colours would be rejected as an unsuitable match for the taupe upholstery of most cars. But there were plenty more motorists where Isserley came from, he seemed to be thinking, so stuff her.

She assessed him while she drove on. Undoubtedly he had more than enough meat on him; too much, perhaps. Fat was a bad thing: not only was it worthless padding that had to be discarded, but it infiltrated deep inside – or so Unser, the chief processor, had once told her. Fat blighted good meat like a burrowing worm.

This hitcher might well be all muscle, though. She pulled off the road, waited for the right time, and carefully executed a U-turn.

The other thing was: he was totally bald, not a hair on his head – which didn't matter, she supposed, since if she took him he would end up hairless anyway. But what made vodsels go hairless before their time? She hoped it wasn't some defect that would affect the quality of the meat, a disease of some kind. A disembodied voice on television had told her once that victims of cancer went bald. This hitcher in the yellow overalls – there he was again now! – didn't strike her as a victim of cancer; he looked as if he could demolish a hospital with his bare hands. And what about that vodsel she'd had in the car a while back, the one who had cancer of the lung? He'd had plenty of hair, as far as she could recall.

She drove past the baldhead again, confirming that he had enough muscle on him to satisfy anyone. As soon as possible, she made another U-turn.

It was funny, really, that she'd never had a totally bald hitcher before. Statistically, she ought to have. His shining hairless head, coupled with his steely physique and queer clothing, might account for these irrational misgivings she felt, as she slowed to stop for him.

'Want a lift?' she called unnecessarily, as he lumbered up to the door she was opening.

'Ta,' he said, trying to ease himself in. His overalls squeaked comically as he doubled over; she released the seat lock, to give him more room.

He seemed embarrassed by her kindness, and, once seated, looked straight ahead through the windscreen while he fumbled with the seatbelt; he had to pull out the strap for what seemed like yards before it would encompass his girth.

'Right,' he said as soon as the buckle had clicked.

She drove off, with him blushing beside her, his face a pink melon set atop a bulging stack of grimy yellow.

After a full minute, the hitcher at last turned slowly towards her. He looked her up and down. He turned back to the window.

He was thinking, My lucky day.

'My lucky day,' he said.

'I hope so,' said Isserley, in a tone of warm good humour, while an inexplicable chill travelled down her spine. 'Where are you heading?'

The question hung in the air, cooled like uneaten food, and finally congealed. He continued staring ahead.

Isserley considered repeating the question, but felt oddly self-conscious about doing so. In fact, she felt self-conscious altogether. Without being aware of it, she was hunching over slightly, leaning her elbows forward, obscuring her breasts.

'Nice pair of tits you've got there,' he said.

'Thank you,' she said. The atmosphere in the cabin instantly began to throb with agitated molecules.

'They didn't grow overnight,' he sniggered.

'No, they didn't,' she agreed.

Her real teats, budding naturally from her abdomen, had been surgically removed in a separate operation from the one that had grafted these puffy artificial ones onto her chest. The surgeons had used pictures from a magazine sent by Esswis as a guide.

'Biggest I've seen for a long time,' the hitcher added, evidently reluctant to leave off mining such a rich conversational seam.

'Mm,' said Isserley, taking note of a road sign and making some quick calculations. One day she would have to tell Esswis that never, in all her far-ranging travels outside his little domain of fields and fences, had she seen a female vodsel with breasts like the ones in his magazine.

'Were you standing long?' she asked, to change the subject.

'Long enough,' he grunted.

'Where are you hoping to get to?' She hoped that perhaps by now, the question might have penetrated his brain.

'I'll decide that when I get there,' he said.

'Well, I'm afraid I'm only going as far as Evanton,' she said. 'It's a change of scene for you, anyway.'

'Yeah,' he sniffed. 'No problem.'

Again the molecules writhed between them invisibly, in silence.

'So what takes you out on the road today?' she said brightly.

'Things to do, that's all.'

'I didn't mean to be nosy,' she went on. 'I'm just curious about people, that's all.'

'S'alright. Man of few words, that's me.' He said this as if this were a special distinction conferred on him by birth, like wealth or good looks. Helplessly, Isserley thought of Amlis.

'You're a bit of a goer, aren't you?' challenged the hitcher.

'I—I beg your pardon?' she said, unfamiliar with the term.

'Sex,' he explained flatly, his big melon head blushing again. 'On the brain. I can spot it a mile off. You love it, don't you?'

Isserley shifted uneasily in her seat and checked the rear-view mirror.

'Actually, I'm always working too hard to think about it,' she said, trying for a casual tone.

'Bullshit,' he retorted passionlessly. 'You're thinking about it right now.'

'I'm thinking about . . . about problems at work, actually,' she volunteered. She hoped he would ask her what her work was. She would be a plainclothes police officer, she'd decided.

'A girl like you don't need to think,' he snorted.

It was about eight minutes' drive to Evanton. She should have said Ballachraggan, which was half the distance, but he might have been annoyed to be taken for such a short ride.

'I bet a good few guys have touched those, yeah?' he suggested abruptly, as if kick-starting a conversation she'd been cack-handed enough to let stall.

'Not very many,' she declared. The precise tally was none, in truth.

'I don't believe it,' he said, leaning back on the headrest, half closing his eyes.

'Well . . . it's true,' sighed Isserley, disconsolately. According to the digital clock, only fifty seconds had passed.

However, the universe seemed at last to have heard her

prayer. The hitcher's eyes narrowed, then shut in what might have been slumber. His head sank a little into the grimy upturned collar of his overalls. Minutes went by, and little by little the purring of the engine and the rolling grey tide of the road reclaimed a reality they had lost. Evanton was only a couple of miles away by the time the baldhead spoke again.

'You know what gets me?' he said, slightly more animated now.

'No, what gets you?' Isserley was sagging in relief, gratefully feeling the air grow less dense, the molecules moving more calmly.

'Them supermodels,' he said.

Isserley thought first of sophisticated automobiles, then thought he must mean the animated drawings which flickered on television early in the mornings: stylized females flying through space wearing elbow-length gloves and thigh-high boots. Just in time, as she opened her mouth to speak, she remembered the true meaning of the term: she'd glimpsed one of these extraordinary creatures on the news once.

'You like them?' she guessed.

'Hate 'em.'

'They earn a lot more than you or me, don't they?' she remarked, flailing, even now, to find some point of entry into his life.

'For doing fuck all,' he said.

'Life can be unfair,' she offered.

He frowned and pursed his lips, preparing perhaps for some arduous unburdening.

'Some of them supermodels,' he observed, 'like Kate Moss and that black one, well . . . it mystifies me. Mystifies me.'

He spoke the word as if it were something very expensive he'd found lying in the street somewhere, which would ordinarily be far outside his purchasing power, but which he now intended to flaunt to everyone.

'What mystifies you?' said Isserley, quite lost.

'Where's the tits on 'em, that's what I want to know!' he exclaimed, cupping one huge hand in front of his own chest. 'Supermodels, and they got no tits! How's that work?'

'I don't know who decides these things,' conceded Isserley miserably, as the atmosphere in the cabin swarmed once more.

'Queers, I bet,' he grunted. 'What would *they* care about tits? That's the answer, I reckon.'

'Could be,' said Isserley in a small voice, barely audible. She was wrung out. Evanton was very near now, and she would need all her remaining energy to ease him out of the car.

'You'd make a fucking good model,' he informed her, looking her up and down again. 'Page three material.'

She sighed, trying to flash a wry grin.

'Maybe I'd need smaller breasts, eh?' she suggested. 'Like them supermodels.' Her awkward imitation of his uncouth phrasing sounded false and pitifully ingratiating; she'd lost her grip. God, what must he think!

'Fuck them supermodels!' he urged her, in a tone almost of gruff reassurance. '*Your* body's way better. They're not natural, them women. They must take stereoids. Like them Russian runners. Shrinks their tits and gives 'em a deep voice and a must-ash. The things that go on in this fuckin' world. There's no limit. And nobody puts their foot down. Mystifies me.'

'The world is a strange place,' she agreed. Then: 'We're almost there.'

'Where?' he demanded suspiciously.

'Evanton,' she reminded him. 'That's as far as I'm going.'

'Oh, I don't think so,' he responded, in a dull, almost inward tone. 'You can go a bit further than that, I'm sure.'

Isserley's heart began to beat harder.

'No,' she insisted, 'Evanton is as far as I go.'

The hitcher reached inside his overalls and pulled out a large grey Stanley knife with its bright triangular blade already unsheathed.

'Just keep going,' he said softly.

Isserley clasped the steering wheel tight, struggling to keep her breathing under control.

'You don't want to do this,' she said.

That got a laugh out of him at last.

'Turn left just before the next road,' he said.

'It would be better . . . for both of us . . .' she panted, 'if we just stopped . . . and I let you out.' Her left index finger was trembling above the icpathua toggle.

He appeared not to have heard her. An old church with windows cemented shut was looming on the left-hand side, with a long gravel path beside it, disappearing into scrubland.

'This is it coming up now,' he advised her quietly.

Isserley looked in the rear-view mirror. The nearest car was perhaps a hundred yards behind her. If she could just bring herself to step on the accelerator, and then slow down at much shorter notice than usual, she could, by the time it caught up, be safely parked in a layby, windows opaque.

She flipped the icpathua toggle.

'Turn *left* here, I said!' the hitcher yelled. 'Left!'

Panic rising up in her like a gas through a liquid, she misjudged the gears of her car and yanked at them with a stomach-churning braying. In the same moment, she glanced down at the passenger seat. The trousers of the baldhead's overalls, she realized now, were as thick as cowhide and covered in an extra yellow layer of something resembling tarpaulin. The icpathua needles had simply failed to make an impression.

She felt a sudden stab of pain in her side. It was the point of the Stanley knife, digging into her flesh through the thin fabric of her top.

'Yes! Yes!' she hissed anxiously, flipping the indicator toggle up and turning into the path he wanted. Gravel clattered under the wheels and thumped loudly against the belly of the chassis. Her hands wrenched at the steering wheel, overcompensating for the sudden turn, and with every heaving breath she felt the sting of the blade in her side.

'OK, OK!' she cried.

He removed the blade and, with his free hand, reached over to steady the steering wheel. His grip was firm but gentle, as if he were teaching her something about driving. His hand was twice the size of hers.

'Please think . . . about this,' panted Isserley.

He didn't reply, but removed his hand from the steering wheel, evidently satisfied that she was doing an adequate job now. The car was puttering through a neglected landscape of low scrub and the rotted remains of hay-bales. Up ahead, a cluster of cheap purpose-built farm huts loomed, skeletons of fragmented concrete and twisted steel. The A9 had all but disappeared from the rear-view mirror, peeping through indistinctly like a distant river.

'Turn right where you see that pile of tyres,' the hitcher instructed her. 'Then stop the car.'

Isserley did as she was told. They had come to rest behind a solid wall three metres high and ten metres long. The rest of the building was gone, but the wall remained.

'Right,' said the hitcher.

Isserley had her breathing under control now. She was trying to concentrate all of herself into her head. Only her wits could save her, for she could not run. She, who had once been able to sprint as fast as a lamb. She could not run.

'I have friends in high places,' she pleaded.

He laughed again, a short dry sound like a cough.

'Get out of the car,' he said.

They each opened a door and stepped out onto the rocky earth. He walked round to her side and closed the driver's door. He pushed her against the flank of the car. Still holding the Stanley knife in one hand, he took hold of her black cotton top in the other, grabbing a handful of the material and yanking it upwards over her breasts. He was so strong that his wrenching of the bunched-up cloth, trapped under her armpits, almost lifted her off the ground. Hastily she raised her arms and allowed the top to be pulled away.

'We can have a . . . a wonderfully pleasurable experience together,' she offered, cupping her breasts in her gently quaking hands, 'if you let me.'

Impassive, red-faced, he positioned himself at arm's length from her. Then, reaching forward, he began to knead her breasts with the hand that wasn't holding the knife, each breast in turn, repeatedly trapping the nipples between thumb and forefinger, rolling them like pellets of dough.

'Does that feel good, yeah?' he said.

'Mmmm,' she replied. There was, of course, no feeling in her breasts at all, but there was plenty of feeling in her spine, which he was pressing against the bowed surface of the car. The cold, electrifying sweat of pain and fear prickled on her shoulders.

He kneaded her breasts for an eternity. His breathing and

hers mingled, cloudy in the frigid air. Far above, a pale sun came out and reflected off his dome-like head. The car's engine made a ticking sound as its parts lost heat and were infiltrated by the chilly weather.

Finally, the hitcher let her nipples go and took a step backwards.

'Get on your knees,' he said. While Isserley was hastening to obey, he ran his free hand down the central slit of his overalls, snapping the fasteners softly to reveal a surprisingly white singlet inside the filthy black and yellow wrapping. The overalls unfastened all the way to his crotch, yawning open. He pulled out his genitals, furry scrotal bulb and all. He stepped forward so that his penis swayed in front of her face.

He held the Stanley knife to the nape of her neck and let her feel the edge of the blade through her hair.

'I don't wanna feel no teeth, understand?' he said.

His penis was grossly distended, fatter and paler than a human's, with a purplish asymmetrical head. At its tip was a small hole like the imperfectly-closed eye of a dead cat.

'I understand,' she said.

After a minute with his urine-flavoured flesh in her mouth, the knife-blade on her neck was lifted slightly, replaced by hard stubby fingers.

'That's enough,' he groaned, squeezing a handful of her hair.

Stepping back, he allowed his penis to slip out of her mouth. Without warning, he grabbed her elbow and pulled it upwards. Isserley didn't have time to tense her muscles into a characteristic vodsel shape, and her arm bent freely at several joints, a zig-zag of unmistakably human angles. The hitcher did not appear to notice. This, more than anything else so far, filled Isserley with nauseous terror.

Once she was standing, the hitcher nudged her further along the car until she was against the bonnet.

'Turn around,' he said.

She obeyed, and he immediately grasped her green velvety trousers and tore them down to her knees with a single jolt.

'Jesus,' he growled from behind her. 'You been in a car accident?'

'Yes,' she whispered. 'I'm sorry.'

For a heady moment she thought he was discouraged, but then she felt the flat of his hand on her back, pushing her forward onto the car's bonnet.

Desperately, she searched for the right word, the word that might make him stop. It was a word she knew, but had only ever seen written – in fact, only this morning, a vodsel had spelled it out. She'd never heard it spoken.

'Murky,' she pleaded.

Both his hands were on the small of her back, the butt of the Stanley knife pressing against her spine. His penis was poking and shoving in between her thighs, straining for entry.

'Please,' she begged, suddenly inspired. 'Let me show you. It will be better for you. I promise.'

Allowing herself to slump flat against the bonnet, her breasts and cheek squashed against the smooth metal, she laid her hands on the cheeks of her buttocks and pulled them apart. Her genitals, she knew, were buried forever inside a mass of ugly scar tissue caused by the amputation of her tail. But the scar lines themselves might resemble the cleft of a vodsel's sex.

'I don't see nothing,' he grunted.

'Come closer,' she urged him, turning her head painfully to watch his domed head looming near. 'It's there. Look.'

In a flash, exploiting the fact that she was balanced on the bonnet of the car, Isserley flung her arms backwards and upwards. She flung them like two whips, and her aim was precise. Two fingers of each hand plunged into each of the hitcher's eyes, right up to the knuckles, right inside his hot clammy skull.

Gasping, she yanked her fingers out again and slammed her hands on the car's bonnet. She managed to right herself just as the baldhead was falling to his knees; in a frenzy, trousers around her ankles, she leapt sidelong out of his way as he pitched forwards, his face rebounding against the bumper with a meaty smack.

'Ugh! Ugh! Ugh!' she cried in disgust, wiping her fingers hysterically on her naked thighs. 'Ugh! Ugh! Ugh!'

She pulled her trousers up and stumbled over to her discarded top, snatching it off the ground where it lay.

'Ugh! Ugh! Ugh!' she cried as she fought her way back into the wet and muddy garment. A slick of grit scraped her shoulders and elbows as she pulled the sleeves down to her quaking wrists.

She scrambled back into her car and switched on the ignition. The engine coughed back to life; she revved it noisily. She reversed away from the baldhead's body, gears clashing, then stalled.

Just as she was about to restart the engine and drive off, she couldn't resist wiping her fingers one more time, with the cloth she used for the windscreen. She noticed that a sizeable wedge of one of her fingernails was missing. She bashed the steering wheel with her palms. Then she got out of the car and went back to the hitcher's body to retrieve what must at all costs not be found and analysed.

It took some time, and required her to improvise tools from the surrounding vegetation.

188 • Michel Faber

When she'd finished, she got in her car and drove away, back to the main road.

Other cars beeped at her as she tried to turn into their midst.

She had her lights on high beam.

If she wanted to join their peaceable procession, that was not allowed.

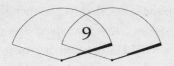

9

ISSERLEY DROVE DIRECTLY to Tarbat Ness, to a jetty she knew there. It was at the bottom of a short and dangerously steep road marked by a traffic sign depicting a stylized car falling into stylized ocean waves.

Isserley drove carefully, parked neatly near the tip of the jetty, pulled the handbrake back as if retrieving something which might get lost otherwise. Then she leaned her arms on the steering wheel and gave herself permission to feel whatever was coming to her. Nothing came to her.

The sea was dead still and steely grey. Isserley stared at it through the windscreen, unblinking, for a long time. Seals were known to play here; there was a sign saying so, somewhere on the road behind her. She stared at the sea for perhaps two hours, determined that nothing should escape her. The sea grew darker, an expanse of tinted glass. If there were any seals hidden below, none broke the surface.

In time, the tide rose silently, licking at the jetty. Isserley didn't know if the water would rise so far that her car would be lifted up and carried into the sea. If the water sucked her under she supposed she would have to drown. She'd been a strong swimmer once upon a time, but that was with a very different body from the one she had now.

She tried to motivate herself to switch on the ignition and drive away to safety, but just couldn't manage it. Thinking of somewhere else she could be was an impossible challenge. *This* was the place she'd decided to go when she'd still had the spirit to make decisions; now that spirit was gone. She would stay here. The sea would either take her or it would leave her be. What did it really matter?

The longer Isserley waited on the jetty, the more she felt as if she had only just arrived, had only been here for a matter of moments. The sun moved across the heavens like the deceptive glow of distant headlights that never got any closer. Water from the North Sea knocked gently on the underside of the car. Isserley continued looking through the windscreen. Something important was eluding her. She would wait here until it came to her. She would wait forever if necessary.

A large cloud in the darkening sky was changing shape all the time. Though she was unaware of any wind, there must be powerful forces up there, shaping the cloud, finding it unsatisfactory, sculpting it into something different. It began as a floating map of a continent, then got compressed into a ship, then grew into something very like a whale. Eventually, towards nightfall, it lapsed into something larger, more diffuse, abstract, meaningless.

Darkness came and Isserley had still not had enough time to decide what to do next. The car rocked slightly, butted from beneath by the haunches of the waves. She would go when she was ready.

The night passed in seconds, surely no more than a few thousand of them. Isserley did not sleep. She sat at the wheel and watched the night pass. Sometime during these dark hours, the sea gave up trying to intimidate her, and slunk away.

At sunrise, Isserley blinked several times. She removed her glasses, but the problem was the windscreen itself, which was misty with condensation. Her own body was steaming hot and clammy, as if she had been sleeping. She could not have been sleeping. It was impossible. She had not let her guard down for an instant.

She switched on the windscreen wipers, to clear the luminous fog. Nothing happened. She switched on the ignition. Her engine coughed feebly and shuddered, then was still.

'If that's the way you want it,' she said aloud. Her voice shook with rage.

She would have to do something about that.

An hour or so later, the windows had cleared by themselves. Isserley became aware of a pain in her side. She brushed at the spot with her fingertips; the fabric of her top was stuck to her flesh with what must be blood. She tugged it loose irritably. She had assumed she was uninjured.

Experimentally, she tried to swivel her hips where she sat, or lift her thighs. Nothing happened. Below the waist, she might as well be dead. She would have to do something about that.

She wound the window of the driver's side down a fraction and peered through the slit. The tide had retreated from the shore, exposing jellified seaweed, half-decomposed jetsam, and bony rocks pimpled with those little molluscs that people – that vodsels – collected. Whelks. That was the word. Whelks.

In the distance, two figures were walking along the shore, towards Isserley's jetty. Isserley watched them advance, willing them to turn back. Her beam of thought, for all its furious intensity, failed to cross the divide. They did not turn back.

At a range of fifty metres or so, Isserley identified the figures as a female vodsel and a dog of unverifiable gender. The female vodsel was small and delicate, dressed in a sheepskin coat and a green skirt. Her legs were stick-thin, sheathed in black, shod in green gumboots. The hair on her head was long and thick, blowing across her face. As she walked along the rocks, she called the dog's name, in a voice wholly unlike a male vodsel's.

The dog wasn't naked; it wore a red tartan coat. It wobbled as it walked, struggling to keep its balance on the slimy rocks. It looked around frequently at the female vodsel.

Eventually, when the two of them had come close enough to Isserley for her to consider putting her glasses on, they stopped in their tracks. The female vodsel waved. Then she turned around and walked away, the dog at her heels.

Isserley exhaled in relief. She resumed watching the clouds, watching the sea.

When at last the car seemed to have dried out in the sun, she tried switching on its ignition again. The engine started obediently. She switched it off. She would go when she was ready.

Turning her head to the passenger side, she stared down at the pock-marked seat as she flipped the icpathua toggle. Two silvery needles stabbed through the upholstery, two thin jets of liquid squirted into the air.

Isserley leaned back in her seat, closed her eyes, and started mewling.

10

ISSERLEY ALWAYS DROVE straight past a hitch-hiker when she first saw him, to give herself time. That's what she'd always done. That's what she would do now. There was a hitcher in her sights. She drove past him.

She was looking for big muscles. Puny, scrawny specimens were no use to her. This one was puny and scrawny. He was no use to her. She drove on.

It was dawn. The physical world did not exist for her, apart from the ribbon of grey tarmac on which she was driving. Nature was a distraction. She refused to be distracted.

The A9 seemed empty, but you couldn't trust it. Anything could happen, any time. That's why she kept her eyes on the road.

Three hours later, there was another hitcher. It was a female. Isserley wasn't interested in females.

Somewhere on the passenger side, above the wheel, a rattle

had started up. She had heard that rattle before. It had pretended to go away, but it had stayed hidden in her car's body somewhere. Isserley would not tolerate this. She would take her car back to the farm, when she had finished work, and she would find that rattle and she would fix it.

Two and a half hours later, there was another hitcher in her sights. Isserley always drove straight past a hitch-hiker when she first saw him, to give herself time. So, she drove past him.

He was holding a large cardboard sign that said PERTH PLEASE. He was not bald. He was not wearing overalls. His body was rather top-heavy, a V-shaped torso on long legs. How thin were those legs? His faded jeans were flapping around them; it must be very windy today.

She drove back and appraised him again. His arms were good. His shoulders were excellent. There was a lot of breast on him, even though his waist was lean.

After her U-turn, she drove towards him a third time. He had curly, unruly red hair and wore a thick knitted jumper composed of many different colours of wool. All the thick-knitted-jumper vodsels Isserley had ever met were unemployed, and lived the life of pariahs. Some authority must actually force them to wear these garments, she thought, as a stigma of rank.

This vodsel beckoning to her now must be an outcast. And his legs would fatten up fine.

She pulled off the road, and he ran to the car, smiling.

Isserley opened the passenger door, intending to call out, 'Do you want a lift?'

It suddenly seemed an absurd thing to say. Of course he wanted a lift. He had a big sign saying PERTH PLEASE; she had stopped for him. Nothing could be more self-explanatory. Words were a waste of energy.

In silence, she watched him strap himself in.

'I . . . This is very good of you,' the hitcher said, grinning awkwardly, combing his hands through his abundant hair, which immediately fell back over his eyes. 'I was getting pretty cold there.'

She nodded gravely, and tried to smile in return. She wasn't sure if she was managing it. The muscles in her face seemed even less connected to her lips than usual.

The hitcher babbled on: 'I'll just leave my sign here at my feet, shall I? You can get to your gears all right, can you?'

She nodded again, and revved the engine. Inwardly, her speechlessness troubled her; she seemed to have lost the power; there was a problem in her throat. Her heart was pounding already, though nothing had happened yet and no decision was on the horizon.

Determined to function normally, she opened her mouth to speak, but it was a mistake. She could sense that the sound rising in her throat would mean nothing to a vodsel, so she swallowed it down again.

The hitcher stroked his chin nervously. He had a soft red beard, so sparse it had been invisible from a distance. He smiled again, and blushed.

Isserley took in a deep, slightly shuddery breath, flipped the indicator and drove off, facing the road ahead.

She would speak when she was ready.

The hitcher fiddled with his sign, trying to catch her eye as he leaned forward. She was not to be caught. He sat back, nonplussed, clasping each of his cold hands inside the other in turn, then sliding them under the fleecy sleeves of his jumper.

He wondered what on earth he could say to put her at ease, and why she'd bothered to pick him up if she didn't want to talk to him. She must have had a reason. The thing was to guess what her reason might be. Judging from the look on her face before she'd turned away, she was completely knackered; maybe she'd just been falling asleep at the wheel, and decided a hitch-hiker would keep her awake. She'd be expecting him to make small talk, then.

It was an alarming thought; he wasn't a 'small talk' kind of person. Long philosophical one-to-ones were more his thing, like the late-night conversations he had with Cathy when they were both a bit stoned. A pity he couldn't offer this woman a joint to loosen things up.

Instead, he thought of commenting on the weather. Not in a cheap way, but saying what he really felt on days like this, when the sky was like . . . like an ocean of snow. It was so mind-blowing the way it could all hang suspended up there, all that solid water, enough of it to bury a whole county in tons of white powdered ice, all of it just floating, way, way up there as easily as a cloud. A miracle.

He looked at the woman again. She was driving like a robot, back straight as a metal bar. He got the impression that the beauties of nature meant nothing to her. There was no common ground there.

'Hi, I'm William,' he could say. Maybe it was a bit late now. But he would have to break the silence somehow. She might be going all the way to Perth. If she drove him a hundred and twenty miles without them exchanging a word, he'd be a basket case by the time he arrived.

Maybe the tone of 'Hi, I'm William' was a little bit crass, a bit American, like 'Hi, I'm Arnold, and I'm your waiter for the evening.' Maybe something more low-key would be better. Like, 'I'm William, by the way.' As if he was mentioning it in the middle of an enthusiastic conversation they were already having. Which, sadly, they weren't.

What was *wrong* with this woman, anyway?

He ruminated for a minute, making an effort to lay aside his own unease and concentrate on her instead. He tried to see her the way Cathy might see her if she was sitting in his seat; Cathy was a genius for sizing people up.

Earnestly striving to connect with his intuitive feminine side, William very quickly came to the conclusion that there must be something badly, badly wrong with this woman. She was in some sort of trouble, some sort of distress. She might even be in shock.

Or maybe he was just being dramatic. Cathy's friend Dave, the writer, *always* looked as if he was in shock. He'd looked like that all the years they'd known him. He was probably born looking like that. This woman, though: she gave off the weirdest vibes. Weirder even than Dave's. And she was definitely not in good shape physically.

Her hair was matted, with streaks of something that looked like axle grease slicked through it, and tufts sticking out at odd angles. Here was a woman who hadn't looked at herself in a mirror for a while, that was for sure. She smelled – stank, really, if he could be so judgemental – of fermenting sweat and seawater.

Her clothes were filthy with dried mud. She'd fallen, maybe, or had some sort of accident. Should he ask her if she was all right? She might be offended if he commented on the state of her clothing. She might even think he was trying to harass her sexually. It was so hard to be friendly, in any genuinely human way, towards female strangers if you were a male. You could be courteous and pleasant, which wasn't the same thing at all; it was the way you'd treat the staff at the Job Centre. You couldn't tell a strange woman that you liked her earrings, or that her hair was beautiful – or ask her how she came to have mud on her clothes.

It was over-civilization that caused that, maybe. Two animals, or two primitives, would never worry about that sort of thing. If one was muddy, the other would just start licking or brushing or whatever was needed. There was nothing sexual about it.

Maybe he was being a hypocrite. He *did* recognize this woman as . . . well . . . a woman, surely? She was a female; he was a male. These were eternal realities. And, let's face it, she was wearing amazingly little clothing for the weather. He hadn't seen so much cleavage in public since well before the snows had set in.

Her breasts were suspiciously firm and gravity-defying for their size, though; maybe she'd had them pumped up with silicone. That was a pity. There were health risks – leakage, cancer. It was so unnecessary. Every woman was beautiful. Small breasts fitted snugly inside your hand and felt warm and complete. That's what he told Cathy, whenever the latest lingerie catalogue came with the junk mail and she went on a downer.

Maybe this woman was simply wearing one of those fiendishly designed uplift bras. Men could be naive when it came to that sort of stuff. He examined her side, from armpit to waist, for tell-tale signs of underwiring or industrial-strength lace. He saw nothing except a small perforation in the fabric of her top, like a snarl from a spine of barbed wire or a sharp twig. The fabric around the hole was tacky with some sort of dried gunge. Could it be blood? He longed to ask. He wished he were a doctor, so he could ask and get away with it. Could he pretend to be a doctor? He knew a fair bit, from Cathy's pregnancies, her motorcycle accident, his father's stroke, Suzie's addictions.

'Excuse me, I'm a doctor,' he could say, 'and I can't help noticing . . .' But he didn't approve of lying. Oh, what a tangled web we weave, when first we practise to deceive, that's what Shakespeare said. And Shakespeare was no fool.

The more he looked at this girl, the weirder she appeared. Her green velveteen trousers were very seventies retro-chic, if you disregarded the muddy knees, but she definitely didn't have the legs of a nightclub babe. Trembling slightly under the thin fabric, so short they barely reached the pedals, they might have been the legs of a cerebral palsy sufferer. He turned his head to glance through the space between his seat and hers, half expecting to see a foldable wheelchair wedged into the back. There was only an old anorak, a garment he could well imagine her wearing. Her boots were like Doc Martens, but even chunkier, like Boris Karloff clogs.

Strangest of all, though, was her skin. Every part of her flesh that he could see, except for her pale smooth breasts, had the same peculiar texture to it: a downy look, like the hide of a cat recently spayed, just beginning to grow back the fur. She had scars everywhere: along the edges of her hands, along her collarbones, and especially on her face. He couldn't see her face now, hidden as it was behind the tangled mane of her hair, but he'd got a pretty good glimpse of it before, and there was scarring along the line of her jaw, her neck, her nose, under her eyes. And then the corrective lenses. They must have the biggest magnification known to optometry, for her eyes to look that big.

He hated to judge anyone by externals. It was the inner person that mattered. But when a woman's external appearance was this unusual, there was every likelihood it would have shaped the whole of her life. This woman's story, whatever it was, would be a remarkable one: perhaps tragic, perhaps inspirational.

He longed to ask.

How sad it would be if he never found out. He would spend the rest of his life wondering. He knew that. He'd experienced it before. Once, eight years ago, he'd had a car himself, and given a lift to a man who'd started weeping, right there in the car next to him. William hadn't asked what was the matter; he'd been too embarrassed, a macho kid of twenty. In time, the man stopped weeping, arrived at his destination, got out of the car, said thanks for the lift. Ever since then, maybe once a week, William would find himself wondering about that man.

'Are you all right?' He could ask that, surely. If she wanted to fob him off, she could put him in his place then and there. Or she could answer in a way that left things more open.

William licked his lips, tried to bring the words to his tongue. His heart beat faster, his breathing quickened. The fact that she wasn't looking at him made things even harder. He considered clearing his throat, like he'd seen men do in the movies, then blushed at how naff that idea was. His sternum was vibrating, or maybe it was his lungs that were doing it, like a bass drum.

This was ridiculous. His heavy breathing was becoming audible now. She would think he was going to jump on her or something.

He took a deep breath and gave up the idea of asking her anything, at least out of the blue. Maybe something would arise naturally later.

If only he could bring Cathy into the conversation, that

might reassure her. She would know then that he was some other woman's partner, the father of two children, a person who wouldn't dream of raping or molesting anybody. How to bring up the subject, though, if she didn't ask? He couldn't just say, 'By the way, in case you might be wondering, I have a partner, who I love dearly'. That would sound so naff. No, worse than naff: positively creepy, even psychotic.

That's what lying had done to the world. All the lying that people had been doing since the dawn of time, all the lying they were doing still. The price everyone paid for it was the death of trust. It meant that no two humans, however innocent they might be, could ever approach one another like two animals. Civilization!

William hoped he would remember all this stuff, to discuss it with Cathy when he got home. He had his finger on something important here, he thought.

Although maybe if he told Cathy too much about this woman who'd given him a lift, she'd take it the wrong way. Talking about his old girlfriend Melissa and the walking tour of Catalonia hadn't gone over too well, he had to admit, even though Cathy had more or less forgiven him by now.

Jesus, why did this girl not speak to him?

Isserley stared ahead of her in despair. She was still unable to speak, the hitcher was evidently unwilling to. As always, it was up to her. Everything was up to her.

A big green traffic sign said there were 110 miles to go before Perth. She ought to tell him how far she was going. She had no idea how far she was going. She glanced into the rear-view mirror. The road was empty, difficult to see clearly under the grey, snow-laden light. All she could do was keep driving, her hands barely moving on the steering wheel, a cry of torment stuck in her throat.

Even if she could bring herself to start a conversation, the thought of how much work it would be to keep it going made her heart sink. He was obviously a typical male of the species; stupid, uncommunicative, yet with a rodent cunning for evasion. She would talk to him, and in return he would grunt, surrender one-word answers to her cleverest questions, lapse into silence at every opportunity. She would play her game, he would play his, on and on, perhaps for hours.

Isserley realized, suddenly, that she just didn't have the energy to play anymore.

Eyes fixed on the bleak road stretching out in front of her, she was humiliated by the absurd labour of it all, this wearisome nudging and winkling at him as if he were some priceless pearl to be drawn out by infinitesimal degrees from his secretive shell. The patience it required of her was superhuman. And for what? A vodsel the same as all the other vodsels, one of billions infesting the planet. A few parcels' worth of meat.

Why must she put so much effort into playing this game day after day? Was this how she would spend the rest of her life? Endlessly putting on these performances, turning herself inside out, only to finish up empty-handed (more often than not) and having to start all over again?

She couldn't bear it.

She looked in her rear-view mirror, then askance at the hitcher. His eyes met hers; he blushed and smirked cretinously, breathing hard. The sheer brute alienness of him hit her like a blow; and, with a heady rush like the nausea after a sudden loss of blood, she hated him.

'Hasusse,' she said between clenched teeth, and flipped the icpathua toggle.

He began to fall towards her; she shoved him back with the flat of her hand. He swayed away from her, his big shoulders tipping like a unstable bale of hay, his head bumping against the passenger window. Isserley flicked the indicator and eased the car off the road.

Safely parked in a layby, her motor still on, she pressed the button to darken the windscreen. It was the first time she'd ever been aware of doing so. Usually she was floating somewhere in space when this moment came; today she was solidly anchored in the driver's seat, her hands on the controls. The glass went deep amber all around her, the world went dark and disappeared, and the little cabin light came on. She leaned her head back against the headrest and removed her glasses, listening to the rumble of distant traffic over the purr of her engine.

Her breathing, she noted, was perfectly normal. Her heart, which admittedly had been labouring a bit when she'd first let the vodsel into her car, was now beating quite tranquilly.

Whatever the problem had been, in the past, with her physical reactions, she seemed finally to have solved it.

She bent down to open the glove compartment. Two tears fell out of her eyes, onto the hitcher's jeans. She frowned, unable to account for it.

Isserley drove directly back to Ablach Farm, trying to fathom, all the way there, what could possibly be wrong.

Of course the events of yesterday . . . or was it the day before? . . . She wasn't exactly sure how long she had spent on the jetty afterwards . . . but anyway, those events . . . well, they *had* upset her, there was no denying that. But it was all in the past now. Water under the bridge, as the vodsels . . . as she'd heard it said.

Now she was driving past the abandoned steelworks, almost home, with a nice big vodsel propped up next to her, just like any other day. Life went on, there was work to be done. The past was dwindling, like something shrinking to a speck in the rear-view mirror, and the future was shining through the windscreen, demanding her full attention. She flicked her indicator at the Ablach sign.

As she drove over Rabbit Hill, she was ready to admit that she was perhaps not in such good shape. But, determined to pull herself together without wasting any more time, she already had a vision of what it would take for her to feel better. Something inside her was trapped. Something small: nothing serious. But still trapped.

To complete her recovery, to get herself back to normal, she needed to release it.

She felt sure she knew how.

Parking in front of the steading, she sounded her car's horn, impatient for the men to come out.

The door rolled open to reveal, as usual, Ensel and the two cronies whose names she'd never bothered to memorize. Ensel, as usual, hurried out to peer through the car's passenger window at what she'd brought home for them. Isserley braced herself for the usual platitude about the quality of the specimen.

'Are you all right?' grimaced Ensel through the glass. He was looking straight at her, ignoring the vodsel slumped under ill-fitting blond wig and sloppily applied anorak. 'You're . . . ah . . . you have some mud on your clothes.'

'It will wash off,' said Isserley frostily.

'Of course, of course,' said Ensel, cowed by her tone. He opened the door and the vodsel, poorly balanced, tumbled out like a sack of potatoes. Ensel leapt back in alarm, then snorted self-consciously and tried to rise above the mishap with panache. 'Um . . . he's a good one, isn't he?' he leered. 'One of the best ever.'

Isserley didn't deign to respond, but threw open her own door and stepped out of the car. Ensel, already busy with the other men dragging the vodsel backwards, registered her approach with a puzzled squint.

'Something wrong?' he grunted as he struggled to lift his burden onto a wheeled pallet. The weave of the vodsel's knitted jumper was very loose and almost useless as a grip-handle.

'No,' said Isserley. 'I'm coming with you, that's all.'

She strode on ahead and leaned against the steading while the men staggered to catch up, pulling the pallet with the vodsel on it.

'Uh . . . is there some problem?' said Ensel.

'No,' said Isserley, calmly watching them bumble through the door at last. 'I just want to see what happens.'

'Oh yes?' said Ensel, bewildered. The other men swivelled their heads to regard each other. Mutely they shuffled across the hangar floor, with Isserley walking beside them.

At the lift, there was an even more embarrassing moment. Clearly, there was only enough room inside for the men and their burden, not for Isserley as well.

'Um . . . you know there's really not that much to see,' simpered Ensel as he jostled with his companions inside the great drum.

Isserley clawed off her glasses and hung them on the frayed neckline of her top, fixing Ensel with a steely glare as the lift began to seal itself shut.

'Don't start without me,' she warned.

*   *   *

Isserley, standing alone in the dimly lit lift, allowed herself to be borne deeper and deeper into the earth. She passed the Dining and Recreation level, descended lower than the men's sleeping quarters.

As she sank through the well-oiled, frictionless shaft, she kept her eyes on the seam that would open when she reached Transit Level. Transit Level was three storeys below the ground. There was nothing lower than Transit Level except the vodsel pens themselves.

She'd expected to feel uneasy, even panicky, going down so far. But when the lift stopped moving and the door slid open, all those arm's-lengths below the ground, Isserley wasn't aware of any nausea. She knew she was going to be all right. She was going to get what she needed.

The Processing Hall was the largest of the linked maze of rooms that made up Transit Level. Its ceiling was high, its dimensions generous, its lighting fierce, leaving no corner in the slightest shadow. It was like an automobile showroom gutted of its contents and sparsely reappointed for more organic purposes. There was plenty of air, breezing out of the many air-conditioning grilles in the whitewashed walls. There was even a hint of marine tang to it.

The hall was lined on three sides with long metal work-benches, unattended just now. Ensel and the other men, as well as Unser, the Chief Processor, were all gathered in the centre of the room, converged around a mechanical contraption Isserley knew must be the Cradle.

The Cradle, constructed from pieces of farm equipment, was a masterpiece of specialized design. Its base was the cannibalized mechanism of an earthmover, welded to a stainless-steel drinking trough. Mounted on top, chest-high to a human, was a two-metre segment of a grain chute, artfully beaten into an amended shape so that its sharp edges were curled harmlessly in on themselves. Gleaming and elegant like a giant gravy boat, the chute was being tilted mechanically on its unseen fulcrum, assuming a perfectly horizontal position.

The person adjusting the balance of the Cradle was Ensel, smug in his responsibility of personally assisting the Chief Processor; his two cronies were engaged in the less precise task of undressing the vodsel, lying nearby.

Unser, the Chief Processor — or the butcher, as he still insisted on calling himself — was washing himself. He was a compact, wiry man, who would have been scarcely taller than Isserley if he'd been a biped. He had massive knobbly wrists, though, and powerful hands, which he was holding aloft as he squatted on his hindquarters next to a metal tub.

He lifted his almost freakishly small, coarse-bristled head and sniffed the air, as if he was smelling the arrival of an unfamiliar scent — Isserley's, not the vodsel's.

'Uhr-rhum,' he said. It was the language of neither humans nor vodsels. He was simply clearing his throat.

Isserley had stepped out of the lift, and it had closed behind her. She waited to be challenged or greeted. The men did neither, carrying on with their activities as if she was invisible. Ensel rolled a small metal trolley of shiny instruments into Unser's reach. The two cronies undressing the vodsel were huffing and puffing with effort, but the sound was smoothed over somewhat by the music all around.

Real music, human music, was being piped into the hall by loudspeakers nestled in the walls. Soft singing and the strumming of instruments imparted a reassuring flavour of home, a pervasive smell of melodies half remembered from childhood. They hissed and hummed soothingly.

The men had already managed to pull off the new arrival's fleecy jumper and were struggling with the rest. The pale flesh was wreathed in many layers of clothing, like layers of cabbage or radish. There was less actual vodsel inside than Isserley had thought.

'Careful, careful,' muttered Unser as the men scrabbled clumsily at the vodsel's ankles to remove tight woollen socks. An animal's shanks were close to where its faeces would fall once it was in the pens; any lacerations would be liable to fester.

Panting from exertion, the men finished their task, tossing the last tiny garment on top of a pile. All these years, Isserley had always been handed the vodsels' clothing and personal effects in a bag, just inside the steading door; this was the first time she'd seen how that bag came to be filled.

'Uhr-rhum,' said Unser again. Using his tail for balance, he waddled up against the Cradle on his hind legs, still holding his arms aloft. His arms were shiny black, as black as Amlis's, in contrast to the rest of his fur, which was grey. However, this was only because his arms had just been washed right up to the shoulders, and the fur was saturated with water, slicked flat.

He looked sharply at Isserley, as if noticing her presence only now.

'Can I help you?' he demanded, squeezing the fur on his forearms a bit smoother still with his encircling hands. Drops of water pattered on the floor at his feet.

'I . . . just came to watch,' said Isserley.

The Chief Processor's suspicious glare burned into her; she realized she was hunching over, her arms folded over her breasts, trying to look as human as possible.

'Watch?' Unser repeated in bemusement as the men struggled to lift the vodsel off the floor.

Isserley nodded. She was only too well aware that she had avoided coming here for four years, had only ever spoken to Unser in the dining hall. She hoped he would at least have noticed, from their rare conversations, that she respected him, even feared him a little. He, like her, was a true professional.

Unser cleared his throat again. He was always clearing his throat; he had a disease, the men said.

'Well . . . keep well back,' he advised her gruffly. 'You look as if you've been crawling through the muck.'

Isserley nodded, and took a step backward.

'OK,' said Unser. 'Put him on.'

The vodsel's lolling body was flopped onto the Cradle, then turned to face the fluorescent ceiling. His limbs were arranged neatly, his shoulders fitted snugly into a special shoulder-shaped indentation which had been sculpted into the metal of the chute. His head came to rest on the lip of the chute, his loose red hair dangling just above the great metal trough.

Throughout all this the vodsel, though placidly flexible, made not the slightest movement himself, except for the autonomic squirming of his testes inside the shrinking scrotal sac.

When the body had been arranged to Unser's satisfaction and the tray of instruments pushed against the edge of the Cradle, the butcher began his task. Balancing on his tail and one hind leg, he lifted his other hind leg up to the vodsel's face and hooked two fingers of his foot into the vodsel's nostrils. An upward tug pulled the animal's head right back and opened its mouth wide. Pausing only to make sure of his balance, Unser flexed his free hands. Then, from the tray beside him, he selected one silver tool shaped like an elongated letter q, and another shaped like a tiny sickle. Both of these instruments were immediately inserted into the vodsel's mouth.

Isserley strained to see, but Unser's big wrists and the twisting motion of his fingers obscured the view as he carved out the vodsel's tongue. Blood began to gurgle out onto the vodsel's cheeks as Unser turned to drop his tools on the tray with a clatter. Unhesitatingly he snatched up an electrical appliance resembling a large star-point screwdriver and, squinting with concentration, guided it into the vodsel's mouth. Flashes of light glowed through the gaps in Unser's nimble fingers as he searched out the incontinent blood vessels and fried them shut with a crackling buzz.

He was already busy sluicing out the vodsel's mouth with a suction pump by the time the smell of burning flesh had permeated the air. The vodsel coughed: the first real evidence that, far from being dead, it was suffering from nothing more serious than icpathuasi.

'That'saboy,' murmured Unser, tickling the Adam's apple to make the creature swallow. 'Uhr-rhum.'

As soon as he was satisfied with the state of the animal's mouth, Unser turned his attention to the genitals. Taking up a clean instrument, he sliced open the scrotal sac and, with rapid, delicate, almost trembling incisions of his scalpel, removed the testicles. It was a much more straightforward job than the tongue; it took perhaps thirty seconds. Before Isserley had registered what had happened, Unser had already cauterized the bleeding and was sewing the scrotum closed with an expert hand.

'That's it,' he announced, tossing the needle and thread onto the tray. 'Finished. Uhr-rhum.' And he looked to his guest.

Isserley blinked back at him across the room. She was

having a lot of trouble keeping her breathing under control.

'I didn't . . . realize it would all . . . be over so soon,' she admitted hoarsely, still crouching and cringing. 'I was expecting . . . a lot more . . . blood.'

'Oh yes,' Unser assured her, combing his fingers through the vodsel's hair. 'The speed minimizes the trauma. After all, we don't want to cause unnecessary suffering, do we? Uhr-rhum.' He allowed himself a faint smile of pride. 'A butcher has to be a bit of a surgeon, you know.'

'Oh, it's . . . very impressive,' complimented Isserley miserably, shivering and hugging herself all the while, 'the way you do it.'

'Thank you,' said Unser, dropping back onto all fours with a groan of relief.

Ensel had made the Cradle tip sideways, and the other men were already hauling the vodsel off it, manoeuvring the body back onto the pallet so it could be rolled to the lift.

Isserley bit her insensate lips to stop herself crying out with frustration. How could it be over so soon! And with so little violence, so little . . . drama? Her heart was hammering in her chest, her eyes were stinging, her fingernails were clawing holes into her clenched fists. She had a need for release raging inside her, swollen to explosion point, and yet the vodsel's ordeal was over; he was already on his way to join his kind down in the pens.

'Don't drag his feet over the fucking *step*,' exclaimed Unser irritably as the men dragged their burden into the lift. 'I've told you a thousand times!'

He cast a knowing glance at Isserley, as if to acknowledge that she, of all people, should have a pretty accurate idea of how many times he could have scolded the men in this way. 'OK, hundreds maybe,' he conceded.

The lift closed with a hiss. Isserley and Unser were alone in the big room with the Cradle and the smell of burning.

'Uhr-rhum,' announced Unser as the silence grew awkward. 'Is there anything else I can do for you?'

Isserley clutched herself tightly, keeping it all in.

'I was just . . . wondering,' she said, 'Are you . . . are there any . . . any *monthlings* still to be . . . processed?'

Unser trotted over to the vat of water and plunged his arms into it.

'No,' he said, 'we've done as many as we need to.'

The agitation of water harmonized with the music issuing from the loudspeakers.

'You mean,' said Isserley, 'there aren't any others that are ready?'

'Oh, there is one left,' said Unser, extracting his arms and shaking the excess water aside with vehement flicks. 'But he'll keep. He can go next time.'

'Why can't he go *this* time?' pursued Isserley. 'I'd love to see' – she bit her lips again – 'to see the way you do it. The end product.'

Unser smiled modestly as he dropped back onto all fours.

'The usual quota has been loaded, I'm afraid,' he remarked with the merest hint of regret.

'You mean,' persisted Isserley, 'there's no room in the transport ship for more?'

Unser was looking down, examining his hands, lifting them from the wet floor one at a time.

'Oh, there's plenty room, plenty room,' he replied pensively. 'It's just that . . . uhr-rhum . . . well, *They*' (he rolled his eyes heavenwards) 'are expecting a certain amount of meat, you know. Based on what we usually deliver.

If we put any more in, they might expect us to deliver the same amount next month, you see?'

Isserley pressed her hands to her breast, trying to calm the hammering of her heart. There was just too much padding in the way.

'It's all right,' she assured Unser, her voice tight with urgency. 'I . . . I can bring in more vodsels. No problem. There's lots of them around just now. I'm getting better at the job all the time.'

Unser stared at her, frowning, puzzled, obviously not knowing what to make of her.

Isserley stared back, half dead with need. The parts of a woman's face she could have used to plead with him, to implore him without words, had all been removed or mutilated. Only her eyes remained. They shone brightly as she gazed unblinking through space.

Minutes later, on Unser's instruction, the last of the month-lings was brought into the Processing Hall.

Unlike the paralysed newcomer who'd preceded him, this one did not need to be carried. He walked upright, meekly, led by two men. In fact, he hardly needed to be led; he shuffled his massive pink self forwards as if in sleep. The men merely nudged him with their flanks whenever he seemed about to stumble or deviate. They accompanied him: that was the word. They accompanied him to the Cradle.

The swollen rigidity of his bulk was such that when he had reached the Cradle and was pushed off-balance, he tipped right over like a felled tree, falling backwards onto the smooth receptacle with a fleshy thwump. He looked sur-prised as his own elephantine weight carried him down the slippery slope of the chute; all the men had to do was guide his progress so that his shoulders came to rest in the designated hollows.

Isserley had edged closer, aching to see his face. The porcine eyes twinkling in his bald head were too small to read from a distance. At all costs she must not miss what was to be written there.

The monthling's eyes were blinking rapidly; a frown was forming on his dome-like forehead. Something was going to happen to him which might be beyond his capacity to stoically endure. He had come to rely on his own bulk, his own indifference to discomfort. Now he sensed he was about to be taken out of his depth. Anxiety was growing in him, searching for expression somewhere among the cells of his fully crammed physiognomy.

Sedated though he was, the vodsel struggled, but not with the men who were holding him; rather, with his own memory. It seemed to him he'd seen Isserley somewhere before. Or perhaps he merely recognized she was the only creature in the room who looked anything like him. If anyone was going to do anything for him, it would have to be her.

Isserley edged forward further still, allowing the vodsel to focus on her. She, too, was trying to place him in her memory. His eyelashes, the only hairs remaining on his head, were remarkably long.

So intently was the vodsel striving now to retrieve his memory of Isserley that he seemed not to notice something being lowered towards his forehead that resembled the nozzle of a petrol pump, attached to the base of the Cradle by a long flexible cable. Unser touched the metal tip of the instrument to the unwrinkled flesh of the vodsel's brow, and squeezed the handle. There was an almost imperceptible dimming of the lights in the building. The vodsel's eyes blinked just once as the current travelled through his brain and down the filament of his spine. A subtle plume of smoke curled up from a darkening smudge on his brow.

Unser yanked the chin up to expose the neck. With two graceful flicking motions of his wrist, he slashed open the arteries in the vodsel's neck, then stood back as a jet of blood gushed out, steaming hot and startlingly red against the silvery trough.

'Yes!' screamed Isserley involuntarily. 'Yes!'

Even as her cry was still ringing out in the Processing Hall, all activity had already stopped dead. A terrible silence fell, made worse by a lull in the piped music. Nothing moved except the unstoppable gush of blood from the vodsel's gaping neck, the frothy liquid glimmering and seething, immersing the vodsel's face and head, swirling his eyelashes in the tide like sprigs of seaweed. The men – Unser, Ensel and the others – stood frozen. Their eyes were all turned on Isserley.

Isserley cringed so low that she was almost falling forward. She was clenching and unclenching her hands in an agony of frustrated anticipation.

The point of Unser's knife was hovering over the vodsel's torso; Isserley knew that the next action must surely be to slit the animal open from neck to crotch, peeling the flesh aside like the front of a pair of overalls. She stared longingly at the knife as it hung in the air for a long moment. Then, devastatingly, Unser withdrew it and allowed it to fall onto the tray.

'I'm sorry, Isserley,' he announced quietly, 'but I don't think it's such a good idea for you to be here.'

'Oh please,' entreated Isserley, squirming. 'Don't let me put you off.'

'We are doing a job here,' the Chief Processor reminded her sternly. 'Feelings don't enter into it.'

'Oh, I know, I *know*,' cringed Isserley. 'Please, just carry on as if I'm not here.'

Unser leaned across the Cradle, obscuring her view of the vodsel's steaming head.

'I think it would be better if you left,' he said, with exaggerated clarity. Ensel and the others looked nervously back and forth between him and the object of his disapproval.

'Look . . .' croaked Isserley. 'What's all the fuss? Can't you just . . . just . . .'

She glanced down at her hands because she sensed they were being stared at. She was shocked to observe her fingers hacking downwards through the air, as if she were trying to claw something out of the atmosphere with her nails.

'Ensel,' said Unser warily. 'I think Isserley may be . . . unwell.'

The men started to move across the wet floor towards Isserley, their reflections vibrating in the brilliant sheen.

'Keep away from me,' she warned.

'Please, Isserley,' said Ensel, still advancing. 'You look . . .' He grimaced awkwardly. 'It's terrible to see you looking like this.'

'Keep away from me,' she repeated.

In the lurid confines of the Processing Hall, it seemed to Isserley that the light had begun to intensify weirdly, its wattage multiplying second by second. The music also seemed to be sagging out of tune, keening nauseously into her spine. Stinging sweat ran into her eyes and down her back. She was, she remembered suddenly, deep inside the ground. The air was vile, recycled through tons of solid rock, with a horrible fake aroma of sea-spray. She was trapped, surrounded by beings for whom this was all normal.

Suddenly sinewy male arms were rearing up at her from all directions, seizing her wrists, her shoulders, her clothing.

'Get your stinking paws off me!' she hissed. But their grip was stronger then her own desperate flails of resistance.

'No! No-o-o! No-o-o-o!' she screamed as they pulled her off her feet.

The instant she fell, everything around her began to contract sickeningly. The walls shrugged themselves loose from their foundations and slid towards the centre of the room, as if attracted by the struggle. The ceiling, a massive rectangular slab of concrete furrowed with fluorescent white, also shuddered loose and loomed down on her.

Shrieking, she tried to roll herself into a ball, but she was caught spread-eagled by many strong hands. Then, the walls and ceiling gulped shut on her and she was engulfed in darkness.

11

BEFORE SHE WAS even properly conscious, Isserley was already aware of two smells, surreally blended: raw meat and recent rainfall. She opened her eyes. The endless night sky was all above her, glittering with a million distant stars.

She was lying on her back, in a vehicle with an open top, parked in a garage with an open roof.

It wasn't her car; it wasn't a car at all, she realized slowly. She was lying inside the splayed flip-top hull of the transport ship, under a yawning aperture in the steading roof.

'I persuaded them the fresh air would do you good,' said Amlis Vess, somewhere not so far away.

Isserley tried to turn her head to find him, but her neck was so stiff it might have been clamped in a vice. Barely breathing for fear of bringing on the pain, she lay very still, wondering what was raising her head up from the metal floor. With her clammy fingers she felt, alongside her paralysed hips, the texture of what lay beneath her: a rough woven mat, of the kind humans liked to sleep on.

'When they brought you out of the lift, you seemed to be choking, almost suffocating,' Amlis went on. 'I wanted to take you outside, but the other men wouldn't let me. And they refused to take you out themselves, either. So I got them to agree to this.'

'Thanks,' she murmured passionlessly. 'I'm sure I would have survived regardless.'

'Yes,' he conceded, 'no doubt you would.'

Isserley examined the sky more closely. There was still a trace of violet in it, and the moon was only just edging into view. It might be six o'clock in the evening, seven at the latest. She tried to lift her head. The response from her body was not so good.

'Can I help you?' said Amlis.

'I'm just resting,' she assured him. 'I've had a very tiring day.'

Minutes passed. Isserley strove to adjust to her predicament, which struck her as both awful and laughable. She wiggled her toes, and then tried to wiggle her hips, unobtrusively. A needle of pain went through her tailbone.

Amlis Vess tactfully refrained from commenting on her sharp intake of breath. Instead he said, 'I've been watching the sky ever since I got here.'

'Oh yes?' said Isserley. Her eyes felt unpleasantly encrusted when she blinked. She longed to wipe them.

'Nothing I imagined really prepared me for it,' Amlis went on. His sincerity was unmistakable, and Isserley found it oddly touching.

'I felt the same, at first,' she said.

'It's pure blue during the day,' he observed, as if she might not have noticed this yet and he was calling her attention to it. Confronted with the sheer earnestness of his enthusiasm, she suddenly felt like shrieking with laughter.

'Yes, it is,' she agreed.

'And many other colours,' he added.

She really did have to laugh then, a snort that was mostly pain.

'Yes, many,' she said through clenched teeth. At last she had managed to lift her hands up, and clasped them across her belly, in a way she found comforting. Inch by inch, she was coming back to life.

'You know,' Amlis went on, 'Some water fell out of the sky not so long ago.' His voice was a little higher than usual, vulnerable with awe. 'It just fell out of the sky. In little droplets, thousands of them close together. I looked up to see where they were coming from. They seemed to be materializing out of nowhere. I couldn't believe it. Then I opened my mouth to the sky. Some droplets fell straight in. It was an indescribable feeling. As if nature was actually trying to nurture me.'

Isserley stroked the fabric of her top over her belly; it was slightly damp, but not very. The rain mustn't have lasted very long.

'The water stopped falling as abruptly as it started,' said Amlis. 'But even now the smell of everything has changed.'

Isserley was able to turn her head slightly now. She ascertained that she'd been laid out in front of one of the ship's refrigerators. The base of her skull was resting on a broad pedal bar at the base of the unit, whose function was to raise the lid when stepped on. Her head wasn't heavy enough to raise the lid; that required the body weight of a man.

To the right of her, on the metal floor almost at her

shoulder, lay two trays of meat covered in transparent viscose. One tray was prime steaks, dark auburn and interleaved. The other, larger tray was densely packed with offal: bleached entrails perhaps, or brains. They smelled strong, even through the wrapping. The men really ought to have finished putting them away before leaving her here.

She turned her head to the left. Amlis was sitting some distance from her, beautiful as ever, his back limbs curled under him, his arms erect, his head raised slightly towards the open steading roof. She caught a glimpse of his sharp white teeth; he was eating something.

'You needn't have stayed with me,' she said, trying to lift her knees without him noticing the effort it took.

'I sit here most of the day and night,' he explained. 'The men won't let me out of the building, of course. But I see the most extraordinary things just through this hole in the roof.' However, he turned his attention to her now, and stood up to move closer to where she lay. She heard the gentle tick of his clawed fingers on the metal floor as he padded along.

He stopped a respectful distance from her body, an arm's length perhaps, and let his haunches drop again, legs curling underneath. His arms remained erect, the tousled white fur of his breast pushing out between them. She had forgotten how black the down on his head was, how golden his eyes.

'All this meat doesn't put you off?' she suggested tauntingly.

He ignored the barb in her comment.

'It's all dead now,' he said simply. 'There's nothing I can do about that now, is there?'

'I thought you might still be working on the minds and hearts of the men, you know,' pursued Isserley, hearing herself overdoing the sarcasm.

'Well, I did my best,' said Amlis, in a self-deprecating purr. 'But I can tell when a challenge is hopeless. Anyway, it's not *your* minds I need to change.' And he glanced round at the contents of the ship's hull, acknowledging the scale of the slaughter and its commercial purpose.

Isserley watched his neck and shoulders, the way his fur was so soft it fluttered in the breeze. Her grasp on her ill-will towards him was growing weak, now that she was imagining him resting his warm fleecy breast on her back, his white teeth gently biting her neck.

'What are you eating?' she demanded, because his jaws seemed to be in constant motion.

'I'm not eating anything,' he declared insouciantly, and resumed chewing.

Isserley felt a flash of contempt: he was like all rich powerful people – smugly comfortable with lying, arrogantly indifferent to the evidence of other people's senses. She pulled a face of disapproval, as if to say, Have it your way. He read this at once, despite the alienness of her features.

'I'm not eating, I'm chewing,' he solemnly protested, but his amber eyes had a twinkle in them. 'Icpathua, actually.'

Isserley remembered now his notoriety on this account and, though intrigued, she affected a look of hauteur.

'I would have thought you'd grown out of that sort of thing,' she said.

But Amlis was not to be baited.

'Icpathua is not a behaviour, adolescent or otherwise,' he pointed out coolly. 'It's a plant, with its own unique properties.'

'Fine, fine,' sighed Isserley, turning her head, shifting her attention back to the starry sky. 'You'll wind up dead, anyhow.'

She heard him laugh but missed seeing it. She regretted missing it, then was irritated with herself for regretting.

'I'd have to swallow a bale of it the size of my own body,' Amlis was saying.

She laughed then, despite herself; the thought of him attempting such a thing was bizarrely funny. She tried to cover her laughter with her hand, but the pain in her back was too vicious and she lay rigid, chortling helplessly, her face naked to him. The more she laughed, the less she could control it; she could only hope he understood she was laughing at a ridiculous vision of Amlis Vess swollen like a pregnant cow.

'Icpathua is an exceptionally effective pain killer, you know,' he remarked gently. 'Why not try some?'

That wiped the grin off Isserley's face.

'I'm not in pain,' she told him frigidly.

'Of course you're in pain,' he said, in a chiding tone which accentuated his pampered vowels. Enraged, she heaved herself up onto her elbows and fixed him with her sharpest glare.

'I'm not in pain, all right?' she repeated, as the cold sweat of agony prickled the flesh of her torso.

For an instant his eyes glowed in antagonism, then he blinked slowly and languorously, as if another trace of sedative had leaked into his bloodstream.

'Whatever you say, Isserley.'

He had not, that she could recall, spoken her name before. Not until now. She wondered what had made him speak it, and whether the same conditions were likely to come around again soon.

But she should really get rid of him somehow. She badly needed to do some exercises to get herself back in shape, and she sure as hell wasn't going to do them in front of him.

The obvious thing would be to excuse herself and walk to her cottage, where he couldn't follow. But she was in too much pain to attempt the half-dozen metal steps between the hull of the ship and the steading floor.

Now that she was on her elbows, she could flex her shoulders and her spine a bit, without it being too obvious. She could distract him by making conversation.

'What do you think your father will do to you when you get back?' she asked.

'Do to me?' The question seemed at first to make no sense to him. Again she had innocently collided with his pampered experience of life. Plainly, the notion of anyone doing anything to him against his will was an alien one. Vulnerability was for the lower orders.

'My father doesn't actually know I'm here,' he said at last, unable to keep a hint of relish out of his tone. 'He thinks I'm in Yssiis, or somewhere in the Middle East. That's where I said I might be heading, anyway, last time we spoke.'

'But you came here in this,' Isserley reminded him, nodding at the meat and the refrigerators all around. 'A Vess Industries transport ship.'

'Yes,' he grinned, 'but not with anyone's official consent.' His grin was boyish, even childlike. He looked up into the sky, and again the fur on his throat rearranged itself like wheat in the wind. 'You see,' he said, 'my father still has this forlorn hope I'll take over the business some day. "Let's keep this in the family," he says. What he means, of course, is that he would *hate* the most valuable new commodity in the world to be poached by a competitor. Right now, the words "voddissin" and "Vess" are inseparable; anyone who yearns for a taste of something unimaginably divine just thinks "Vess".'

'How convenient for the both of you,' said Isserley.

'It's nothing to *do* with me – well, not since I was old enough to ask questions, anyway. My father treats me like a sassynil. "What's to know?" he says. "This stuff grows, we harvest it and ship it home." But he's not *quite* as secretive with me as he is with everybody else. I only have to show a glimmer of interest in the business, and you can see him weakening. Still hoping I'll see the light. I suppose that's why he's always given me access everywhere – including the Vess docking bays.'

'So?'

'So what I'm trying to say is . . . On this trip I was a . . . what's the word? A stowaway.'

She laughed again. The bones and muscles in her arms gave way and she landed on her back once more.

'I suppose the richer you are, the further you have to go to find thrills,' she remarked.

He took offence, at last.

'I had to see for myself what's going on here,' he growled.

Isserley tried to raise herself again, and covered her failure with a sigh of condescension.

'There's nothing so unusual going on here,' she said. 'Just . . . supply and demand.' She spoke these last words in a sing-song, as if they were an eternal, inseparable pairing like night and day, male and female.

'Well, I've confirmed my worst fears,' he went on, disregarding her claim. 'This whole trade is based on terrible cruelty.'

'You don't know what cruelty is,' she said, feeling all the places on and inside her body where she had been mutilated.

How lucky this cosseted young man was, to have a 'worst fear' that concerned the welfare of exotic animals rather than any horrors he himself might have to face in the struggle for survival.

'Have you ever been down in the Estates, Amlis?' she challenged.

'Yes,' he said, with his exaggeratedly perfect diction. 'Of course. Everyone should see what it's like down there.'

'But not for so long that it starts to get uncomfortable, huh?'

Her retort roused him to exasperation; his ears stiffened.

'What would you want me to do?' he said. 'Volunteer for hard labour? Get my head smashed in by thugs? I'm *rich*, Isserley. Do I have to get myself killed to atone for that?'

Isserley declined to answer. Her fingers had found the crust around her eyes. It was a fragile limescale of dried tears, wept in her sleep. She wiped it away.

'*You* came here,' said Amlis, 'to get far away from a harsh life, isn't that so? *I* never had to suffer a harsh life, for which I'm very grateful, I promise you. Nobody wants to suffer if they can get away with it. Surely, as human beings, we want the same thing.'

'You'll never know what I want,' she hissed at him with a vehemence that surprised even her.

The conversation froze into stillness for a while. Gusts of cold wind blew in through the steading roof; the sky darkened further; the moon rose, a circular loch of floating phosphorescence. In time, the wind carried a single leaf into the building; it fluttered down into the hull and was immediately pounced on by Amlis. He turned it over and over in the space between his hands, while Isserley struggled to turn away.

'Tell me about *your* parents,' he said at last, as if inviting her to fulfil her side of the most benign and easy bargain imaginable. Isserley felt a nudge against a hard mass of undigested hatred in her guts.

'I don't have any parents,' she warned him stonily.

'Well, the way they *were*, then, when they were alive,' he amended.

'I don't talk about my parents,' stated Isserley. 'Ever. There's nothing to say.'

Amlis looked into her eyes, and immediately accepted that this was an area where, despite being Amlis Vess, he was not going to be granted access. He sighed.

'You know,' he said, almost dreamily, 'I sometimes think that the only things really worth talking about are the things people absolutely refuse to discuss.'

'Yes,' snapped Isserley, 'Like why some people are born into a life of lazing around and philosophizing, and others are shoved into a hole and told to fucking get busy.'

Amlis chewed on his icpathua, his eyes narrowed in anger and pity.

'There's always a price attached, Isserley,' he said. 'Even for being born rich.'

'Oh, yes,' she sneered, miserable with desire to stroke the white plush of his chest, to follow the line of his silky flank. 'I can see how it's damaged *you*.'

'Not all damage is obvious,' he said in a soft voice.

'No,' she retaliated bitterly, 'but it's the *obvious* damage that gets those heads turning, don't you find? The brand everyone recognizes, eh, Mr Vess?'

Alarmingly, he reared up, stood at her shoulder, and lowered his head close to hers, shockingly close.

'Isserley, listen to me,' he urged her, the black down of his face bristling, the warm breath from his mouth tickling her neck. 'Do you think I can't see that half of your face has been carved off? Do you think I haven't noticed that you've had strange humps grafted onto you, your breasts removed, your tail amputated, your fur shaved off? Do you think I can't imagine how you might feel about these things?'

'I doubt it,' she wheezed, her eyes stinging.

'Of course I can see what's been done to you, but what I'm really interested in is the inner person,' he pressed on.

'Oh *please*, Amlis: spare me this shit,' groaned Isserley, looking away from him as the tears squirmed out of her eyes and ran down one cheek to disappear inside the ugly stoma of her mutilated ear.

'Do you think nobody is capable of noticing you're a human being underneath?' he exclaimed.

'If your kind had noticed I was a fucking human being they wouldn't have sent me to the Estates, would they?' she yelled back at him.

'Isserley, *I* didn't send you to the Estates.'

'Oh no,' she raged, 'nobody has any individual responsibility, do they?'

She turned violently away from him, forgetting to brace herself for the pain. It shot down her spine, like a skewer piercing her from ribcage to rectum. Amlis was at her side the instant she screamed.

'Let me help you,' he said, wrapping one arm around her shoulders, and his tail around the small of her back.

'Leave me alone!' she wept.

'Let's get you sitting up first,' was his response.

He helped haul her to her knees, his velvety, bony forehead brushing against her throat, then immediately he backed away, allowing her to find her centre of gravity.

She flexed her stiff limbs, feeling the spastic tension deep inside her flesh, the lingering thrill of his touch on the surface. Her shoulder-blades cracked dangerously as she rotated them; she couldn't afford to worry about what sort of impression she made now. She looked around for Amlis, saw he'd just made a brief foray deeper inside the hold.

'Here, have some of this,' he said, approaching her on three limbs, holding up a clump of something vegetal in his free hand. He seemed quite serious, which struck Isserley as unaccountably funny.

'I don't approve of drugs,' she protested, then immediately burst out laughing, her fragile defences unhinged by pain. Wiping fresh tears from her cheeks, she accepted a mossy sprig of icpathua from him and put it into her mouth.

'I just chew it, do I?'

'Yes,' he said. 'After a while it turns into a sort of cud, and you don't even have to think about it anymore.'

Half an hour later, Isserley felt much better. A feeling of anaesthesia, even well-being, was disseminating through her body. She was doing her exercises, right in front of Amlis Vess, and she didn't mind. He was going on and on about the evils of meat-eating, and everything he said seemed to her pathetic and amusing. He really was a very amusing young man, if you didn't take his sanctimonious ravings too much to heart. Enjoying the low tones of his voice as it droned, she gyrated her limbs slowly, trying to focus on her own body, chewing the bitter weed over and over.

'You know,' Amlis was saying, 'since people have started eating meat, some mysterious new diseases have been reported. There have been unexplained deaths.'

Isserley smirked; his preachings of doom were solemnly hilarious.

'Even the Elite are hinting there may be dangers,' he insisted.

'Well,' she replied airily, 'All I can say is that everything is done to the highest standards at this end.'

She snorted with laughter again, and, to her surprise, so did he.

'How much does a fillet of voddissin cost, anyway, back home?' she enquired, stretching her arms up towards the night sky.

'About nine, ten thousand liss.'

She stopped her gyrations to look at him in disbelief. Ten thousand liss was, for an ordinary person, a whole month's worth of water and oxygen.

'Are you joking?' she gaped, her hands falling to her sides.

'If it costs less than nine thousand, you can bet it's been adulterated with something else.'

'But . . . who can afford that?'

'Almost no-one. Which makes it fantastically desirable, of course.'

Amlis sniffed thoughtfully at a stack of scarlet meat under viscose wrapping, as if trying to decide whether he'd smelled it, back home, in its final form. 'If someone wants to bribe an official, flatter a client . . . seduce a woman . . There's no better way.'

Isserley still couldn't quite grasp it.

'Ten thousand liss . . .' she marvelled.

'In fact,' Amlis went on, 'meat is *so* valuable that they're actually trying to make it grow in laboratories.'

'Do me out of a job, huh?' said Isserley, getting back to her exercises.

'Maybe,' said Amlis. 'Vess Industries spends a fortune on transport.'

'I'm sure they can easily afford it.'

'Of course they can. But they'd rather not bother, all the same.'

Isserley stretched her arms out horizontally and slowly skimmed them through the air.

'Rich people will always want the real thing,' she declared.

Amlis played with his leaf, manipulating it as much as he could without destroying it.

'There are plans,' he said, 'to market meat to the poor, in a debased form. My father's cagey about it, of course. But I happen to know there have been some pretty weird experiments done. It's business. My father would chop the planet into pieces if he thought there was profit in it.'

Isserley was spinning slowly on her feet, like a propeller or a weather-vane. It was something she could not have done if her body hadn't been tampered with. In a shy way, she was showing off to Amlis.

'There's a rather nasty snack food,' he was explaining, 'that's very popular in the Estates — very thin slices of a starchy tuber fried in fat and then dried to a crisp. Vess Incorporated has been flavouring these with some kind of vodsel by-product. The demand is phenomenal.'

'Trash will eat trash,' said Isserley, stretching to the skies again.

There was a hissing sound from outside the ship. Isserley and Amlis peered over the edge of the hull down into the steading, and watched Ensel and another man step out of the lift. The other two men gazed back at them across the empty expanse of concrete.

'Just checking,' called Ensel, his coarse voice reverberating hollowly against the metal walls, 'to see if you were all right.'

'I'm fine, Ensel,' replied Isserley, barely acknowledging him. 'And Mr Vess is quite safe.'

'Uh . . . right,' said Ensel. 'Right.' And without another word he turned tail and re-entered the lift, followed by his companion. Another hiss, and they were gone.

Amlis, at Isserley's shoulder, spoke quietly.

'Ensel really cares about you, you know.'

'Well, he can go fuck himself with his own tail,' said Isserley, and licked the icpathua cud back out of her cheek for further chewing.

Above their heads, it had started raining again, just lightly. Amlis looked up into the blackness, in wonder and puzzlement. The stars were gone; a haze had replaced them, and the luminous floating disc had moved almost out of sight. Droplets of water pattered against his fur, disappearing instantly into the dark smooth parts, glistening and trembling on his woolly white breast. Hesitantly, he reared up on his hind limbs, leaning back on his tail, and opened his mouth. Isserley had not seen his tongue before. It was as red and clean as the petal of an anemone flower.

'Isserley,' he said, swallowing. 'Is it true about the sea?'

'Mmm?' She was enjoying the rain on her face; she wished it would pour down.

'I heard the men talk about it,' Amlis continued. 'A body of water that sort of . . . lies right next to the land and stays there permanently. They've seen it in the distance. They say it's vast, and that you go there all the time.'

'Yes,' she sighed. 'It's true.'

The aperture in the steading roof was starting to roll shut; Ensel had evidently decided she'd had quite enough fresh air.

'And when I was letting those poor vodsels go,' said Amlis, 'even though it was pitch dark, I saw . . . what looked like . . . *trees*, except absolutely enormous, taller than this building.' His plummy accent was pitiable now; he was like a child, trying to sum up the grandeur of the universe in the stilted language of the playpen.

'Yes, yes,' she smiled. 'It's all true. It's all out there.'

The steading roof had been shut now, though; the outside world was gone.

'Take me out to see it, please,' Amlis said suddenly, his voice echoing faintly in the hangar.

'Out of the question,' she responded flatly.

'It's dark,' he urged her. 'We wouldn't be seen.'

'Out of the question,' she repeated.

'Is it vodsels you're worried about? How dangerous can those dumb animals possibly be?' he pleaded.

'Very dangerous,' she assured him.

'To life and limb, or to the smooth running of Vess Industries?'

'I don't give a shit about Vess Industries.'

'Then take me,' he entreated. 'In your vehicle. I'll behave myself, I promise. I just want to look. Please.'

'I said no.'

Minutes later, Isserley was driving slowly under the tangled bower of tree-branches, past Esswis's farmhouse. The lights were on, as usual. Isserley's car lights were off. She could see well enough by the light of the moon, and she didn't have to bother with her glasses. Besides, she had travelled this path hundreds of times on foot.

'Who built these houses?' asked Amlis, squatting on the passenger seat, his hands on the edge of the dashboard.

'We did,' said Isserley evenly. She was pleased no houses were visible beyond the farm, and that her own decrepit cottage looked like something that might have been cobbled together from bits of stone and debris lying about. Of Esswis's far grander dwelling she said: 'That one was built for Esswis. He's sort of my boss. He mends the fences, organizes the animal feed, that sort of thing.'

They passed close by Esswis's house, close enough for Amlis to see the condensation-clouded windows, with their chunky wooden ornaments on the sills.

'Who carved those?'

Isserley glanced at the sculptures.

'Oh, Esswis,' she said, automatically as they drove past. But the lie might, she suddenly realized, be the truth after all. Glowing, fading, in her mind's eye was a row of driftwood shapes, whittled and honed to a skeletal elegance, frozen in balletic attitudes of torture, lined up side by side behind the double glazing. Maybe this was how Esswis filled the lonelier hours of winter.

Isserley drove through the open fields, where massive round hay-bales lay scattered like black holes in the horizon. One field lay fallow, the opposite one was lush with the dark secretive greenery of potatoes. Here and there, bushes and trees that served no agricultural purpose sprouted up towards the heavens, displaying hardy flowers or long fragile twigs, each according to its kind.

Isserley knew what Amlis must be feeling: here was plant life that did not need to be grown in tanks or grubbed out of chalky, slimy soil, but that grew straight up into the air like a gush of joy. Here was acre upon acre of tranquil fecundity, taking care of itself with no apparent help from humans. And he was seeing Ablach's fields in winter: if only he could see what happened here in spring!

She drove very, very slowly. The path to the shore wasn't designed for two-wheel-drive vehicles and she didn't want to damage her car. Also, she was nagged by an irrational fear that a bump in the track might jolt her right hand off the steering wheel and she'd trip the icpathua toggle by mistake. Although Amlis wasn't belted in and kept shifting around on the seat in his excitement, the needles might still get him.

At the great gate at the end of the Ablach path, not far short of the cliffs, Isserley stopped the car and turned off the engine. From here there was a clear view of the North Sea, which was silver tonight, under a sky whose eastern reaches were grey with advancing snow, while the west was still bright with the moon and stars.

'Oh,' said Amlis feebly.

He was in shock, more or less, she could tell. He stared straight ahead at the immense, impossible waters, and she stared at the side of his face, secure in the knowledge that he was unaware of her longing.

After a long time, Amlis was ready to ask a question. Isserley knew what it was going to be before he even opened his mouth, and answered him before he could speak.

'That thin line of brightness there,' she pointed. 'That's where the sea ends. Well, it doesn't really end there, it goes on forever. But that's where our perception of it ends. And above that: that's where the sky begins. You see?'

It was almost cruelly poignant, but delightful too, the way Amlis seemed to regard her as the custodian of an entire world, as if it belonged to her. Which, perhaps, it did.

The terrible price she'd paid *had* made this world her own, in a sense. She was showing Amlis what could be the natural domain of anyone willing to submit to the ultimate sacrifice – a sacrifice no-one but she had dared to make. Well, she and Esswis. But Esswis rarely left his farmhouse. Too devastated, probably, by his disfigurement. The beauties of nature meant nothing to him; they were insufficient consolation. She, by contrast, kept pushing herself out there to see what there was to be seen. She exposed herself daily to the great impartial skies, glad to be consoled.

In time, a flock of sheep walked single-file along the fringe of cliff at Ablach's boundary. Their fleeces glowed in the moonlight, their black faces almost invisible against the tenebrous gorse.

'What are those?' marvelled Amlis, his nose almost squashed against the windscreen.

'They're called sheep,' Isserley told him.

'How do you know?'

Isserley thought fast.

'That's what they call themselves,' she said.

'You speak their language?' he goggled as the creatures trotted past.

'Not really,' she said. 'A few words.'

He watched them, every last one of them, his head moving closer and closer to Isserley's as he followed their slow progress out of his experience.

'Have you tried using them for meat?' asked Amlis.

Isserley was dumbfounded. 'Are you serious?'

'How do I know what you people have got up to?'

Isserley blinked repeatedly, fumbling for something to say. How could he even *think* of such a thing? Was it a ruthlessness that linked father and son?

'They're . . . they're on all *fours*, Amlis, can't you see that? They've got fur – tails – facial features not that different from ours . . .'

'Listen,' he began testily, 'if you're going to eat the flesh of a living creature . . .'

Isserley sighed; she yearned to just place her forefinger against his lips and quieten him.

'Please,' she implored, as the last of the sheep vanished into a tunnel of gorse. 'Don't spoil this.'

But, typical man, he was not to be dissuaded from wrecking the perfection of the moment; he only chose a different tack.

'You know,' he said, 'I've talked to the men quite a lot.'

'What men?'

'The men you work with.'

'I work alone.'

Amlis took a deep breath; began again.

'The men say you're not yourself.'

Isserley snorted contemptuously. This would be Ensel he had in mind. Ensel, all mange and scars and swollen balls, spilling his guts to the visiting big shot. Man-to-man confessions.

Sensing the poison of hatred trickling back into her system, she was sad, almost ashamed: what a relief it had been to be without it, if only for a little while! Could this little cud she'd been chewing really have such a placating effect? She turned to Amlis, and smiled awkwardly.

'Have you got any more . . . uh . . .' Don't make me say the word, she thought.

Amlis handed her another sprig of icpathua, from the clump he'd brought along.

'The men are saying you've changed,' he said. 'Has anything bad happened to you?'

With his gift to her still in her hand, Isserley did her best to keep her bitterness in check.

'Oh, the odd stroke of bad luck, from time to time. Wealthy young men promising they'll take care of me, then standing by as I get sent down to the shithole. My body being carved up. That sort of thing.'

242 • Michel Faber

'I mean just recently.'

Isserley leaned her head back against the seat, adding the icpathua to what she still had in her mouth.

'I'm fine,' she sighed. 'I have a difficult job, that's all. It has its ups and downs. You wouldn't understand.'

On the horizon, a cloud of snow was gathering with great speed. She knew he hadn't a clue what it was, and cherished this knowledge.

'Why not quit?' he suggested.

'Quit?'

'Quit. Just stop doing it.'

Isserley rolled her eyes up to heaven, or the ceiling of her car. The upholstery of that ceiling was, she noticed, in some decay.

'I'm sure Vess Incorporated would be most impressed,' she sighed. 'Your old man would send me his personal best wishes, I'm sure.'

Amlis laughed dismissively.

'You think my father is going to come all the way out here and bite you in the neck?' he said. 'He'll just send somebody to take your place. There are hundreds of people begging for the chance.'

This was news to Isserley – horrifying, sickening news.

'That can't be true,' she breathed.

Amlis went quiet for a moment, as he tried to find his way safely through what had opened up between them: the jagged traps of her grief.

'I don't for a moment want to minimize what you've suffered,' he said carefully, 'but you must understand there are rumours back home about what this place is like – the skies, the visibility of the stars, the purity of the air, the lushness of everything. There are even stories about giant bodies of water – about how they go on and on for' (he laughed) 'a mile at a stretch.'

He said no more for a while, waiting for her to be ready. She was leaning back in her seat, her eyes falling shut. In the moonlight, her damp eyelids were silvery and intricately patterned, like the leaf he had admired in the steading.

She *is* beautiful, he thought. In her own strange, strange way.

Eventually, Isserley spoke again.

'Look, I couldn't just quit,' she pointed out. 'My job provides me with a home . . . food . . .' She struggled to come up with more.

Amlis didn't wait. 'The men tell me you basically live on bread and mussanta paste as it is,' he said. 'Ensel says you seem to live mostly on thin air. Are you telling me there's nothing growing in this world you couldn't survive on? And nowhere you could make a home for yourself?'

Isserley gripped the steering wheel angrily.

'Are you suggesting I live like an animal?'

They sat in silence for a long time, while the snow-clouds gathered on the firth and then drifted over the farm. Isserley, taking surreptitious glances at Amlis, noted that his awe and excitement were now tinged with unease: the unease of having hurt her, the unease of what was happening above him. To his inexperienced eyes, the snow-clouds no doubt resembled the noxious smogs of home, the kind that were sometimes so foully toxic that even the Elite were forced underground.

'Are . . . are we going to be all right?' he asked at last, just as the moon was being extinguished by the swirling grey haze.

Isserley smirked. 'No adventure without risk, Amlis,' she chided him.

Snowflakes began to whirl through the air, careering wildly, trembling, spiralling, diving against the windscreen. Amlis flinched. Then a few flakes blew in through the open passenger window, settling on his fur.

Isserley felt him shudder next to her, smelled a new odour on him. It was a long time since she'd smelled human fear.

'Relax, Amlis,' she purred serenely. 'It's only water.'

He pawed nervously at the alien substance on his breast, then murmured in wonder as it melted between his fingers. He looked at Isserley as if she had organized this whole display herself; as if she had just up-ended the whole universe for him, in case it might charm him for a moment.

'Just watch,' she said. 'Don't talk. Just watch.'

Together they sat in Isserley's little car as the sky unburdened its load. Within half an hour all the land around them was dusted with white, and a brilliant crystalline lather was climbing up the windscreen.

'This is . . . a miracle,' Amlis said at last. 'It's as if there's another sea, floating in the air.'

Isserley nodded eagerly: how intuitively he understood! She had often thought exactly the same thing herself.

'Just wait till the sun comes up! You won't believe it!'

Something happened in the air between them then, something molecularly disturbing.

'I'm not going to see it, Isserley,' Amlis said sadly. 'I'll be gone by then.'

'Gone?'

'I'm leaving tonight,' he said.

Still she seemed unable to grasp what he could possibly mean.

'The ship,' he reminded her, 'is leaving in a couple of hours. I'm going to be on it, of course.'

She sat very still, taking the information in.

'It's not like *you* to do what you're told,' she joked feebly, after a while.

'I *need* to get back home,' explained Amlis, 'to talk about what I've seen here. People need to be told what's being done with their blessing.'

Isserley laughed harshly. 'So it's Amlis the Crusader,' she sneered, 'bringing the light of truth to the whole human race.'

He grinned, hurt twinkling in his eyes. 'You're a cynical creature, Isserley. Listen, if it's easier for you to digest, you could say I've got no ideals really. You could say I just want to go back and annoy the hell out of my father.'

She smiled wearily. The snow had almost completely obscured the windscreen by now; she would have to shift it soon, or she'd start feeling claustrophobic.

'Parents, eh?' griped Amlis awkwardly, trying to maintain a fragile bridge between them. 'Fuck 'em.' The vulgarism sounded forced and self-conscious coming from him; he'd misjudged his tone, lost his grip a little. And, shyly, he reached across and laid a hand gently on her arm.

'Anyway,' he said, 'it would be very easy to get seduced by this world. It's very, very . . . beautiful.'

Isserley lifted her arms up to take hold of the steering wheel. His hand slipped off her as she found the ignition unerringly in the gloom. The engine thrummed into life, the headlights came on.

'I'll drive you back to the steading, then,' Isserley said. 'Time's getting away.'

*   *   *

Back at the steading, the great aluminium door was open a crack, and Isserley could see Ensel's snout already poking through. He'd have been sweating, she could well imagine, all through the hours of Amlis's absence; he was probably on guard duty. Let's see him come out now and tell her that this catch of hers was the best ever, the little creep.

Ensel stayed right where he was, however, waiting.

Isserley reached across Amlis's body to open the passenger side door, the mechanism of which was defeating him. Her forearm brushed momentarily against his fur, and she smelled the warm flesh underneath. The door swung open, letting in a blast of cold air and feathery snowflakes.

'Aren't you coming in?' Amlis asked.

'I have my own place to go to,' Isserley told him. 'And I've got work in the morning.'

One last time he locked eyes with her, a flash of antagonism sparking between them. Then:

'Take care of yourself,' he muttered, lowering himself out of the car onto the white ground. 'There's a voice inside you. Listen to what it says.'

'It says fuck off,' she said, but she was smiling crookedly, and crying too.

He padded through the snow, towards the door which was rolling open for him.

'I'll come back sometime,' he called, turning his head over his shoulder as he walked. Then, grinning: 'If I can get transport, of course.'

Isserley drove to her cottage, parked the car in the garage, walked herself into the house. Since she'd last been home, mysterious trespassers had slipped some glossy leaflets under her front door. An assortment of vodsels far too puny to make the grade wanted her to vote for them in an election;

Scotland's future was at stake and the power lay in her hands. There was also a note from Esswis, which Isserley did not attempt to read. Instead, she went straight to bed, covered her naked body in blankets, and wept and wept for hours.

The little numbers on her depleted digital clock had stopped flashing altogether, but she estimated it was about four in the morning when the transport ship finally launched itself with its characteristic groan.

Afterwards, she listened to the roof of the steading rolling shut. Then, soothed by the music of the waves playing in the stillness of Ablach, she rocked herself to sleep.

12

FOLDING HER ARMS across her breasts, palms on shoulders, and closing her eyes, Isserley allowed herself to slip under the water. Giving the sorely punished muscles and bones of her neck permission to let her head go, she felt her hair swirl up towards the surface as her heavy little skull sank like a stone. The world disappeared into darkness, and the familiar sounds of Ablach Farm were swallowed up into a numb aquatic murmur.

The rest of Isserley's body sank more hesitantly than her head, at first trying out a new centre of gravity, attemping to float, before it too descended towards the bottom. Bubbles leaked out of her ears and nose. Her mouth was slightly open, not breathing.

After a minute or two, she opened her eyes. Through the shimmering water and the waving seaweed of her hair, she could see a glow of sunlight, distorted, like a distant glimpse of an open door at the end of a dark corridor. As her lungs began to hurt, this light began to dilate, then throb in rhythm with her labouring heartbeat. It was time to come up for air.

Pushing up from the bottom, she splashed through the surface with her head and shoulders, gasping fresh oxygen, wiping her streaming hair back from her face, blinking and snuffling. Her vertebrae shifted and clicked, a sickening gristle sound trapped deep inside the flesh, as the weight settled back on her shoulders.

In the world outside the water, the sunlight had ceased to shimmer and pulsate: it shone through the soiled window of the bathroom, warm and constant. The nozzle of the shower was lit up like a lamp, and ceiling cobwebs luminesced like wisps of sheepswool caught on a barbed-wire fence. The ceramic top of the toilet cistern was almost too bright to look at, so Isserley let her eyes rest on its waxy torso. The pale blue letters tattooed there, ARMITAGE SHANKS, were as incomprehensible as ever, despite Isserley's years of learning the language. The hot-water tank gulped and belched, the way it always did when Isserley had a bath instead of a shower. At her feet, the rusted brass taps gurgled and hissed. The green plastic bottle of shampoo said EVERYDAY USE. Everything was back to normal. Amlis Vess was gone, and she remained, and it was already tomorrow. She should have known from the beginning that it would end like this.

Isserley leaned her head back, resting the base of her aching skull on the ceramic lip of the bath. On the ceiling directly above the tub, the pus-coloured paint hung in intricate shards and blisters, eroded by years of steam. Several coats of paint, like thin geological layers, had been penetrated by this attrition. It was the closest thing Isserley had yet found, in this world, to the landscape of her childhood. She lowered her eyes.

Her body was invisible below the reflective surface of the water, except for the tips of her toes and the curves of her breasts. She stared down at those alien mounds of flesh, easily imagining them as something other than what they were. Marooned like this in the sunlit water, they reminded her of rocks in the ocean, revealed by the tide. Stones on her chest, pushing her down. Amlis Vess had never seen her without these artificial tumours bulging out of her; would never know that she had once had a smooth breast worthy of his. Hard and sleek, with glossy auburn fur which men could hardly keep themselves from stroking.

She closed her eyes tightly, enduring the exquisitely unpleasant sensation of water trickling out of her mutilated ears. As if taking advantage of this lapse in vigilance, a dribble of scalding water leaked abruptly from the hot tap onto her left foot. Isserley hissed in surprise, and clenched her toes into a fist. How strange, she thought, that such tiny, trivial discomforts could still matter, when Amlis was gone and she was ready to die.

In the rusty soap dish hooked onto the side of the bathtub lay several new razor blades wrapped in cardboard. She unsheathed one of them, flicking the cardboard away. Reaching down to the grimy tiled floor, she picked up the mirror she'd brought downstairs with her. She held it above her, angled it to get the best light, looking herself straight in the face.

She tried to see herself as a vodsel might.

Even at a glance, she found it difficult to believe how much she had let herself go. It seemed like only a few days ago that she'd last done what was necessary to push herself across the dividing line into bestiality; it must have been much longer ago than that. What a bizarre sight she must have been to the vodsels who'd seen her recently. It was a good thing, really, that the last couple were safely out of circulation, because she had to admit she didn't pass muster now; her fur was growing back everywhere except in the places that were so severely scarred or artificial that nothing could grow there. She looked almost human.

Her hairline was barely discernible anymore; downy fuzz covered her forehead and connected up with the thicker fur on her brows. Her lower eyelashes had almost ceased to be defined as such, merging with the stubble on her cheeks, brown stubble that was softening as it grew. Her shoulders and upper arms were lined with a tentative fleece of auburn.

If Amlis Vess had stayed a little longer, he would have seen something of why men from the Elite had always promised her that they would keep her where she belonged, that they would put in a good word for her when the time came, that they would make sure she was never sent where a girl as beautiful as her should never be forced to go. It would be a crime against nature, one of them had told her once, as he stroked her flank, straying inwards towards the soft genital slit.

Isserley wielded the razor blade with great care. She'd dabbed shampoo onto her cheeks, but because the fur went right up to the rims of her eyelids, she must be careful not to push the soapy froth onto her eyeballs. Her eyes were sore enough from having to wear glasses so much of the time. And, of course, from weeping over Amlis, and life in general.

With delicate, tender scrapes, she shaved the fur off her face, leaving a few wisps for eyelashes. She tried to stop frowning, to make her forehead smooth as she dragged the razor across it. With every scrape she rinsed the blade in the bathwater; soon her fur was floating all around her, borne on a flotilla of shampoo scum.

When she was finished, Isserley picked up the mirror again and examined herself. A droplet of watery blood was trickling down her forehead; she wiped it away before it could run down into her eye. It would heal in a minute.

Instead of a straight hairline, windscreen-style, she'd given herself a slight V-shape, as a sort of experiment. She'd seen it on vodsels sometimes and thought it looked quite attractive.

The rest was straightforward. Unsheathing a fresh blade, she shaved her arms and legs, her shoulders, her feet. With a grunt of effort she swivelled her arms behind her back and shaved there, one hand angling the mirror, the other wielding the blade. Her abdomen needed only a few touch-ups; the scarred flesh from her amputated teats was dimpled and tough, like the torso of a lean, well-muscled vodsel who kept away from alcohol and fatty feed. The tangle of knotted flesh between her legs she didn't touch or examine; it was a lost cause.

The water had gone cold around her, and looked like a pond stagnant with brown algae. She stood up and gave herself a quick blast of hot water from the shower nozzle to flush off the loose fur. Then she stepped out of the tub onto the cold tiles, next to her shabby little pile of discarded clothes. Grasping them in her toes, she tossed them into the bath and pushed them under the water, which was instantly filthy.

Amlis Vess was gone, and there was nothing to do but go to work.

The midday news came on the television while she was doing her exercises. For the first time in years, it had some relevance to her.

'A search is under way for missing Perthshire man,

William Cameron,' said a concerned female voice, as the grubby screen in Isserley's bedroom displayed a picture of the red-maned, knitted-jumper vodsel she'd picked up days before, 'who was last seen attempting to hitch-hike home from Inverness on Sunday.' A different photograph replaced the first, this one showing the vodsel relaxing in front of a caravan, hugging between his legs a sleepy-eyed female with thick glasses. Two chubby toddlers, out of focus, were frozen in the extreme foreground, wide-eyed with surprise at the camera flash. 'Police say there is as yet no evidence of any connection between Mr Cameron's disappearance and the murder of Anthony Mallinder on Sunday.' The red-mane and his family were extinguished and a grainy image of the monstrous baldhead in yellow overalls was superimposed, instantly making Isserley's flesh creep. 'They acknowledge, however, a possible connection with the disappearance of German medical student Dieter Genscher, last seen at Aviemore.' The disturbing sight of the baldhead was mercifully replaced by a snapshot of a harmless-looking vodsel Isserley couldn't recall seeing before. Then, after what seemed like only a fraction of a second, there was some high-quality film footage of the A9, the camera mounted low on the ground, to show the passing cars from the perspective of a hitch-hiker.

Isserley continued her exercises as the news progressed to other things: huge herds of starving vodsels in a foreign country, the misbehaviour of a singer who wasn't John Martyn, sporting events, weather. Driving conditions were likely to be quite good, if the forecast was accurate.

Exercise and the sun beaming in through the window had dried her hair. She appraised herself in her little mirror, frowning. Her fresh black top – the freshest-looking of the ones in her wardrobe – was a little frayed. Still smart, but a little frayed.

You shouldn't have taken that red-haired vodsel, she said to herself, suddenly. William Cameron.

Pushing the thought away, she tried to return her attention to the matter at hand. Where was she supposed to get more clothes? Donny's Garage didn't sell clothes. For years, she'd resisted the temptation to wear items of clothing she'd come by in the course of her work, fearing that they would be recognized as belonging to individual vodsels, but maybe . . .

You shouldn't have taken him, she told herself again. You're slipping. It's over.

Her trousers were fine, the green velvet glossy and clean. A bit patchy on the seat, perhaps, but no-one ever saw that, all being well. Her shoes were polished and seemingly indestructible. The cleavage of her bosom glowed in the sunlight like something from the cover of a vodsel magazine. The tiny cut on her hairline had healed already; she picked the crust off, and it didn't resume bleeding. She ran her fingers through her hair, all ten fingernails securely in place. She breathed deeply, sucking the cool clean air through her nostrils, keeping her spine straight. Outside her window, the earth's atmosphere was bright and blue, obscuring the eternities of space beyond.

Life goes on, she insisted to herself.

On her way out of the house, she found the note from Esswis, which she'd forgotten all about. By the looks of it, it had been lying under her door for days. She held its damp and faded text up to the light. Esswis's tortuous scrawl didn't make things any easier, but one thing was immediately clear: this wasn't a personal letter. He was merely passing on a message from Vess Incorporated, which, because Esswis was Isserley's superior, had been conveyed to him first.

As far as Isserley could decipher, Vess Incorporated was wondering if there was any possibility she could bring in a few more vodsels than usual. Twenty per cent more per annum would be fine. If there was any difficulty, the Corporation could send someone to help her out. In fact, it was seriously considering sending someone anyway.

Isserley folded the note into a pocket of her trousers, even though she hadn't read it all. Vess Incorporated would have to learn that it couldn't fuck with her like this. She would send them a little message on the next transport ship. In the meantime, she would think about what changes needed to be made to her working life.

Isserley's arrival in the dining hall caused much guttural murmuring among the men. They obviously hadn't expected her to reappear so soon after her humiliation, but that was because they were stupid and understood nothing. Wouldn't they just love to have had a bit longer to gossip about her! What a stir her breakdown and her expulsion from the Processing Hall must have made in their stagnant little world! How the legend would have grown if she'd hidden away for days in her cottage, paralysed with shame, until at last she was so weak with hunger she was forced to crawl down to them! Well, she refused to give them the satisfaction. She would tough it out, show them what she was made of.

She cast her eyes disdainfully over the entire herd of them. Compared to Amlis Vess, they were scabrous grotesques, pea-brained savages. She should never have felt shame about her own deformity; she was no uglier than they were, surely, and infinitely better bred.

'Is the high-quality meat all gone?' she enquired, rummaging among the pots and bowls on the serving tables. The memory of her one little taste of the divine marinated steak that Hilis had prepared in honour of Amlis was suddenly haunting her.

'Sorry, Isserley, it's in here,' said the squinty one with the mouldy face whose name she always forgot. He patted his mangy, distended belly and wheezed with laughter.

Isserley beamed pure contempt at him. They ought to feed you on straw, she thought, then turned her back and busied herself with her old standby of bread and mussanta paste. Better to eat that, bland though it was, than take a risk with the blistered fatty sausages and limp wedges of pie: there was no telling what sort of trash was in them.

'Plenty of pie,' somebody assured her.

'No thanks,' she smiled insincerely, as she leaned against one of the benches, ignoring offers to sit down on the floor with this man or that. Holding one hand under the thinly pasted bread to catch any crumbs that might fall, she began to eat, staring over the men's heads, planning her day.

'That fancy meat sure was good,' recalled Yns the engineer, then, sniggering, quipped: 'We'll just have to get a few more visits from Amlis Vess, won't we?'

Isserley looked down at him, as he grinned back at her with decayed teeth and a glisten of gravy on his snout. Yet despite her distaste, she understood all of a sudden that he was harmless, an impotent drudge, a slave, a disposable means to an end. Imprisoned underground, he was living out an existence scarcely better than what he would have known if he'd stayed in the Estates. To be brutally honest, all these men were falling apart, hair by hair and tooth by tooth, like over-used pieces of equipment, like tools bought cheap for a job that would outlast them. While Isserley roamed the airy spaces of her unrestricted domain, they remained trapped below the barns of Ablach, labouring mindlessly, grubbing in tungsten-lit gloom, breathing stale air, eating whatever offal was too gross to be of value to their masters. Amid much fanfare about escape and pioneering, Vess Incorporated had simply dug them out of one hole and buried them in another.

'I'm sure there could be some changes made around here,' Isserley said, 'without needing a visit from Amlis Vess to justify them.'

This caused more guttural murmurings, meaningless insurrections mumbled by creatures without hope. Only one man spoke up.

'There's a rumour Vess Incorporated wants bigger shipments,' said Ensel. He was eating a mash of green vegetable from a dish, and washing it down with fresh water rather than the ezziin favoured by the others. Isserley realized, with a pang of pity, that he was trying to take care of himself, to keep up some sort of standard. Perhaps, all this time, he'd been saving himself for her, conscientiously discouraging his fur from falling out, fur that was the colour of unrinsed potato and the texture of . . . of an old anorak hood.

'I'm sure Vess Incorporated would love us all to work harder,' she remarked.

Everyone ate in silence for a while.

You shouldn't have taken the red-haired one, thought Isserley again. *It's over.*

She grimaced, and disguised the grimace by biting into her bread. Don't be so gutless, she chided herself. In a week, it'll all be forgotten.

As the food dwindled, disappearing serve by serve, its individual smells waned and were replaced by a rising fug of male sweat and fermented alcohol. It was an atmosphere almost guaranteed to inspire disgust in Isserley, but today she was able to rise above it. In fact, she actually began to relax as it sank in that the men who were here now were the only ones she would need to confront. Unser, whom she'd dreaded running into so soon after her disgrace, was nowhere to be seen and the food was vanishing fast. Hilis was absent, too, as he always was by the time the meal was laid out. That was good: that suited her.

She should never have allowed herself to be led into his kitchen, looking back on it now; Hilis had tried to get too intimate with her, had carried on as if they were two of a kind. She wasn't anybody's kind – the sooner he understood that, the better it would be for both of them. As for Unser, he'd humiliated her when she was at her most vulnerable, the bastard. She wished she could wipe him off the face of the planet, for having abused his power like that. It was just as well he wasn't showing his face.

Mealtime was drawing to a close; one of the men had wandered off already, and others were licking and slurping the inner reaches of their bowls and pitchers. Isserley's relief about Hilis and Unser turned, at last, to curiosity – where were they? Then it dawned on her that it must be all a matter of hierarchy and privilege. Unser and Hilis were a cut above these brawny specimens littered around the dining hall; probably the two of them ate together in some cosy retreat – enjoying a better class of food too, no doubt. What were the two of them feasting on? She'd like to know. Those sealed supply crates that came with every monthly shipment: was it really just stuff like serslida and mussanta in them, or were there secret luxuries she never got to sample? And what about the way Vess Incorporated conveyed its messages to her via Esswis, despite the fact that everything revolved around her?

Men and their little power games! She'd tackle these inequalities soon enough.

Isserley spread another slice of bread and mussanta, then helped herself to a bowl of the same green vegetable Ensel had chosen. She was determined always to go off well-fuelled from this day onwards, to make sure she never again succumbed to the humiliating helplessness of hunger far from home. She drank water by the cupful and felt her stomach swelling inside her.

'We hear another woman might be coming,' blurted the mouldy-faced man, then sniggered awkwardly under Isserley's glare.

'I wouldn't hold your breath,' she advised him.

Blinking, the mouldy-faced man went back to his pitcher of ezziin, but Ensel wasn't so easily cowed.

'What if they do send someone, though?' he said thoughtfully. 'It'd make a big difference to your life wouldn't it? The way it's been till now, it must get lonely for you sometimes. All that territory to cover, and just you to cover it.'

'I manage,' said Isserley evenly.

'There's nothing like friendship, though, is there?' Ensel persisted.

'I wouldn't know about that,' warned Isserley.

She was out of the dining hall and back on the surface within two minutes.

Mist was rolling in from the invisible horizon as she drove her car onto the A9. The road itself was still clear enough, but the fields on either side were already half lost, silos sinking into the fog, cows and sheep meekly allowing themselves to be swallowed up. A tide of white haze lapped at the grassy shores of the motorway.

This is another thing Amlis would have killed to see, Isserley thought. The clouds coming down to earth. Pure water floating through the air like smoke.

There were a million things Amlis would never experience, privileged though he was, beautiful and unscarred though he was. He was a prince returning home, but his kingdom was a slag-heap compared to Isserley's own domain. Even the Elite, sheltered from the worst of the ugliness, were like prisoners in opulent cages; they would live out their lives without even imagining the beauty that Isserley saw all around her every day. Everything they devoted themselves to was sealed indoors: money, sex, drugs, outrageously expensive food (— ten thousand liss for a fillet of voddissin!). All to distract them from the awful desolation, the darkness, the putrefaction, lying in wait for them just outside the thin skin of their homes.

Here in Isserley's own private world, that was all reversed. What went on inside the houses — mere specks under the vast sky — was insignificant; the dwellings and their inhabitants were like tiny shells and shrimps nestling on the seabed under an ocean of pale blue oxygen. Nothing that happened on the ground could ever compete with the grandeur of what happened above. Amlis had glimpsed this, had stolen an incredulous look at the sky for a few hours, and then had to let it go; she had made a sacrifice, and had gained the whole world forever.

No-one else must ever come here, she told herself.

In the distance, a hitcher stood on her side of the road, gesturing hopefully to whoever she might prove to be. She slowed down, to take a good look at him. Behind her, another car revved its engine and tooted its horn, impatient to pass. She ignored it. It could complain all it liked, as long as it left this hitcher alone until she'd made up her mind.

The hitcher was big, dressed in a suit without a raincoat over the top, and bareheaded. He wasn't bald: in fact, he had a halo of grey hair fluttering in the breeze. He was standing right next to the sign that said **P**, reassuring drivers that he wouldn't be any bother to stop for. That was about as much as Isserley was able to take in, what with the other car tooting and growling behind her.

Passing the hitcher, she veered into the parking area to allow the angry vehicle its way through. Of course the hitcher thought she was pulling over for him, but it was too soon for Isserley to make such a commitment; she wasn't going to make any more mistakes. As soon as the coast was clear, she accelerated back onto the road, and the hitcher, who'd shambled into a half-run towards her car, slumped to a standstill as she left him in the pall of her exhaust.

On the second approach, passing by on the opposite side, she noted that he was quite shabbily dressed. The clothes themselves were of good quality – he was wearing a dark-grey suit with a light-grey pullover underneath – but they had a greasy sheen, and hung like loose hide on his hulking frame. The slits of his coat pockets sagged open like extra orifices, the knees of his trousers were baggy and pale, the hand that waved limply at the passing traffic looked dirty. But what was he like inside?

He turned to look at her car as she passed, because there was so little traffic on either side of the road. If he recognized her as the driver who'd almost stopped for him a minute ago, he gave no sign; his face was a stoical mask, hard and wrinkled. Isserley had to admit he wasn't the most impressive specimen she'd ever seen. He was getting a bit old; his hair was grey, he had a taupe beard with flecks of silver in it, he didn't stand very upright. He had plenty of muscle on him, but a fair bit of fat too. Among vodsels, he was no Amlis Vess, that was for sure, but he wasn't an Yns, either. He was average.

On the third approach, she decided to take him. Why not, after all? What difference would it make in the end? What right did Vess Incorporated have to make her task more difficult than it already was? If they had their way, she would be vetting the inhabitants of the entire world, endless millions of them, rejecting almost every single one, in an insane search for perfection. It was time they realized what was really out there. This hitcher was what was really out there.

She pulled over into the same parking area as before, gently tooting her horn in case he was afraid of being fooled a second time. Raindrops began to spatter on the windscreen as he walked towards her; within the few seconds it took him to reach the passenger door, a downpour was setting in.

'Where are you going?' she asked, as he swung into the car next to her, a rumpled grey mass with a grim head screwed into the shoulders.

'Nowhere fast,' he said, staring straight ahead.

'I beg your pardon?'

'Sorry,' he said, acknowledging her with a faint smile, though his bloodshot eyes were humourless. 'Thanks for stopping. Carry on, carry on.'

She looked him quickly up and down. As well as being shabby, his suit was covered in loose hair — not his own, but black and white. His own hair had been cut severely in the past, and the basic shape of the design could still be seen, but all around the old edges, a moss of more recent hair had sprouted: a wiry thicket on his neck, wayward fuzz on his jaws, and then the bristles which covered virtually all his flesh from his cheeks to the grubby collar of his pullover.

'But where do you want to go?' insisted Isserley.

'I don't really care,' he said, an edge of irritability poking through his dull monotone. 'Know any exciting places? I don't.'

Isserley tried to listen to her instincts, to judge if there was any danger in him. Strangely, she couldn't detect anything. She gestured to the seatbelt, and his brawny hands, whose nails were black with grime, fumbled for the clasp.

'Take me to the moon, how's that?' he suggested testily. 'Take me to Timbuktu. Take me to Tipperary. It's a long way, they say.'

Isserley looked away from him, puzzled. The rain was pelting down. She flipped the toggles for the windscreen wipers and the indicator.

Even as he was strapping himself in, the hitcher was thinking there was still time to change his mind. What on earth was the point of going through with this? Why not just get right out of the car, go right back where he'd come from, and keep his . . . his *poison* to himself? There was something so sick about doing this day after day, going out on the road and seeing if he could trap some poor sucker into giving him a lift. Then, as soon as he had a captive audience, of course he would let them have it, right in the guts, right between the eyes, always the same thing. Why do it? Why? He never felt any better afterwards – worse, usually. The drivers who picked him up felt worse, that's for sure – if they were able to feel anything at all. What a way to treat people who were only trying to do a good turn!

Maybe he'd behave differently with this one, because she was a girl. Getting picked up by a female was pretty rare, especially such a young one. She looked like she'd suffered, too, in her short life: she hadn't had it easy. Pale, sitting stiffly, trying to put on a brave face. He'd seen it before. Too much too young. Tits on display to show she wasn't ready to give up being sexy yet, but the rest of her beaten and worn down, prematurely old. Did she have two screaming toddlers waiting for her at her parents' place? Was she some sort of addict? A prostitute struggling to find an alternative way of making ends meet? The skin of her scrawny clenched hands was dry and scarred. He couldn't see her face now, but at a glimpse it had seemed like a battleground of bitter experience. God, if only he could spare her what he was going to put her through – make a superhuman effort to keep it all in. But fat chance. He'd let her have it like all the others. Until something happened to make him stop. Until, finally, it was all over.

He could see her little nose, sniffing, poking out from behind the curtain of her hair. She was sniffing him, all right. They all did. It had begun.

'I'll open a window, shall I?' he offered wearily.

Isserley flashed an awkward smile, embarrassed at being caught out.

'No, no, it's raining,' she protested. 'You'd get wet. I – I don't really mind the smell, actually. I was just wondering what it is.'

'It's dog,' he said, staring straight ahead of him.

'Dog?'

'Pure aroma of dog,' he affirmed. 'Essence of spaniel.' He clenched his fists against his thighs, and agitated his feet against the floor; Isserley noticed he wasn't wearing any socks. Grunting repeatedly as if being teased with a sharp implement, he grimaced into his lap, then suddenly asked, 'Are you a dog person or a cat person?'

Isserley thought that one over for a minute.

'Neither, really,' she said, still unsure of her footing in this bizarre conversation. She racked her brains to retrieve what little she knew on the subject of cats and dogs. 'I don't know if I could take good care of a pet,' she admitted, noting another hitcher on the next hill, wondering if she'd made a mistake choosing this one. 'It sounds complicated, from what I've heard. Don't you have to keep pushing a dog off your bed, to show him who's boss?'

The vodsel grunted again, in pain this time, as he tried to cross one leg over the other irritably, and hit his knee on the underside of the dashboard.

'Who told you that?' he sneered.

Isserley decided against mentioning the dog breeder, in case the police were looking for him. 'I think I read it somewhere,' she said.

'Well, I don't sleep on a bed,' said the shabby vodsel, folding his arms across his chest. His voice had lowered to a monotone again, a strange mixture of prickly insolence and unfathomable despair.

'Really?' said Isserley. 'What do you sleep on?'

'A mattress in the back of my van,' he said, as if she was trying to argue him out of it but he'd ceased to care. 'With the dog.'

Unemployed, thought Isserley. Then, immediately: it doesn't matter. Let him go. It's over. Amlis has gone away. No-one loves you. The police are moving in. Go home.

But she had no home to go to, not really. Not unless she did her job. Pushing back defeatist thoughts, she tried instead to reason with the vodsel at hand.

'If you own a van,' she challenged him politely, 'why are you hitch-hiking? Why not drive yourself?'

'Can't afford the petrol,' he muttered.

'Doesn't the government give you . . . um . . . an allowance?'

'No.'

'No?'

'No.'

'I thought everybody who's unemployed gets an allowance from the government.'

'I'm not unemployed,' he retorted. 'I own a business.'

'Oh.' Isserley saw, out of the corner of her eye, a peculiar change coming over his face. Colour had risen to his cheeks, and his eyes glistened, with a feverish enthusiasm perhaps, or tears. He bared his teeth, which were punctuated by the creamy Polyfilla of old food.

'I pay myself a wage, y'see?' he declared, his enunciation suddenly clear. 'Whatever I can afford. Once I've paid my employees.'

'Um . . . so how many people have you got working under you?' asked Isserley, perturbed by the rictus of his grin, the intensity of his concentration. He seemed to have been roused from a coma, drastically infused with a potent cocktail of fury, self-pity and hilarity.

'Well now, there's a question, there's a question,' he said, thrumming his fingers against his thighs. 'They may not all be turning up at the factory, y'see. Might have got discouraged by the locked gates. Might have got discouraged by the lights being off. I haven't shown up there myself, for the last few weeks. It's in Yorkshire, y'see. Lot of petrol to get to Yorkshire. And then, I owe the bank about three hundred thousand pounds.'

The rain was easing off now, allowing Isserley to orient herself. She could set him down in Alness, if his craziness got out of hand. She'd never had anyone quite like him before. She wondered, alarmingly, if she liked him.

'Does that mean you're in trouble?' she asked, meaning the money.

'In trouble? Me? No-o-o-o,' he said. 'I haven't broken any laws.'

'But aren't you a . . . a missing person?'

'I sent my family a postcard,' he fired back immediately, grinning, grinning all the while, sweat twinkling in his eyebrows and on his moustache. 'Peace of mind for the cost of a stamp. Saves the police from wasting valuable time, too.'

Isserley stiffened at the mention of police. Then, having ordered her body to relax, she got suddenly worried in case she'd let her arms sag into an angle impossible for vodsel musculature. She glanced down at her left arm, the one nearest him. It looked fine. But what was that horrible squeaking noise near her face? Oh: it was the windscreen wipers, scraping dry glass. Hastily, she switched them off.

Give up, it's over, she thought.

'Are you married?' she said, after a deep breath.

'Now there's a question, there's a question,' he responded, seething, virtually rising off his seat. 'Am I married. Am I married. Let me think now.' His eyes shone so fiercely they looked ready to explode. 'Yes, I suppose I was married,' he decided, as if conceding, with grisly good humour, a point someone else had just scored at his expense. 'For twenty-two years, as a matter of fact. Until last month, as a matter of fact.'

'And now you're divorced?' pursued Isserley.

'So I'm told, so I'm told,' he said, with a wink like a violent tic.

'I don't understand,' said Isserley. Her head was starting to ache. The car was full of the heady stink of dog, the radio-active glare of psychic torment and the sudden blaze of noonday sun right in her eyes.

'Have you ever loved anyone?' the vodsel challenged her.

'I — I don't know,' said Isserley. 'I don't think so.' She would have to take him soon, or let him go. Her heart was starting to labour, and her stomach seemed to be going into spasm. There was a roaring sound somewhere behind her, which a glance at the rear-view mirror confirmed was another vehicle — a mammoth campervan, tilting from side to side impatiently. Isserley checked her own speed and was un-nerved to find it was thirty-five miles an hour — slow even for her — so she drove a little closer to the edge.

'I loved my wife, y'see,' the dog-smelly vodsel was saying. 'I loved her very much. She was my world. The full Cilla Black.'

'I beg your pardon?'

As the campervan swept past, dragging its shadow over Isserley's car, the vodsel began to sing, loudly and unin-hibitedly.

'*Sh'was my world, she was my night, my da-a-ay; sh'was my world, sh'was every breath, I ta-a-ake, and if our love, ceases to be-e-e, then it's the end of my world, for me-e-e!*' He shut up as abruptly as he'd begun, and was again grinning at her fiercely, tears leaking down his grizzled cheeks. 'Get the picture?'

Isserley's head throbbed as she eased the car back towards the middle.

'Are you under the influence of mind-altering drugs?' she said.

'Could be, could be,' he winked again. 'Fermented potato juice, made in Poland. Tough on pain, tough on the causes of pain, all for six pounds forty-nine a bottle. Bit of a disappointment in bed, though. And conversation's a bit one-sided, I feel.'

The A9 was clear for several hundred yards in front and behind, the campervan having sped half-way to the horizon. Isserley let one finger rest on the icpathua toggle. Her heart wasn't beating as hard as it usually did; instead, she felt sick, as if she might throw up any minute. She took a deep breath of dog-flavoured air, and made an effort to tie up the one last loose end.

'Who takes care of your dog when you go out hitching?'

'No-one,' he grimaced. 'She stays in the van.'

'All day and night?'

She'd posed the question without accusatory emphasis, but it seemed to wound him deeply. His manic energy flowed out of him in a gush, and he was left listless and dispirited.

'I never stay out that long,' he argued, monotone again. 'I need my walkies too. She understands that.'

Isserley's finger trembled against the icpathua toggle, then she hesitated, swallowing down a surge of nausea.

'It's a pretty big van,' the vodsel muttered defensively.

'Mm,' Isserley reassured him, biting her lip.

'I need to know she'll still be there when I get back,' he pleaded.

'Mm,' said Isserley. Sweat was stinging the fingers of her left hand and her wrist ached. 'Excuse me,' she whispered. 'I . . . I have to pull over for a minute. I'm not . . . feeling so good.'

The car was already travelling at a crawl. She allowed it to roll into the nearest parking area and brought it to a halt. The engine shuddered and was still. Supporting herself with one quivering fist against the steering wheel, she wound open a window with the other.

'You're not a well girl, are you?'

She shook her head, unable to speak.

They sat in silence for a while, as the fresh air blew in. Isserley breathed deeply, and so did the vodsel. He seemed to be struggling with something, just as she was.

Eventually he said, in a low desolate tone, but very distinctly:

'Life is shit, you know that?'

'I don't know,' sighed Isserley. 'This world is very beautiful.'

He grunted disdainfully.

'Leave it to the animals, I reckon. Leave the whole fucking lot to the animals.' That seemed to be his final word on the subject, but then when he saw that Isserley had begun to cry, he lifted his filthy hand and hesitantly pawed the air near Isserley's shoulder. Thinking better of it, he folded both his hands into his lap and looked away, out of the passenger window.

'I've had my outing for today,' he said softly. 'How about you just let me out here?'

Isserley looked him straight in the eyes. They were shiny with unwept tears, and she could see a tiny Isserley reflected in each one.

'I understand,' she said, and flipped the icpathua toggle. The vodsel's head tipped against the glass of the passenger window and rested there. The wispy grey hair growing out of his neck fluttered in the breeze.

Isserley wound up her window and pressed the button to make the glass turn dark. As soon as the interior of the car was dim and private, she pulled the vodsel back from the side window and turned his face to the front. His eyes were closed. He looked peaceful, not shocked and apprehensive like the others. He might have been sleeping, snoozing an over-long journey away, a slumber of a thousand light-years.

Isserley opened the glove box and selected a wig and a pair of spectacles. She fetched the anorak from the back seat. She dressed her fellow-traveller carefully, smoothing his dull, faded hair under a mop as black and glossy as his own might once have been. His brows were warm and bristly against the scarred flesh of her palms.

'I'm sorry,' she whispered. 'I'm sorry.'

When he was ready to go, she lightened the windows and started the car. She was less than twenty minutes from home, traffic permitting.

Back on Ablach Farm, Ensel was first out of the steading as usual, to greet her. Everything, it seemed, was back to normal.

Isserley opened the passenger door, and Ensel appraised what was sitting there.

'A beauty,' he complimented her. 'One of the best ever.'

That's when Isserley finally lost it.

'Don't *say* that!' she screamed at the top of her voice. '*Why* must you always fucking *say* that!'

Flinching at the violence of her response, Ensel seized hold of the body between them. Isserley seized hold too, struggling to keep him upright as he was dragged along the seat into the outstretched arms of the waiting men. 'He's *not* the best,' she raged as she clutched and pushed. 'He's not the worst. He's just a . . . just a . . .' Slipping from all their grasps, the body fell heavily on the stony ground. Isserley shrieked in fury, 'Fuck *you!*'

Leaving the scabrous beasts to their bumbling and grunting, she drove to her cottage in a cloud of dust.

*   *   *

Two hours later, just as she was starting to calm down, she found Esswis's note in her pocket, and re-read it, this time forcing herself to decipher the last few lines. Vess Incorporated had just one extra request of her, it seemed. They were wondering if she could perhaps see her way clear to supplying them with a vodsel female, preferably one with intact eggs. There was no need to process the female. Just wrap her up carefully, send her along, and Vess Incorporated would take care of the rest.

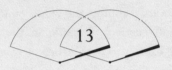

13

NAKED AND AFRAID of sleep, Isserley roamed her house from room to room, in the dark, hour upon hour. Her route was spiral, beginning in her bedroom, then along the landing to the other bedroom she never used, then downstairs to the rotten-floored hallway, the empty master bedroom, the front room filled with twigs and branches, the gutted kitchen, the clammy bathroom. She paced each one, going over and over in her mind the story of her life so far, and what she could do in the future.

Among the things she considered, to take her through until the morning at least, was knocking down the inner walls of the cottage. The idea came to her in the front room downstairs, when she'd suddenly picked up a big stick and swung it with all her strength against the nearest surface. It was very satisfying: the plaster exploded on impact, exposing a dark cavity and a rib of rough wood. She hit it again, and more fell away. Maybe she would turn the house into one big room. Maybe she would knock the whole fucking place down.

After bashing the wall for twenty minutes or so, she had a hole barely big enough to crawl through, and wielding the stick had ceased giving her the satisfaction of the first few blows. The scar-line where her sixth finger had been amputated was throbbing in pain, and the savagery of her swings was doing something bad to her spine. So, she gave up, and resumed pacing. Her bare feet collected debris. She moved from room to room, tapping the walls with her nails. The house creaked and rustled. Outside in the trees of Ablach Farm, owls were calling to each other, screaming like human women in orgasm. The wind was swollen with the sound of waves crashing on the sea-shore. Somewhere in the farther distance, a foghorn blew.

It was well after midnight when Isserley finally went to bed, too tired to think any more. She had a number of half-formed plans now, and she hoped she'd stayed awake long enough to make sure the sun would be up by the time she awoke.

She slept deeply, for what seemed like a very long time, but when she resurfaced, gasping in terror, it was still pitch dark. The sheets were tangled tightly around her legs, damp and humid, slightly abrasive with grains of plaster, fragments of twig, dirt. She touched herself all over: the flesh of her arms and shoulders was as hot as meat newly fetched from the oven, but her legs were stone cold. Of all the phases of sleep to be woken from, this was the worst.

Cruelly, even though her system hadn't got round to restoring its equilibrium, it had still managed to squeeze in her usual nightmare about being buried alive, abandoned, condemned to die in an airless prison.

And yet . . . *was* it her usual nightmare? Glimpsing its after-image as it faded from her mind, she realized there was something different about it. The way it had made her feel was the same as always, but for the first time, the creature at the centre of the drama seemed to be someone other than herself. Not at the beginning, no: at the beginning it was unmistakably Isserley, being led down into the bowels of the earth. But by the end she seemed to have changed shape, size and species. And in those last anxious seconds before waking, the dream hadn't been about a human being anymore, but a dog, trapped inside a vehicle in the middle of nowhere. Her master wasn't coming back, and she was going to die.

As soon as she was fully awake, Isserley disentangled herself from the bedclothes, hugged her cold legs in her warm arms, and began to argue herself back from the brink of panic.

Of course the dog she'd dreamed of was yesterday's vodsel's dog, but there was no need to be having nightmares about it. The animal would be just fine. Its master would have left the windows of his van open a fraction, surely. And even if he hadn't, vehicles weren't exactly vacuum-sealed, and the weather was cool. As for imagining the dog was going to starve to death, well, that was stupid. When the dog got hungry, it would start barking, and eventually people would get irritated by the noise and search out where it was coming from. In any case, what was so important about the fate of a dog? Dogs died every day. She'd seen the flattened carcasses of lots of them on the A9, had driven over the remains herself, rather than swerve dangerously. They made a barely perceptible bump under the tyres. Their consciousness was rudimentary.

Isserley rubbed her eyes and looked up. She'd put fresh batteries in the clock yesterday, as part of reclaiming a grip on her life: it now glowed 4:09. Maybe it would have been better not to know how many hours she still had to wait for sunrise. Maybe it would have been better not to wake up at all.

She crawled out of bed, crippled as usual. What heaven it would be to get revenge on the surgeons who'd done this to her! She'd never even seen their faces: she'd been drugged into oblivion by the time they'd stuck their knives in. And now they were probably boasting to Vess Incorporated how much they'd learned from their mistakes, how there was no comparison between the miracles they could perform now and the crude experiments that had been Esswis and Isserley. In a fair world, she would be given the opportunity, before she died, to tie those surgeons to a slab and do a bit of experimenting of her own. They could watch, tongueless, as she carved their genitals away. To keep their noise down, she'd give them big chunks of their own severed tails to chew on. Their anuses would clench as she penetrated their spines with iron skewers. Their eyes would blink blood as she sculpted brave new faces for them.

Isserley switched on the television and began her exercises.

'I can't endure a lifetime without love,' a voice whispered into her dark bedroom. The image materialized, a black-and-white little female clinging onto a broad-shouldered male looking away from her, towards the sky.

'Don't be silly,' he chided her gently. 'You won't have to.'

Isserley reached out her foot to change the channel just as a sleek aeroplane flew off into dramatic gloom, propellers twirling.

Warm colours suffused the screen, abstract and mutable. The camera image pulled back, sharpening into an iridescent circle of wet glass held between a giant thumb and forefinger, like a single spectacle lens smeared with soup.

'Cultures such as this one,' said an authoritative voice, 'may literally be growing a cure for cancer.'

Isserley stood staring into the fire she had made, almost mesmerized. She'd built a much larger pyre of twigs and branches than usual, and the flames blazed gold and apricot in the dawn. With effort she roused herself and walked past her car, which was already clear of the shed and facing out of the farm, engine running. Isserley limped across to the steading, her shoes scuffing awkwardly along the stony ground. There was something wrong at the base of her spine which exercise hadn't yet managed to fix.

'Isserley,' she spoke into the intercom.

No-one answered, but the great metal door rolled open. Just inside, as expected, sat the black plastic bag filled with the personal effects of the last vodsel. She grabbed it and left the steading immediately, just in case whoever was on duty was coming up from the earth's depths for a chat.

Back at the fireside, she pulled the vodsel's shoes, pullover and dog-haired suit out of the bag, and examined the rest. There wasn't much there: he'd evidently worn nothing but a stained T-shirt under his pullover, and no underpants. His jacket was empty, and in the pockets of his trousers, apart from car keys and a wallet, there was nothing.

Laying the pullover on the bonnet of her car to keep it off the dewy grass, she sprinkled the jacket, T-shirt, trousers and shoes with a christening of petrol, then tossed them onto the fire. There was a surprising amount of dog-hair on her hands, which she didn't want to wipe on her own clothing. With any luck, it would wear off naturally.

Grunting in discomfort, she knelt to look through the wallet. It was a fat one compared to other wallets she'd seen, but there was little variety inside. Instead of the usual assortment of laminated plastic cards, official concessions and licences, addresses, tickets and sales dockets, there was only money and one sheet of card folded small like a miniature map. The fatness was caused by the sheer bulk of the cash. As well as a few coins, there was a wad of banknotes, mostly twenties with a few tens and fives, adding up to £375. Isserley had never seen so much money before. It was enough to buy five hundred and thirty-five litres of petrol, or a hundred and ninety-two bottles of the blue shampoo, or more than a thousand razor-blades . . . or . . . fifty-seven bottles of the fermented potato juice the vodsel had mentioned. She transferred the banknotes to her trousers, distributing them between both pockets to minimize the bulge.

The sheet of card was a large colour photograph, folded many times. When opened and smoothed out, it showed the vodsel, much younger, embracing a female in a gauzy white dress. Both of them had glossy black hair, rosy cheeks and big crescent smiles. Isserley's vodsel was clean-shaven, unwrinkled, grime-free. There was no old food on his teeth, and his lips were wet and pink. No doubt she was extrapolating, but she fancied she could tell just from his expression that his happiness was genuine. She wondered what his name had been. There was an ornate signature, *Pennington Studio*, inscribed on the bottom right-hand margin, which struck Isserley as a foreign name, though the vodsel hadn't sounded foreign to her.

Even as Pennington's clothes burned, Isserley was toying with the idea of rescuing him. Amlis had had no trouble setting a few vodsels free; she could surely do it with just as little bother. The men down there were imbeciles, and most of them would still be asleep.

But of course it was too late. Pennington would have had his tongue and his balls removed last night. He hadn't much wanted to live anyway, and he was hardly likely to have changed his mind by now. He was better left alone.

Isserley stirred the bonfire with a stick, wondering why she was bothering to be so thorough. Force of habit. She tossed the stick onto the flames, and walked to her car.

As Isserley drove along the A9, the sun was rising higher above the horizon, recovering from whatever it had suffered behind the snow-capped mountains during the night. Unclouded and at large, it shone with abrupt intensity, casting a generous golden light over all of Ross-shire. Just by being in the right place at the right time, Isserley was part of that landscape too; her hands turned gold on the steering wheel.

Light as beautiful as this was worth everything, she thought – or damn near everything. Outside the twisted bones and scarred flesh of one's own body, life wasn't shit at all.

Pennington's pullover still felt a little odd against her skin, but she was getting used to wearing it. She liked the way the cuffs wrapped snugly round her wrists, the tarnished fibres luminescing in the sun. She liked the way she could glance down her breast, and, instead of seeing that repugnant cleavage of artificial fat, get an impression of furriness, an illusion of her natural self.

Not far up ahead, a hitcher stood beckoning at the roadside. He was young and thin, and held a battered cardboard sign saying NIGG. Isserley drove past without even slowing down. The vodsel made a 'fuck you' sign in her rear-view mirror, and then turned to be ready for the next car in line.

* * *

It was easy to find the spot where she'd picked Pennington up. The carriageway was especially narrow on the stretch leading up to it – that's why the cars had banked up behind her – and of course there was the **P** sign to look out for. When she'd found it, she parked her car exactly where she'd stopped the day before, give or take a few feet. She stepped out, locked the doors, and went in search of the nearest farm path into the fields.

Pennington's van, too, was easier to find than she'd expected. It was tucked away where she herself would have parked a vehicle if she'd been wanting to hide on this bit of farmland. Shaded by a row of tall trees there stood a ruined mill, roofless and skeletal, against which bales of hay had been piled. The hay had been spoiled by unseasonal weather and left to rot. From the perspective of motorists driving on the A9, there was nothing to be seen except a glimpse of ruins and hay. From the perspective of the farmhouse, half a mile distant, there was only the cluster of trees, sparing the farmer a reminder of blighted resources which would cost money to remove. In the space between the trees and the mill, visible only by trespass, stood Pennington's van.

It was a much more luxurious vehicle than Isserley had imagined. She'd pictured a rusty, battered, barely roadworthy thing, dark blue perhaps, with faded writing on the side. Instead it was a glossy cream, finished in polished chrome and unperished black rubber, like one of the brand-new ones on display in Donny's Garage.

Inside its lustrous hull, Pennington's captive dog was jumping from seat to seat, barking frenziedly. Isserley could see that the animal was whooping its lungs out, but through the closed windows the noise was low-pitched and muffled – an ugly racket at close quarters, but one which she doubted would carry very far, even in the dead of night.

'Good boy,' she said, stepping up to the vehicle.

It did not occur to Isserley to be afraid as she used Pennington's keys to unlock the van's side door. The dog would either run away or attack her; so, either she would watch it scampering into the distance, or she might be forced to kill it. Either way, her conscience would be at rest.

She swung the door open, and the dog sprang out with what seemed like the velocity of an exhaust backfire. It landed in the grass, almost rolling head-over-heels, then whirled to face Isserley, trembling and twitching. Pure black and white, like a miniature Amlis in animal form, it glowered at her, confused, a rubbery frown wrinkling the down of its dark forehead.

Isserley left the door of the van open, and walked away, back towards the A9. She was not really surprised when the dog followed her, sniffing at the waist of Pennington's pullover, which hung down to Isserley's thighs like a dress. The spaniel's nose nudged her hip repeatedly, then she felt its wet tongue licking one of her hands. With a groan of distaste, she lifted both her arms into air, surrender-style, as she hurried to her car.

Pennington's dog managed to lick her hand one more time while she was making sure she didn't slam its snout in the car door. It stared up at her through the glass, uncomprehending, as she turned on the ignition.

'You're on your own now, doggy,' Isserley said, conscious of course that the dog had no language in common with her.

Then she drove away, leaving the animal sitting at the side of the road.

On the homeward journey, Isserley found herself thinking all the same thoughts she'd thought endlessly during the night, about what she was going to do with the rest of her life.

Of course, there were any number of ways she could go, depending on how much courage she could muster, or how much physical misery she was game to endure. Each plan promised its own sweet rewards, and carried with it its own frightening consequences. But she was tired of weighing one future against another; she'd thought too much.

It was time to let instinct decide. She would let her fingers dangle within reach of the controls, and if they pressed the toggle down, well . . . that was how it would be.

Within minutes, she was approaching the road-sign that said *B9175: Portmahomack and Seaboard Villages*. She checked her rear-view mirror and the road up ahead: no-one coming in either direction, to push her forward or hold her back. Her fingers hovered over the indicator. Her foot seemed paralysed on the accelerator. The sign flashed past, the turn-off was swallowed up in the trees, and she was still driving north. The decision was made. She would never see Ablach Farm again.

A while later, still travelling northwards, Isserley turned her car onto the Dornoch Bridge, and immediately got a queasy feeling in her guts. It wasn't hunger, though she was certainly feeling that by now. It was premonition. Something was waiting for her on the other side.

She pulled over, half-way across the bridge, in a parking area provided for tourists. There was a tourist there already, staring over the railings at the glittering firth, binoculars ready for seals or dolphins. Isserley brought her car to a standstill behind his luxury caravan, and cautiously opened her door. The tourist turned to acknowledge her arrival. He was obese and short, with spindly legs: a definite failure to make the grade.

'Hi there.' He waved, squinting into the sun.

'Hi,' echoed Isserley, keeping her car between them. Satisfied he would stay where he was, she turned away from him and looked down the length of the bridge to the mainland. Shielding her face with one cupped hand, she removed her glasses and peered into the distance, focusing her huge eyes on the traffic that seemed to be banked up at the roundabout, a little herd of vehicles hesitating to move, as if undecided between the Clashmore and Dornoch roads.

Then she spotted the headgear of police, ducking and weaving among the vehicles.

Isserley swung back into her car and revved it into motion. With more skill and boldness than she would have predicted herself capable of, she executed a U-turn in the middle of the bridge – a highly illegal act, no doubt, but one which those tiny far-off police were in no position to pursue. She glanced over her shoulder to check the tourist at the railing: he was staring at her in awe as she drove away, but he wasn't using his binoculars, so he probably wasn't trying to fix her appearance or her licence-plate number in his memory.

I want to go home, she thought, but her decision had been made: she had no home anymore.

Within a few minutes she was driving southwards past Tain, ignoring the temptation to reconsider. If she'd been willing to turn off the A9 and drive through the centre of the town, she could have come out the other end and followed an alternative route to Portmahomack – and Ablach Farm. But Ablach Farm was closed to her now. Vess Incorporated wouldn't take care of her if she didn't deliver the goods, she knew that; it wasn't going to house and feed her out of the goodness of its heart.

As for Amlis, he'd said he'd return . . . but his kind were

always lavish with the promises, weren't they? What about all the men who'd promised to keep her safe as she neared the grading age? 'The Estates? A beautiful girl like you? Just let them try, Iss, and I'll have a word with my father.' Spoilt little poseurs, the lot of them. Fuck them, fuck them all.

It would be very easy to get seduced by this world, Amlis had said, when he touched her arm. It's very, very beautiful. What had he meant? Could he have been meaning to imply that *she* was beautiful, too? Why else would he have touched her at that moment? His fingers . . . But no, of course he hadn't meant that. He was seeing an ocean and a snowy sky for the first time, with a mutilated cripple sweating next to him. The charms of her scarred flesh could hardly compete with a naked new world, could they?

There was a pain in her heart. She missed Ablach's shore already. All that time she'd spent roaming the empty confines of her cottage last night, she could have spent there, walking the moonlit water's edge, or along the cliffs. But even then she'd probably already known that saying goodbye would only make things harder.

One of the impossible futures she'd considered, while pacing the rooms of her cottage, was living in a cave on the Ablach shore. There were several caves there, which she'd never explored because of her claustrophobia – which was precisely the problem, of course, with the idea of her living in a cave.

Also on the beach there was a stone hut ('the fishing bothy', Esswis had once called it, with the air of a man who knows everything). Its doors were so weathered and rotten that they swayed in the wind like curtains; its windowless interior was mucky with tar and decomposing sheep turds. The main obstacle to living there, though, was that there was also a large piece of machinery bolted to the floor, a cast-iron mechanism the size of a cow, designed to haul boats onto the seashore. Of course it might not be functional anymore, but there was no way of being certain. There would have been big problems if she was stretched out naked in a corner of the bothy, asleep, and suddenly a boatload of fishermen walked in.

She'd also considered building herself a little dwelling on the Ablach cliffs somewhere, made of branches, driftwood and maybe those big sheets of corrugated tin she often saw washed up on the shore. But Esswis would surely have noticed if the farm sprouted an extra dwelling, especially if Isserley was missing and he was searching for her. And, as soon as Vess Incorporated was aware she'd run away, that was surely what Esswis would be sent to do.

Isserley frowned, remembering the police. She couldn't afford to be stopped by them, because her car was decorated with out-of-date tax stickers, and she had no licences for anything. She must find a place to hide, and stop driving for a while. It was no big challenge; it would be easy. She wasn't bound to the A9 anymore, after all, but could explore the out-of-the-way roads, where there was little traffic and long stretches of uncleared forest. She could disappear into the trees like a pheasant.

Three days later, Isserley woke from dreams of sexual release, clutching fur in her fists. It was the hood of the anorak, pillowing her head on the back seat of her car. She was in so much discomfort, yet still filled with the fantasy of orgasm, that she wanted to laugh.

Her car was nestled in a bower of ferns near the edge of a loch. The tips of twigs actually touched some of the windows, and tiny birds hopped from roof to tree and back again, their fragile claws pattering on the metal. Unseen creatures, possibly ducks or swans, would rustle the tideless water nearby, particularly in the late afternoons. Overhead, the cover was so dense that snowfalls would never reach the ground, and there was more sunlight reflecting off the loch than through the trees.

All in all, this bower was such a good place to hide that, when Isserley had first eased her car into it a couple of days ago, she'd found another one there already. Fortunately it wasn't inhabited. It was a mere skeleton of a car: gutted, wheel-less, rusted all the colours of the forest, overgrown with moss. Isserley parked hers right alongside, taking advantage of the extra camouflage.

Undeniably, the first night had been difficult. The back seat was just a few inches shorter than she was, and those few inches proved crucial to her body's needs. But she'd survived, and the next two nights were slightly better.

She hadn't wanted to sleep in her car, but until she found another place to live, she had no choice. The notion of sleeping under the stars, curled up in a field somewhere, was all very romantic and defiant, but deep down she knew her spine would punish her for it next day. She needed a bed, or at least something soft to lie on. The back seat of her car was at least padded and smooth. And if one morning she woke up in really serious trouble, she could always pull herself up by the headrests of the front seats.

The ideal place to sleep, the perfect home, if she could have any place in the world she wanted, would be an abandoned lighthouse. But did lighthouses ever get abandoned? She wished they did. They stood on the very edge of the land, right next to the open sea, and their spires reached almost to the clouds. She could imagine herself up there, right at the top, sleeping on a soft mattress with windows all around her, letting the sunlight in as soon as it arrived.

Right now, she was lying low, growing weak with hunger. She really would have to eat something today, something more substantial than the raw turnip she'd stolen from a field the night before last.

As soon as she'd done her exercises, she waded into the icy shallows of the loch and washed herself. Then she shaved, mirror in one hand, blade in the other, dipping shampoo froth into the shimmering water. She hoped the shampoo wouldn't do any harm to the things that lived in the loch. A few drops of chemical soap into such a vast reservoir of natural purity wouldn't have much effect, surely?

For her first hot meal since leaving the farm, she drove to a service station she knew, where she'd bought petrol in the past.

One day she might conquer her fears and actually drive into a large town, park her car amongst hundreds of other cars, and walk into a supermarket, the way vodsels did when they needed food. That day was far off yet. Only recently, she'd driven past a giant Tesco right next to the A96 to Aberdeen, wondering if she dared venture in. It was so close to the road, she could almost see inside its tinted glass doors. Everything she'd ever seen on television was probably jammed inside that massive concrete steading, with a plague of vodsels picking at it, jostling and lunging for the choicest morsels. No, she wasn't ready.

At the service station, she bought twenty pounds worth of petrol. She also selected a pre-packaged meat meal from a self-serve metal and plastic display labelled HAPPY TUM'S®

ROADSIDE DINER. There were three choices: Hot Dog, Chicken Roll, and Beef Burger. Each was wrapped in white paper, so that she couldn't see the contents. She chose the Chicken Roll. She'd heard the television say that Beef was dangerous – potentially deadly, even. If it could kill vodsels, she didn't like to think what it might do to her. As for the Hot Dog, well . . . there was something bizarre about going to a lot of trouble to save a dog from death and then eating one a few days later.

She picked the paper parcel up in her hand and placed it in the microwave oven, then followed the instructions for what buttons to press. Forty-five seconds later, she had her Chicken Roll, steaming hot in her palm.

Forty-five minutes later, she was huddled in the grass behind a parking area in Saltburn, straining to vomit. Her mouth was stretched wide open, saliva drooling off the point of her tongue, but when the gush finally came, it went up her nose instead, spraying and bubbling out of her constricted nostrils like carbonated gravy. For a minute she thought she was going to choke to death, or that the vomit was going to scald its way up her tear ducts and drip out of her eyes. But these were delusions of panic, and the spasms subsided before long.

When it was all over, Isserley removed, with trembling hands, the screw top of a large bottle of Aqua Viva – water, apparently. She'd bought it at the same time as the Chicken Roll, just in case the unfamiliar meat didn't agree with her. She'd strongly suspected it wouldn't, but she'd given it a chance. The riddle of what she could safely eat would not be solved in a day. Trial and error would teach her what she could get away with. In the meantime, she sucked at the plastic nub of the water bottle, gulping the soothing clear liquid down.

She wouldn't starve. There were potatoes growing in the fields, turnips scattered for the sheep, apples on the trees. These were all perfectly fit for human consumption, as the men on Ablach Farm proved every day in the Dining Hall. It wasn't enough, but she would survive. In time, she would discover foods she couldn't yet imagine, foods which would remind her of the delicacies of her childhood, foods which would make her feel languorous and satisfied and complete.

It was all out there somewhere, she was sure.

Driving back towards her bower by the loch, along the narrow road through the forest, she was alarmed to see a vodsel up ahead, gesturing extravagantly for her to stop. He wasn't a police officer, he was a hitcher, but he was very agitated, almost dancing on the carriageway itself. She swerved in an attempt to avoid him, but he sprang into her path, spreading his arms wide, forcing her to brake to a sudden halt.

He was a massive specimen, young and superbly muscled beneath his leather jacket, but his face was wild.

'Ah'm soarry! Ah'm soarry!' he cried, slamming his palms down on the bonnet of her car, fixing her with an imploring stare. 'But Ah hud tae make yi stoap!'

'Please get out of the way!' called Isserley through the windscreen, revving her engine threateningly. 'I don't pick up hitchers!'

'Mah girrilfriend's huvin' a bebby!' he bawled back at her, waving one meaty arm at an invisible point beyond the forest. 'Fer pity's sake! Ah've come a hunnert fifty miles, and Ah've goat aboot five fuckin' miles tae go!'

'I can't help you!' shouted Isserley.

'Jesus fuckin' Christ!' he grimaced, slapping himself on the forehead. 'Ah'm nae gonny pit a hand on yi. Ah'll jest sit! Yi kin tie me up, pit a knife tae mah throat, Ah dinnae care whit yi dae – mah girrilfriend's huvin' a bebby! Ah'm gonny be a faither!'

It was obvious he wasn't going to let her go, so she opened the passenger door and let him in.

'Thanks,' he said, sheepishly. 'Yir a pal.'

Shona, he was thinking. Hold on, Shona.

Isserley didn't reply, but jerked the car into motion with an awkward grind of gears. Five miles, and she could be rid of him. And if she didn't speak, maybe he wouldn't either.

'I cannae tell yi whit this means tae me,' he said hoarsely after a few seconds.

'It's OK,' said Isserley, staring intently at the road ahead. 'Just let me drive.'

'I love her so much,' he said.

'Good,' said Isserley.

'She rang me up last night, when Ah wis already in mah bed, on the rig, y'ken. "Jimmy, Ah'm in labour," she says. "It's come on a week early. Ah know yi cannae get home. Ah jest wanted yi tae know." Ah wis oaff that rig like a rocket!'

'Good,' said Isserley.

There was a pause as the car pootled along, at forty-five miles an hour as usual. To Isserley's eyes, the trees were flashing by on either side, a blur, though she had to admit the deserted road ahead looked static.

'Kin yi nae drive a wee bitty faster?' the vodsel asked at last.

'I'm doing my best,' Isserley warned him. Even so, she

nudged her foot against the accelerator. Then, to take his mind off the car's speed, she asked him:

'Is this your first child?'

'Aye. Aye,' he enthused, then breathed deep. 'Immortality.'

'I beg your pardon?'

'Immortality. That's whit weans are, y'ken? An endless line of weans through history, y'ken? All this life efter death stuff disnae make sense tae me. Dae *you* believe in it?'

Isserley was having so much trouble decoding his accent and certain key words that she failed to grasp what he was really asking her.

'I don't know,' she said.

He was not to be stopped, however. A raw nerve had been touched, even though he was the one who'd touched it.

'The Wee Free Church says mah bebby's gonny be a bastard,' he complained, 'because me and mah girril's nae married. Whit's that all aboot? Fuckin' prehistoaric, y'ken?'

Isserley pondered this for a second, then smiled and shook her head in defeat.

'I don't understand a word you're saying,' she confessed.

'Whit religion are you?' he immediately asked her.

'I haven't got any religion,' she said.

'Yir parents, then?'

Isserley thought a moment.

'Where I come from,' she replied carefully, 'religion is . . . dead.'

The vodsel hummed in sympathy, then carried on with his incomprehensible sermon as they plunged deeper into the forest.

'Reincarnation quite appeals tae me,' he said, straining to suppress his excitement. 'Shona – mah girrilfriend – says it soonds daft, but there's sumpn in it, Ah reckon. Everythin's goat a soul, and yi cannae destroy a soul. Plus yi get tae huv anither try – dae better next time.' He laughed loudly, showily, as if inviting her to join in. 'Who knows, eh? Ah might come back as a wumman, or a wee beastie!'

Rounding a corner, they sped downwards into a small valley, and Isserley eased her foot down on the brake, simultaneously turning the steering wheel. Without warning, the rattle in the chassis reappeared, beating much louder than ever before, and the whole vehicle shuddered. An instant later, the car reached the lowest point of the slope, and its locked wheels made contact with a grey slick of frost.

Almost in a dream, Isserley felt her vehicle sliding free of the tarmac's friction, as if it were launching itself on water or into the air. Two big male hands clasped over her own on the steering wheel, and helped her wrench it round, but it made no difference. The car flew smoothly off the edge of the road and, with a ferocious smack, collided with a tree.

Isserley was unconscious only for a second, or so it seemed. Her spirit fell back into her body as if from a height, like it had always done when she'd just stung a vodsel. If anything, the impact of landing seemed gentler than she was used to. Her breathing wasn't as laboured, and her heart wasn't hammering. The trees of the forest were almost supernaturally vivid in front of her eyes, until she realized that both her glasses and the windscreen were gone.

She looked down. Her green velvet trousers were sprinkled with broken glass and saturated with dark blood, and a twisted wedge of metal was taking up all the space where she would have expected her knees to be. She felt very little pain, and she guessed this must be because her spine was shattered. The crescent of the steering wheel had penetrated her breasts, leaving her torso uninjured. Her neck, though, felt better than it had for years, and this realization jerked a hysterical sob of laughter and grief from her. Something warm and gelatinous, trapped inside her top and Pennington's pullover, slid down her abdomen and into her lap. She shuddered in revulsion and fear.

The vodsel was no longer next to her. He'd been thrown through the windscreen. She couldn't see his body from where she sat.

The torn fabric of one of her trouser legs started making a little flapping, sucking noise, and she felt desperately sick, but managed to look away. She noticed then that the icpathua needles were sticking out of the upholstery of the passenger seat. There'd been a malfunction. Knowing it was absurd, Isserley punched the edge of the seat feebly with a bloodied fist, trying to make the needles retract. They didn't.

Suddenly, somewhere behind her on the road, a car screeched to a halt, and a car door slammed. Footsteps scattered gravel.

Acting automatically, Isserley reached over to the glovebox and fetched out the first pair of glasses to hand. She jammed them onto her face, and was immediately half-blinded by them: they were real optical lenses, of course, not clear glass.

A figure was looming close to her, leaning towards where the driver's window had been; a small figure with a haze of pink throat, bright yellow clothing and a halo of dark hair.

'Are you all right?' said a tremulous female voice.

Isserley laughed helplessly, snorting a dribble of wetness from one of her nostrils. She wiped it on her wrist, recoiling a little in surprise from the distorted magnification of her arm and unfamiliar feel of wool against her cheek.

'Don't move,' said the female voice, toughening up. 'I'll get help. Just sit tight.'

Isserley laughed again, and this time the other woman laughed with her, a nervous hiss.

The blur of colours flitted out of Isserley's range of vision, and she heard the crackle of undergrowth in front of the car. The woman's voice came again, louder, almost businesslike.

'Is this . . . your partner?' she called, from what sounded like quite a long way away.

'A hitcher,' said Isserley. 'I didn't know him.'

'He's alive,' said the woman. 'He's breathing.'

Isserley leaned her head back on the seat and inhaled deeply herself, trying to decide how she felt about the vodsel's survival.

'Take him with you, please,' she said after a moment.

'I can't,' said the woman. 'We've got to wait for the ambulance men.'

'Please, please take him with you,' said Isserley, squinting into the green and brown haze in search of her.

'I really can't,' insisted the woman, calm now. 'He's probably got spinal injuries. He needs expert attention.'

'I'm worried my car will catch fire,' said Isserley.

'Your car won't catch fire,' the woman said. 'Don't panic. Just stay calm. You're going to be fine.'

'At least take his wallet,' Isserley pleaded. 'It'll tell you who he is.'

The undergrowth crackled again, and the bright colours swam back into Isserley's field of vision. Again the woman was standing at the hole in the driver's window. A warm, small hand laid itself against Isserley's neck.

'Listen, I have to leave you for a few minutes while I find a phone. I'll be back as soon as I've rung an ambulance, OK?'

'Thank you,' said Isserley. Out of the corner of her eye, she glimpsed pale collarbones and a curve of bosom inside a peach-coloured top, as the woman leaned over Isserley's shoulder to lift something off the back seat.

'The Mercy Hospital isn't far,' the woman reassured her. 'You'll be away in no time.'

Isserley felt the warm hands on her again, and realized belatedly that her own flesh was frigidly cold. The woman was wrapping her up in the anorak, gently tucking it around her shoulders.

'You're going to be all right, OK?'

'OK,' nodded Isserley. 'Thank you.'

The woman disappeared then, and the sound of her car driving off faded into silence.

Isserley removed the spectacles and dropped them into her lap, where they landed with a patter of windscreen glass. She blinked, wondering why things were still out of focus. Tears ran down her cheeks, and her view through the shattered windscreen cleared.

Isserley checked the top of the dashboard, where Yns, at the same time as he'd set up the icpathua network, had installed the other little alteration to the car's original design: the button for the aviir. Unlike the icpathua connections, which involved fragile electrics and hydraulics that had obviously been damaged in the accident, the connection between the dashboard button and the cylinder of aviir was one simple, sturdy tube, waiting only for a squirt of something foreign into the oily liquid.

The aviir would blow her car, herself, and a generous scoop of earth into the smallest conceivable particles. The explosion would leave a crater in the ground as big and deep as if a meteorite had fallen there.

And she? Where would she go?

The atoms that had been herself would mingle with the oxygen and nitrogen in the air. Instead of ending up buried in the ground, she would become part of the sky: that was the way to look at it. Her invisible remains would combine, over time, with all the wonders under the sun. When it snowed, she would be part of it, falling softly to earth, rising up again with the snow's evaporation. When it rained, she would be there in the spectral arch that spanned from firth to ground. She would help to wreathe the fields in mists, and yet would always be transparent to the stars. She would live forever. All it took was the courage to press one button, and the faith that the connection had not been broken.

She reached forward a trembling hand.

'Here I come,' she said.